KNAVES

KNAVES: A Blackguards Anthology

Outland Entertainment | www.outlandentertainment.com

Founder/Creative Director: Jeremy D. Mohler

Editor-in-Chief: Alana Joli Abbott

Publisher: Melanie R. Meadors

Senior Editor: Gwendolyn Nix

Published by Outland Entertainment

5601 NW 25th Street

Topeka KS, 66618

Paperback: 978-1-947659-47-6

EPUB: 978-1-947659-35-3

MOBI: 978-1-947659-37-7

PDF-Merchant: 978-1-947659-38-4

Worldwide Rights

Created in the United States of America

Editor: Melanie R. Meadors and Alana Joli Abbott

Cover Illustration: Daniel Rempel

Interior Illustrations: Nicolás R. Giacondino

Cover Design & Interior Layout: STK•Kreations

CONTENTS

INTRODUCTION

Howard Tayler

AT LEAST SIX hundred," she told me. "But no more than a thousand."

They're just words, I told myself. It's no crime to stake a few hundred of them, ink-fixed, to the pages of a book. It's not as if they were ever alive to begin with. And since it's no crime to pen them, it's no crime to take money for the penning.

But I was hesitant.

"I only know a few of the authors," I said. "Shanna, Cat, Maurice, Misty"

"*Mercedes,*" she said. "And four out of fourteen isn't bad."

"I need more to work with. I can't write an introduction on nothing but reputation and a knack for hackery."

"I've seen you do more with less."

She had me there.

"But I can send you some manuscripts," she said. "Tell me you'll do it?"

"I'll do it."

WEEKS PASSED, AND tens of thousands of words flitted freely through my mind, oblivious to the possibility that I might snatch them from the streams of consciousness and cement them into the ignominy that is an introduction: likely unread, easily outshone, a page of word-cemetery past which readers will drive quickly, their breaths held lest some of their own words get buried alongside noble unfortunates like 'ignominy' and 'oblivious.'

The manuscripts gave me far more than I needed, but they also showed me exactly how rewarding it would be for readers to speed by a few hundred inky corpses on their way to true tales of villainy, mass graves of text in which thousands upon thousands of words lie forever bound bearing narrative testimony of those heroes of their own stories who, if they were ever unfortunate enough to find themselves in stories of actual heroes, would cower in shame at their misdeeds.

Shame not unlike what my words would feel as they lay out in front of these stories.

MORE WEEKS PASSED. I considered the blank page, and which of my words would be forced up against it, like the first against the wall when the revolution someday comes. I wondered how few words would need to die before the work could be done. *"This is a good book about bad people, and you should read it"* says everything that needs to be said, but those thirteen words need support. *"No, really. I mean it"* is unlikely to prop them up enough to convince the reluctant reader. Throwing "really" down a few more times would have the opposite effect, though murdering a few adverbs in the introduction might prevent them from finding their way into things people actually read.

And then I wondered if that's where the slippery slope of self-justification begins. Sure, it would be sloppy and ineffective to kill "really" a dozen times, but I'm being paid to put words in the ground, and killing that one over and over could be a service to humanity. And it might be fun. And there's money in it. And as long as I'm killing things that end with "ly" I could line "actually" up in front of the laser jets a few hundred times and really make the world an actually better place. So I began to write...

If there is to be a happy ending there must somewhere be an unhappy ending. Otherwise "happy" is simply implied. This collection gives us that opposition, helping us to understand good by letting us inside the head of evil, encouraging us to tread the grey roads that weave precariously between darkness and light, and showing us the perils and precipices that lie along the middling twilight paths of amorality. If the ends can justify the means, then the several endings found herein may serve as justification for a wide range of means, from the golden means of classical beauty to the meanest means of petty cruelty, and beyond, into the ever-questioning realm of "is that what this means?"

It's really, really good. Seriously, it's actually good enough for that much really. It's really actually really really actually that good.

"Really?" she said.

"Is it too much?"

"That last stretch was, well... quite a stretch. But I'll let it slide because dropping a few actuallys down the well makes me smile."

Then she smiles, and it's that editor smile which says I've missed something. It's the smile which suggests that maybe all those dead words I glossed over in my contract hid something that was still alive. Something coming up behind me.

I look behind me and see nothing.

When I turn back around there is another contract on the table, squarely between the two of us. A veritable killing field of words bleeds black from the uppermost page of several.

I stare in what I hope looks like thoughtful silence, but which probably comes across more accurately as mute horror and despair.

She slides the new contract closer. "You kill words quickly, and without compunction. That's useful to us. And you seem to enjoy it, which might prove useful to you..."

THE FERRET IN THE QUEEN'S PURSE

Kenny Soward

THE ALE AT the Bald Stallion tasted flat and stale. The air smelled like rotten hay, and the bard sang in a voice that reminded me of two old cats having a row. But it was my kind of place. The kind of place where opportunities were made.

"Have another?" The warty-faced proprietor leaned on the bar and fixed me with his pale eyes. It was clear he did not recognize me, but I did not take offense. It would not spoil my ruse.

"Of course, good Kine," I winked. "I'll have another, and another after that most likely."

"I like your enthusiasm," Kine grinned, "as long as you've got the coin to back it up. You just passing through?"

"I've heard good things about your fine ale," I said with a nod. "So here I am. And now I have the added honor of drinking alongside Slithora's finest soldiers."

I gestured toward a table where three tired-looking men dressed in gray uniforms brooded over their ales.

"Whatever suits you," Kine said as his eyes flashed to the soldiers and then back at me. "I'll get your drink."

"Many thanks." I turned, leaned my elbow on the bar, and admired the infamous soldiers of the Gray Watch.

The big slow one named Mart let loose a deep-throated belch while the wiry Jansford scratched at his scruffy beard. Their leader, a tall rugged man called Thoms, appeared lost in his ale.

I'd learned the soldiers' names from a little girl who ran around the place snatching up loose coins from tables. She was a dirty little scrub, but I admired her industriousness. She reminded me a lot of myself.

"Here's your ale," Kine said, and I heard him place the tankard on the bar with a dull *thud*.

"Thanks, kind sir." I turned and tossed a few coppers down. Then I took my ale and found an empty table near the soldiers. I slouched into a chair and picked up on their conversation.

"What's eating at you, Thoms?" Mart asked in a dullard's voice.

"It's the damn rumors about the Ferret," Thoms replied. His eyes shot a quick look around the place.

"We've all heard them," Mart confirmed with a nod. "They say the Ferret and his men are going to try and steal Queen Gruna's jewel."

"Let me anywhere near the Ferret," Jansford said with a sneer, "and I'll slit the bastard's throat."

"I'm sure you will." Thoms looked doubtfully at his friend. "If you even see him coming. I hear he moves like a shadow."

"And he's deadlier than a snake," Mart said.

"Well, a ferret ain't like no snake, you idiot." Jansford tossed a stale piece of bread at the bigger soldier. It bounced off Mart's chin and hit the table. "A ferret is all soft and cuddly, while a snake is sleek and poisonous. *I'm* more like a snake than the Ferret."

"I'm just saying," Mart said, his brow furrowed, "that they're both fast. Fast and deadly."

"Well, the Ferret ain't going to get the Queen's Jewel," Jansford said as he scratched at his scruffy beard some more, "because we've got a hundred men guarding the tower where it's locked up."

The little girl ran by my table just then, and her sharp green eyes flashed at me like two hot gemstones.

"Hey, want to see a trick?" I asked as I held up a coin and grinned.

The little girl stopped in her tracks and returned to the table with both hands on the edge, her gaze stuck to the coin I held. Then her eyes shifted to mine, and she nodded.

"Very well," I said as I lifted an old black sash from my coat and waved it in the air.

The girl's dirt-smeared face brightened, and the hint of a smile crept onto her lips. I held up the coin in front of her, then covered it with the old black sash. I'd gotten the piece of cloth from an old witch who lived in an outlying swamp, and she'd taught me the magic words of nothingness after I'd payed an outrageous price in coin. I would be sure to get my money's worth in the end.

I mumbled the phrase she'd taught me then ripped the sash away. The coin was gone.

I turned my hand back and forth to prove it had vanished completely. The girl studied my fingers with growing concern as she realized the coin was gone forever. I chuckled as her confused expression turned into an angry glare. Then she huffed and flew away in a flurry of old skirts and dirty legs.

I continued smiling as I tucked the coin into my pocket and turned back to the soldiers. They were still discussing rumors about the Ferret and his desire to have Queen Gruna's jewel.

"It's just sad," big Mart said, shaking his head. "The Queen's been kicked around enough."

"That depends on your point of view," Jansford said.

"What do you mean?" Mart asked.

"The barbarian hordes don't think she's been kicked around enough," Jansford said. "Looks like they got tired of her pushing them out of their native lands and decided to shove back."

That much was true. Queen Gruna had driven the barbarians out of the Eastern Wolds ten years ago, and the barbarians had just returned the favor. They'd expelled the Queen out of their lands all the way here to the Slithoran outpost of Lindy, where she enjoyed the protection of her husband, King Edmond.

"She's just so beautiful." Mart shook his head like a big dumb bull. "To think those barbarians almost had her."

"She'll be fine in Lindy," Thoms assured the big man. "King Edmund loves her, and we're King Edmund's men, so we're bound to love her, too."

"Yes, that's good," Mart nodded. "As long as we're here to protect her, she'll be fine."

Mart's adoration of Queen Gruna almost made me throw up in my mouth. I didn't blame the barbarians for kicking her ass out of the Eastern Wolds. She'd been a cruel ruler to the barbarian folk, torturing anyone who resisted her and taxing farmers into poverty. She'd treated the barbarians almost as bad as she treated her own soldiers. King Edmond was the only one who could control her wrath, and everyone feared the day he died and passed complete rule of Slithora to her.

On that note, I stood and turned to the three soldiers.

"Greetings, men of the Gray Watch." I flipped my dyed-yellow hair over my shoulder and bowed. "I could not help but overhear you speaking of that dastardly Ferret and his evil intentions."

"And just who the bloody hell are you?" Thoms asked as his hand slid to a plain steel dagger resting on the table in front of him.

"Allow me to introduce myself," I said as I straightened and grinned. "I am called Barrett the Golden, and I am at your service in defense of the Queen's honor."

"What does that mean?" Mart said to Jansford with a confused look.

"Shut up, you oaf," Jansford sneered at Mart, but the wiry man's intense eyes never left me.

"You're Barrett the Golden?" Thoms asked with a doubtful look. "You hardly look like a hero of the realm."

"What do you mean, sir?" I asked with an offended expression as I flipped my hair again.

"Well, first of all," Thoms said as he pushed his chair back and stood to his full six feet three inch height. "Barrett the Golden is rumored to be huge. You're far too small. And your clothes are shabby for a man who is supposed to be swimming in coin."

"Have you ever seen Barrett the Golden up close?" I asked.

"Admittedly not." Thoms shrugged. "But I've heard enough to know he ain't you."

"I can explain my clothing," I said. "I'm just back from a mission for King Edmund, and I thought to stop here at the Bald Stallion for a proper ale before I start my last leg home."

"A proper ale?" Jansford laughed. "At the Bald Stallion? Do you know where you are, sir?"

"I have travelled throughout the Kingdom of Slithora and beyond many times," I said in an apologetic tone, "but this is my first time in the Stallion."

"Well, your thirst has led you astray, I'm afraid." Jansford chuckled and shook his head. "Nothing but piss water here."

"I heard that, Jansford," Kine called from behind the bar.

"You said you just returned from a mission for King Edmund?" Thoms pressed me. "What was the mission?"

"My mission was to scout the very hordes that drove Queen Gruna from her the Easter Wolds and back into the arms of her dear husband, our King," I said in a hushed tone. "Hence, the condition of my clothing. Crawling around in ditches does not lend itself to staying clean."

"That's hardly the mission of a champion." Thoms narrowed his eyes at me.

"True," I nodded, "but King Edmund assured me it was of the utmost importance. The barbarian hordes are now on our own doorstep, incited by the Queen, and he wants to know everything about them. When it comes to proper scouting, there is no one better than me."

"Oh, no," Mart said with a crestfallen expression. "The barbarian hordes are going to kill us all."

"Shut up, you oaf," Jansford said. "The barbarian hordes will do no such thing. And if you ask me, I say the Queen should never have left our lands in the first place."

"Well, she is rather rambunctious," I said as I picked some dirt from beneath my nail. "Always keen on invasion and making enemies and whatnot."

"What you're saying makes sense enough," Thoms said as he studied me. "But you're missing one thing."

"What's that?"

"Barrett the Golden is called that for more than just his golden locks." Thoms gestured at my belt. "Where is your golden sword?"

"Oh, that." I gulped. "You want *that* sort of proof."

"Indeed, we do." Jansford rose to stand next to Thoms.

My eyes moved back and forth between the two challengers before falling to the slack-faced Mart. I noticed the little girl standing behind the soldiers with her arms crossed and a smug look on her face. The soldiers would take great pleasure in tossing me out of the Bald Stallion if I didn't produce the sword, and the little girl would enjoy my misfortune just as much. The soldiers might also be the sort to beat me up or toss me in a dungeon to rot. I was sure Jansford lived for such moments.

"Very, well," I said as my gaze shifted back to Thoms. "Behold, the golden sword!"

I cast my cloak aside from where it had hidden my legendary weapon. I grabbed the golden hilt and pulled it half out of its sheath to reveal a similarly-colored blade.

"It's true," Mart said with an expression of dumbfounded awe. "It really is Barrett the Golden."

———————

IT WAS WELL past midnight when I grew weary of the Bald Stallion and its terrible ale. I allowed my body to drag and slouch a bit as I settled up with Kine and then turned to leave. The place had cleared out except for a few lonely denizens who wallowed in some thought or another, and I didn't have the heart to tell them the ale would solve nothing for them.

The soldiers had gone two hours before.

I staggered three or four steps toward the door when the little girl darted from beneath a table and stood in front of me. Her jade green eyes studied me with open curiosity, and I couldn't help but admire her boldness.

I stood straighter and then tossed her a coin with a wink. She caught it with practiced ease, turned it over in her hand, and darted off.

I chuckled as I fake-stumbled to the door and placed a hand on either side of the frame to steady myself. I peered into the cobbled streets of Lindy and licked my dry lips.

Houses and businesses were crammed together in a strange array of wood and brick, leaving plenty of nooks and crannies for robbers to hide. Gas lanterns lit the streets, but most of those had soot-covered shutters that hadn't been cleaned in weeks.

I stepped carefully into the gloom and turned down Axenfeld Way whilst maintaining an air of drunkenness. I stumbled past dark alcoves and stoops searching for any sign of movement, and I strained my ears to hear any odd sound.

My stomach churned with anticipation as I waited for the attack to come, but the moments ticked on without the slightest stir. The street curved upward into a nicer part of town called the Garden District that boasted polished cobblestones and glass storefronts.

That's when they struck.

A sword cut at me from an alley on the left. I leaped into the center of the street to avoid having my head cleaved from my neck, then I threw back my cloak and whipped my sword from its sheath.

Thoms rushed from the darkness and swept at me with his sword again. I parried, then nicked his hand with the tip of my blade. The Gray Watchman cursed and danced away.

Heavy footfalls stormed at me from behind. I knew it had to be Mart. I spun to my left in a full circle and swatted the big man's ass with the flat of my blade as he charged by. Mart slammed into Thoms in a painful collision, and both soldiers went down in a heap.

"That was a very poor hammer and anvil," I quipped as my eyes darted around to find Jansford.

I heard a scritch of boots on the roof above me, and I spun away as Jansford landed where I had just been standing. He held a blackjack in his hand, and he would have clobbered me in the back of the head had I been slower.

"Gotcha," I said as I lunged forward with my sword and tagged him hard on the hip with the flat of my blade.

The wiry fellow drew his sword and skipped forward on quick feet. The tip of his blade flew at me like a steel hummingbird, and it was all I could do to parry him.

I sensed someone rushing me from the left, so I stepped back just as Mart lunged by in another failed attempt to tackle me. I brought my sword around and down to slap his other ass cheek. The big man dropped to his knees with a howl.

I jerked my sword to counter Thoms's thrusting blade, then I brought my weapon around to deflect a reverse swing from Jansford meant to cut me in two. Thoms and Mart seemed to be playing nice, but Jansford wanted to destroy me.

A spike of anger gave surge to the blood rushing through my veins, and I leaped into action. I deflected another of Jansford's cuts, then I nicked his wrist with a flick of my sword, causing him to drop his weapon with a yell.

Mart loomed up on my right, and I crouched quickly to avoid being hit by his big, meaty fist. I countered with a kick to his ribs that drove the wind from his lungs but stopped short of cracking his bones.

A thrown cobblestone glanced off my left shoulder, and I grunted as pain shot down my arm. I reeled to see Thoms charging at me with steely eyes, but I leaped into the bed of a parked carriage and delivered a kick to his chest that sent him careening onto his back.

I looked around to see that Jansford still had some fight left in him. The wiry soldier approached me with a plain steel dagger in his hand. He flipped it up and caught it by the blade before flashing me a grin.

"Go ahead," I said, grinning back. "Throw it—"

"Enough," Thoms growled as he got up from the street and bent over to catch his breath. When Jansford did not stop right away, he added a bit of warning to his tone. "I said, enough, Jansford!"

Jansford froze in place with the dagger held high, then he shrugged and spun the blade back into the sheath at his waist.

"What's the meaning of this?" I asked with an offended tone. "Do Gray Watchmen always attack well-known heroes?"

"I'm sorry," Thoms said with a wave of his hand. "I just had to be sure you're really Barrett the Golden."

"Why?"

"Because we might have a job for you," Thoms said.

"I am Barrett the Golden," I said firmly. "But what kind of job could the Gray Watchmen offer me?"

"You said you would defend the Queen's honor with your life." Thoms stood up and put his hands on his hips.

"I did—" I started to say, but then my voice caught in my throat. My eyes caught the gleam of something on the ground where I had been parrying Jansford so enthusiastically.

Several specks of gold plate lay in the dim glow of a nearby gas light.

I glanced down at my golden sword and saw several chips in the hilt. My gut grew heavy, and my eyes lifted to the soldiers, but it did not appear that anyone else had noticed. I sheathed my sword and stepped down from the back of the carriage with my boot covering the golden flakes.

"I did say that," I repeated. "But I only take orders from King Edmund directly."

"Please follow us back to our guardhouse," Thoms said as he found his own sword and returned it to its sheath. "You can talk to our captain. He'll tell you all about it. Please."

"It seems you are honorable men," I gave them an agreeable nod, "if a little over enthusiastic in your duties. I would hear what your captain has to say. Lead on, good Watchmen."

Thoms nodded, then started up the hill with Mart in tow. Jansford gave me a surly look before falling in behind his comrades. I scraped my boot across the golden flakes so that they would be less noticeable in the light, then I followed the soldiers up the curved lane into the Garden District.

I'd never actually been in the Garden District before, even though it was a place Barrett the Golden would likely frequent. It was well past midnight, but many establishments stayed open late to serve those who reveled at night. My eyes took in tavern signs drawn up in fanciful scripts like pieces of artwork, and the smells of cooked meats and spiced meads made my mouth water. The patrons inside brimmed with affluent energy, and my boots tread upon pristine cobblestones that were recently scrubbed. I would have much rather spent my evening here than at the Bald Stallion.

Thoms led us down some alleys where we passed several other soldiers changing shifts or running errands, and their eyes lingered on me as they passed. My stomach turned beneath their scrutiny, but I grinned back as if it was quite natural for me to be in the company of soldiers.

We finally came to a large guard tower on the eastern wall, and Thoms gave a knock on the thick, wooden door. The steel portal opened, and a grizzled soldier looked out.

"Thoms, what are you doing here?" the guard asked. "You're not due for a shift until tomorrow."

"We need to speak to the Captain," Thoms said.

"What for?"

"We've got Barrett the Golden here," Thoms said in a hushed tone. "Was thinking maybe the Captain might need him for the, uh… you know… the *thing*?"

"Oh, right," the guard said. "The thing. You sure the Captain would approve of an outsider knowing about the *thing*?"

"What if the Captain found out we had the greatest swordsman in all the land in our company but failed to introduce them?" Thoms growled.

I wasn't sure if I was the greatest sword fighter in all the land. Still, I was at least in the top five, and I appreciated Thoms's support.

"Maybe you're right about that." The guard stared at me as I flipped my golden hair. "All right. Let's see what the Captain has to say about him."

Bolts slid aside, and the door opened. I followed my escorts inside without hesitation, but my gut sank when twelve pairs of eyes turned in my direction. The soldiers of the Gray Watch sat around three rows of tables playing cards or eating. One soldier stared at me as soup dripped from his beard.

I desperately hoped that none of these men had ever seen Barrett the Golden before. I could be in trouble if they had. But common soldiers seldom mixed with heroes, so I did not think it was likely. In any case, I could not show any fear despite that my skin itched with warning.

"Greetings, mates," I called out with a big smile. "And hail to the King and Queen."

"Hail to the King and Queen," they muttered and then went back to what they were doing.

I sighed softly in relief.

Thoms told Mart and Jansford to stay put, then he motioned for me to follow him up a set of stone stairs that wove around the inside of the tower.

"Enthusiastic lot," I quipped, referring to the soldiers.

"It's been hell ever since the Queen came to town," he said. "She brought her lot back from the front all wounded and underfed with the barbarians in hot pursuit. Us Watchmen are doing double shifts on the walls and taking extra night patrols. We're exhausted, and the pay isn't that great."

"Luckily, the walls you're guarding are quite impenetrable," I said.

"Yeah, but there's another problem," Thoms said.

"What's that?"

"Rumor has it the Ferret's got two hundred mercenaries at his disposal, and he covets the Queen's jewel above all else," Thoms said.

"The Ferret is a rat-faced weasel," I said with a dark look.

"This is technically true," Thoms agreed. "Since ferrets and weasels are the same thing."

"Are they?" I asked with a tilt of my head. "And more to the point, why are the Ferret and his two hundred men any more dangerous than the barbarians?"

"I'll let the Captain tell you," Thoms said.

We came to a door at the top of the stairs, and Thoms knocked. Another guard answered much the same way the first one had. Thoms told me to wait on the stairs while he went inside to speak with the Captain.

I looked down at the men below me as I waited. There was a lot of steel between myself and the exit, but it was too late to turn back now. I took a deep breath and tried to calm my speeding pulse. Then the door swung open, and Thoms motioned me inside.

"Come on," he said, "the Captain will see you."

"Ah, good." I nodded and then stepped across the threshold.

The Captain's quarters took nearly the entire diameter of the tower, although it was mostly full of extra armor and weapons. A few oil lamps cast a warm light in the room, and a map of the surrounding lands was spiked to the table with daggers.

The Captain was a stocky man with wide shoulders and a head shaved down to the skin. His eyes held an expression of curiosity and doubt as he came to stand in front of me with his hands on his hips.

"So you're Barrett the Golden?" he asked. "You don't look like much."

"That's what I told him," Thoms said. "But he beat me, Mart, and Jansford pretty easily. And we even had the jump on him."

They had not actually gotten the jump on me, but I played along.

"I am Barrett the Golden," I tossed my yellow hair and bowed to the Captain. "And your soldiers were right to test my mettle. With men like the Ferret around, we can never be too sure who to trust."

"I'm sorry if they caused you any trouble," the Captain said. "I know you are a friend of the King."

"And the Queen," Thoms said. "Barrett declared his loyalty and devotion to Queen Gruna, so I thought he might be good to have along for the, um, thing."

"Oh, yes." The Captain glanced at Thoms.

"What is this *thing* I keep hearing about?" I asked.

The Captain seemed reluctant to go on about it, but something in my curious expression must have convinced him I was worth trusting.

"We're moving the Queen and her jewel to the capital city of Vijale," he said, "under heavy guard."

"I see." I raised an eyebrow. "And you're afraid the Ferret will get to her jewel?"

"Aye," the Captain said.

"I figured it would be good to have Sir Barrett along to help protect us from the Ferret and his mercenaries," Thoms said to the Captain. "Like I said, he beat all three of us without breaking a sweat. And I figured you'd want someone along who had experience with a scoundrel like the Ferret."

"Yes, well, we could always use another sword," the Captain said with more enthusiasm. "What say you, Barrett? Would you be willing to assist us in escorting Queen Gruna to the safety of Vijale? There would be a hundred silver in it for you."

"I'm on my way to Vijale anyway," I said, "so it would be a favor to the Queen and our own blessed King Edmund. No payment necessary."

"That is honorable of you, sir," the Captain said. "We leave on the morrow. Can you be ready?"

"I'll be here at the break of dawn," I said as I nodded my golden head.

———

THE ROAD TO Vijale was a comfortable ride. As the greatest fighter in all the land, they honored me with a seat atop Queen Gruna's carriage. A line of fifty soldiers on horseback stretched out before me, and there were another fifty behind. These were some of Slithora's best fighters, all heavily armored and watchful. The Captain rode at the front of the line while Thoms, Jansford, and Mart mixed in with the rest of the soldiers.

We passed hamlets and fields full of grazing cattle. I had very little contact with Queen Gruna except when she disembarked to stretch her legs or go piss in the woods. She was not an ugly woman, but Mart's declaration that she was a beauty was a stretch.

And she proved herself to be shrewd, crass, and intolerable at every stop. Once she slapped a cup of water out of a servant's hand and declared the woman "slacking." Another time she made a guard get on his hands and knees so she could sit on his back with a glass of wine in her hand. And the last disgusting straw was when Queen Gruna openly scolded the Captain as a nitwit for not stopping to hunt a succulent wild boar for her supper.

The fact that she would not even acknowledge the presence of the greatest sword fighter in the land did not deter me from keeping a watchful eye on her carriage and the priceless jewel inside.

Rumors of the Ferret and his men spread like a plague through the ranks, and the Gray Watchmen grew nervous as we entered the deepest part of the forest, some fifty miles outside of Vijale. Trees pressed in around us, and strange sounds made dark music in our ears. The tension grew to an unbearable level, and even I began to sweat with the thought of some invisible foe watching us from the woods.

Still, I kept up my banter with the men by telling jokes and bolstering their spirits, and everyone breathed a sigh of relief when we exited the forest a half day later. The gleaming walls of King Edmund's capital city of Vijale loomed in the distance like a beacon of hope.

The Queen seemed especially confident now that she was so close to the fortified city. She had avoided capture by the barbarians, survived the dark forest, and now looked forward to a plush life back home with her King Edmund.

We stopped in the late afternoon not ten miles from Vijale at the Queen's command. She climbed from her carriage with a smug grin and declared that she would take a short walk to relieve the stress in her legs so that she would look fresh for her husband. Then off she strolled off with a dozen heavily armed soldiers along a deer trail.

It was then that I became personally acquainted with the Queen's jewel.

The theft itself took only a moment or two. I climbed down from the carriage and pretended to check beneath it for any road damage. Then I leaned inside the open door as if tidying the Queen's comforts. No one questioned Barrett the Golden's motives. The Captain trusted me, the Queen trusted me, and I was well-liked among the men, even though we'd only been travelling the better part of a day.

I found the Queen's jewel inside a locked box on the floor. There were no magical wards or traps protecting it. I only had to pick the lock, exchange the jewel with a rock, and then slip the priceless artifact into a pouch at my waist.

I backed out of the carriage, grabbed the carriage door, and worked it back and forth as if testing the hinges. Soldiers went about their business all around me, but no one suspected a thing.

"You there," the Queen called, just as I was climbing back atop the carriage.

My heart stuck in my throat as I turned to see her coming out of the woods and pointing right at me. I expected the next words out of her mouth to be, "kill that man," but she only smiled, reached into her purse, and tossed me a coin.

I caught the flying coin and pressed it between my fingers. It was a copper piece with a hole in the middle.

"The Queen thanks you for your service," said one of her bodyguards as his mistress climbed into the carriage.

"Thank you, my Queen," I gave her a courteous nod and tucked the coin into an inner pocket.

We continued on the last leg of our journey as the white walls of Vijale grew massive and gleaming before us. I could have made my escape some time ago, but I could not resist sitting right above the Queen with her prized possession resting snugly against my hip. It was my nature to test fate.

I chuckled on the inside, but outwardly I played the part of a hero whose only concern was the security of the realm. I stood up, scanned the horizon with a narrow-eyed glare, and dared the Ferret and his men to test us.

I secretly hoped that the Queen would take a peek at her jewel and then go into hysterics when she found it missing. I imagined her screams as she tumbled from her carriage to search for the thief. Perhaps I would flaunt the jewel in front of her before making my getaway.

But the Queen did not find her jewel missing, nor did she give me the pleasure of hearing her anguished cries. We arrived at the gates in perfect peace.

A mechanism inside the walls churned and the gates swung open. I fully expected a welcoming committee of Vijale's finest soldiers to escort the Queen to her plush lodgings, but what came out was a glorious knight trotting on a splendid white steed.

My heart beat like a fist in my chest as I took full measure of the man.

Barrett the Golden, the *true* Golden, was a full six feet five inches tall, and he weighed twice as much as me easily. His chainmail armor was all silver and gold, and his golden sword hung from his hip. His yellow hair hung in feathered waves around his head, and his chin was bold and strong.

The Captain and his soldiers split to let him pass, and many looked between the two of us with expressions of confusion. A division of King Edmund's own Vijale soldiers rose from their hidden positions along the side of the road and fixed their arrows upon me.

I was double surrounded, but I gulped down a tremor of fear and held my smile.

"Hello there, Barrett." Barrett the Golden waved and stared at me with eyes as blue as the sea. "Or should I say, hello Ferret?"

There were gasps as everyone around me realized what must be the truth. I was not Barrett the Golden at all, but some imposter with nefarious intentions. I was possibly even the Ferret himself.

"Hey, we trusted you," I heard Mart shout from somewhere behind me, and my heart broke a little at that. But Mart did not know how cruel Queen Gruna was, and it was up to me to ensure that people like her got what they deserved.

"You have me dead to rights," I said to the big blond man on the horse. "I am indeed Hanser the Ferret, and I have stolen your Queen's jewel."

A scream shook the carriage, and the Queen slammed the door open and stumbled out. Then she spun and fixed me with a wicked glare. Her face was so red and bloated with rage that she could not utter a single word, and I closed my eyes and sighed as the pure moment washed over me.

"Hanser the Ferret." Barrett broke me from my reverie with a flip of his golden hair. "Hand over the jewel, and I'll ask the King to go easy on you. Perhaps a dozen years in the dungeon would suffice."

"I'll not be going to any dungeon today," I said with a glorious toss of my own golden locks. "But I do have a question. How did you find me out?"

"I'm good friends with King Edmund." Barrett shrugged. "I was here when the advance riders came to report that the Queen was less than a day's ride away and in the good hands of Barrett the Golden."

I blinked at him.

"I should have planned this better," I admitted. "I had no idea you would be in Vijale. But maybe it's good that you're here. I want you to witness me pull off the greatest theft of this century."

"Give back the jewel," Barrett growled.

"Yes," the Queen hissed as she made grasping motions with her hands. "My jewel. Give it back."

"I think not," I said, and I shook the black sash loose from an inner pocket and started to wrap it around my hand. "For it is time to bid you farewell."

I held up my hand and whispered the magic words the swamp witch had taught me, then I waited for the magic sash to make me disappear, just like it had done to the coin back in the Bald Stallion. I had tested it a hundred times before, and it never failed me.

Yet I remained perfectly visible. The magic had failed, and my stomach sank as the danger around me grew all too real.

"I… I don't understand," I sputtered.

"See this necklace?" Barrett laughed and tapped on a gem that hung around his neck. The jewelry clicked against his chainmail collar. "This negates all magic within a hundred yards. You won't be disappearing today, Ferret."

"Well, that's inconvenient," I said with a frown. "And hardly fair. There's all of you and just one of me."

"Speaking of fair." Barrett dismounted from his horse, tore his sword free from its sheath, and pointed it at me. "You have another option. Come down off that carriage and face me like a man."

"That seems dangerous," I said, "compared to simply disappearing like a ghost."

"I'm tired of this banter," Barrett strode boldly toward the carriage as he gestured to the archers on my right. "Come face me, Ferret, or be riddled with arrows like the coward you are."

Someone ushered Queen Gruna out of the way as a dozen soldiers pulled their bowstrings tight. Their arrows were nocked and ready, and I was in their sights.

It was at times like these I could not afford to give two shits about my own safety. To second guess myself would only amount to a quick death. I had learned long ago to act upon my instincts and not be intimidated by large, well-muscled men with flouncy yellow hair. Especially when my own hair was just as flouncy.

I drew my sword and leaped from my seat onto the back of a carriage horse. An arrow sprang towards me, but I swatted it away with the flat of my blade. Then I leaped over the horse's head to land in a crouch before Barrett.

Barrett swung his massive blade in my direction. I parried his sword high and launched into a dazzling flurry of sweeps and stabs. I was faster than him, but he was flexible and patient. Our swords *clanged* in the settling light, and my shoulder jolted every time our steel clashed.

Try as I might, I could not score a hit.

He dodged my sweeping blade and brushed off my lightning quick attacks. He used his armor to deflect my much weaker weapon and forced me to move in a wide circle. Sweat stung my eyes, and my heart pounded like mad in my chest.

Barrett was sweating and panting, too, but not half as much as me. And I had not put a single scratch on his armor. I stepped back to catch my breath as the soldiers around us chuckled and grinned.

"Not bad," Barrett laughed as he swung his sword back and forth with easy grace. "But not the unbeatable Ferret we're all so used to hearing about."

"Well, you're every bit as handsome as I'd heard," I replied, simply because I could think of nothing else say. "And I'm honestly a bit jealous."

The golden knight laughed and pressed my guard.

I shifted my feet and sidestepped to my right as I delivered a series of low thrusts at his gut. He parried each one easily, but he crouched a bit more each time, and his guard fell lower and lower. I continued to work at his body until our swordplay grew hypnotizing and my weapon was whittled down a worn-out chunk of steel.

Then I saw my opportunity.

I sprung high and stabbed the magical gem hanging from Barrett's neck. The stone shattered against his hard chainmail, and chips flew in every direction.

Barrett the Golden bellowed as I vanished into thin air.

It was not easy to get away from the soldiers, even when they could not see me. Barrett swept his big sword in every direction, and the soldiers stumbled and reached around like blind mice trying to find a piece of cheese. Queen Gruna wailed like a mad ghost on a windy night.

I wove my way through the throng of grasping hands. I walked away from Queen Gruna and her sobbing. I left behind the "hero" who called himself Barrett the Golden. I walked to the edge of the woods without looking back and then stepped into the peaceful trees.

I took easy strides along deer trails and through open fields. The effects of the sash wore off with every step I took. I lifted my hand and saw parts of myself become visible again, even as the sash fell to pieces, and then to dust.

Soon, I came upon a stream where three weary men washed their faces in the cool water. I hid behind a tree and listened to their conversation.

"Why did our friends turn on us?" Mart asked in a hurt tone that made me bite my lip with regret.

"They think we were part of it," Thoms said. "They think we were working with the Ferret."

"Yeah, bloody Mick tried to hack my head off," Mart said. "And he's been my mate for years."

"That's what we get for trusting people," Thoms said.

"But why would he do that to us?" Mart asked. "Why would he trick us that way?"

"Because people are evil, Mart," Thoms said. "If you haven't learned that by now, you never will."

"I should have seen through his ruse," Jansford said with a disgusted look. "I'm supposed to be the sneakiest bastard alive, not that weasley Ferret."

"Ferrets and weasels really are the same thing." Mart frowned.

"Never mind, you big oaf." Jansford patted Mart on the shoulder affectionately. "Just fill your skin so we can be off."

"But where should we go?" Mart asked. "My whole family is here in Slithora."

"I'm not sure," Thoms said as he filled up his own skin. "But Queen Gruna won't stop until she's got our heads on spikes."

I thought about walking away, but something in my heart broke for these unfortunate men. I was the scoundrel. I was the one who had caused them this trouble. I was the one who had changed their lives forever. All they had done was try to be good soldiers.

I let out a long sigh and stepped out from behind the tree.

"Good men of the Gray Watch," I called with a wave of my hand. "I am Hanser the Ferret, and it seems that I owe you an apology."

ALL MINE

Mercedes Lackey & Dennis Lee

THE GIRL WAS very young and thin. She could have been any age from eleven to fourteen. She might have been biracial, but her dark, straight, short hair gave no clues, and her coloring could have been due to Mediterranean descent, Greek or Italian, or even Spanish. Dr. Marcus Dufresne only knew her as "Subject 0067." The hospital scrubs all the subjects in the Program wore were baggy on her slender frame. From here, he could not see her eyes.

She stared fixedly at a small, foam ball resting between hands flat on the surface of the table where she sat. Every visible line of her radiated tension and effort. Watching her was, frankly, boring. Finally, she let out her breath in a sigh. "I can't," she said, or rather, whispered, apologetically.

"Yes, you can Sixty-seven," came from a speaker in the room; a stern, harsh voice. "Two hours ago, you threw a pitcher full of water at Eighty-eight's head. Now you claim you can't lift a tiny foam ball. You aren't trying."

In another child, that might have elicited an angry response. Not from this one. The girl looked up at the speaker, and a slow tear trickled down her face. Now Marcus could see that her eyes were a sad, deep dark brown, like the eyes of a beaten puppy. "I *am* trying," she whispered. "My head hurts, I'm trying so hard."

"No, you're not!" the voice snapped. *"You're useless! Worthless!"*

Instead of rebelling, the girl shrank into herself, and her features froze into a mask of terror. Her mouth opened and closed, but no sound emerged.

Through the one-way mirror, Marcus watched as another slow tear ran down the girl's face. There was something there. Something familiar. It sparked a brief twinge of despair, a distant memory. He pushed the thought away and glanced back at his tablet, intent on recording the brain wave activity that blipped steadily from the device attached to Subject 0067's cranium.

"There you have it," said the Project Lead, Dr. Joseph Garvey. He was an ugly man, and his looks were not improved by facial and cranial scarring. He had clearly had some cosmetic surgery, but the ropy keloid scars that remained testified he had at one point been severely burned. The injury had to have been substantial; enough that his left arm was either completely cybernetic or in a cybernetic sheathe. The arm hummed at times, and when Garvey lifted something heavy, it whined. Hydraulics, perhaps. It threw Garvey off-balance when he walked, but it was strong enough Marcus had once seen Garvey crush the edge of a metal table during a heated discussion with another of his underlings. "She's perfectly capable of throwing cinder-blocks at people when she's frightened enough, but she can't seem to lift a grain of rice otherwise. And her psychometry is erratic and weaker than we'd like. She can only backtrack about a week before it becomes useless. Think you can do anything with her? You did wonders with Fifty-nine and Seventy-two."

"I'll have her up to speed by your deadline," Marcus murmured, still studying the oscillating waves on his tablet. "This one is different, to be sure. Look here." He turned the tablet towards Garvey and pointed. "There's a strong undercurrent to her efforts. She might not have the baseline strength others have, but she's still developing. Still, look at the regularity of it. She's displaying a resonance that no one else has before. It's solid. I can work with this."

Garvey studied the tablet. "That resonance may be the problem. Something's holding her back. Can you turn it off?"

"I suppose I could," Marcus said. "Not the first thing I would propose though."

"And why's that?"

"It might play havoc with her natural development. You run the risk of it strengthening her ability now, only to have it burn out." Marcus paused. "Oh, and it might kill her."

"What's your point?" Garvey said. "If she dies, we can get more."

"It just seems a waste of a perfectly good subject. Call it instinct. I think there may be much more to this one than a common foot soldier. I'm thinking of the long game here."

Garvey sniffed at Marcus's objections. "When has that ever been an issue? We need working operatives *now*, not at some nebulous point in the future. Besides, children obey; teenagers rebel. They're better for our purposes when either young or old enough to be trained to respond to commands by a superior."

"This one might be different," Marcus argued, although he kept his tone flat and uninflected. "There's potential there for more. Her behavior suggests you might mold her well into adulthood as the perfect operative. If you play this right, she'll follow your orders until her dying breath."

Garvey waved that away. "Operatives *now*, Doctor. Not in the future. Invisible, obedient operatives. No one ever pays a damn bit of attention to children. No one thinks of them as metas."

Marcus shrugged. "As you wish. I can start her on the cocktail immediately." He swiped at his tablet a few times and began to input notes.

"Test Subject 0067," Marcus said, as the tablet dutifully began to record his voice. "Note vitals and tailor the usual cocktail to her specifications. Standard monitoring apparatus." He paused, and shrugged again. "Ignore elevated risks of compromising her immune system, shock, and death. Subject 0067 is expendable."

———•———

VIRTUE HUDDLED IN the corner of her bed farthest from the door. The room was scarcely big enough to hold the bed and a tiny bedside table with a tablet. She had wrapped herself in her blanket and was hugging her pillow, knees to her chest. *They* never allowed her any tissues unless she was actually sick, because they had discovered the little fairies she'd made from them hidden under her mattress. So her sleeve had to do for her sniffles and her pillow to dry her tears.

A gentle tap on her door made her stiffen. "*Querida*, it's me," said a soft, accented voice, and she relaxed, relief flooding through her.

"Ramon!" she exclaimed. "It's okay—"

She didn't need to go any further. The door opened long enough for a lean, tall, Hispanic man in a janitor's coverall to slip inside. He was carrying a teddy bear and a box of tissues.

She reached for the bear first, as he sat down on her bunk, slipped his arm around her shoulders, and held her, pulling out a tissue for her. "Were they very terrible today, *chiquita?*"

"They keep saying I don't try," she said plaintively into his shoulder. "But I *am!* I *am* trying!"

"You do not need to convince me. I know you are," Ramon replied. "I wish I knew how to help you," he added, in frustration. "But I do not. I wish I could take you away. You could be a sister to my little Maria."

"I'd like to have a sister," Virtue said, for what was probably the millionth time.

"Well, you know I am taking night classes to make my English better, and I have just read a story in my English class about sisters," Ramon replied, drying her eyes gently with a tissue. "Once upon a time, there was a beautiful queen. She wanted a child very badly. One day, while a fairy was listening, she stuck her finger while she was embroidering—"

"What's embroidering?" Virtue interrupted.

"It is making pictures on clothing with colored threads and a needle," Ramon said patiently. "It makes clothing prettier."

Virtue examined the hem of her scrub sleeve and sighed. She would never have pretty clothing...

"So she was embroidering, and stuck her finger, and before the blood could soil the sleeve, she held her hand outside the window, so the drop of blood fell on the snow outside instead."

Virtue did not ask what "snow" was. Ramon had explained that to her, and she had looked up pictures on her tablet.

"*Oh*, the queen said. *I wish I could have a little daughter with lips and cheeks as red as blood, and another with skin as white as snow*, she said, and the good fairy, who was listening, and knew she was a good and virtuous queen, nodded, and said, *Let it be so...*"

MARCUS LET THE cold water run over his hands and felt that familiar surge of numbing clarity as the chill set in. He wondered if it was enough, and considered the prospect of a good long shower in freezing water. It had been another bad day, but numbing it away was hardly going to solve his problems. He had just spent hours fruitlessly trying to stimulate Test Subject 0067's brain activity with a diverse barrage of challenges, ranging through electrical, chemical, and even emotional triggers. Nothing seemed to elicit more than a passive blip on his monitors. The remnant spikes he observed in her brain activity after her rare episodes of explosive power suggested she was on the cusp of something unprecedented. There was something in that subject that defied prediction, as if she was on the verge of actually *evolving* into something entirely new. Maybe not *homo superior*, but certainly no longer mere *homo sapiens*. The sharp, staccato spikes that streamed across the screen of his tablet suggested something more to him than neuronal synapses dutifully firing off. They seemed to cry out in a muted rage, shackled and tethered mere inches away from a satisfying and violent release.

He sniffed in distaste. Violence was chaos; it was unrestricted emotion vented out through destructive channels. He had always preferred the calculated order he could impose on his reality. He was a scientist. He loved the elegant task of posing questions and systematically designing and executing experiments to prove or disprove them. Done correctly, conclusions drawn from experimentation could be absolute and overpower any counterpoints founded upon flimsy, nebulous beliefs and pre-existing notions. Any truth could be uncovered by the collection of hard facts. Marcus had never let something as prosaic as morals or emotion lend its voice to the process.

Until the day Emily had told him she was sick, the day Marcus had discovered another part of himself.

Marcus grunted as he pushed the thought away. He didn't have time for it. He had promised Garvey a working assassin before the end of the month, and he was no closer to that goal than he was to his own freedom. It was a long-standing joke in academic circles how most scientists were little more than indentured servants—slaves really—but having now served under not one, but *two* well-funded madmen, Marcus had to wonder when his life had crossed that undefined line from lampoon to full-fledged horror show. He had barely escaped the clutches of Dominic Verdigris III with little more than the shirt on his back, but—he *had* escaped. And he still drew breath. That was something at least, an achievement of sorts, something he was incredibly lucky to have, and he knew it. But there was the problem. How had he been so euphoric from his escape, so grateful for his new-found freedom, that he had stumbled so carelessly into the hands of another crazed scientist?

Still, at least here he was able to continue his own work, to some degree. While Marcus could draw many similarities between Dominic Verdigris III and Dr. Jacob Garvey—in their paranoia, their obsession with success, their indifference to human life—at least Garvey was less hands-on in his approach. He more-or-less trusted his subordinates to do the work and get his results. Their lives depended on it, after all. Verdigris had never been so trusting. It really was a miracle that Marcus had managed to escape.

Be grateful for small "favors."

It helped that Garvey didn't seem to want to be here either. It wasn't just his disdain for his researchers or his impatience for positive, repeatable results. Marcus suspected Garvey approached all aspects of his life in a similar fashion. He could feel it coming off the ugly man in waves. There were more important things to attend to than the unpredictable surges of power in filthy, disgusting, *unreliable* children! Garvey wanted adults who were *like* children in that they could be easily controlled, but were otherwise responsive and predictable. Marcus had long suppressed the notion of correcting Garvey's misplaced notions.

The last thing anyone, man or child, could be was *controlled*, at least in any real way that mattered. Frightened, perhaps, cowed into a superficial state of submission to escape the threat of pain. But short of lobotomizing them, Marcus couldn't see any way to fully control a sentient being. People were too damn stubborn for their own good. Marcus often wondered what the world would be like if people simply obeyed their betters, trusting that the smarter person knew what was best for them.

Emily had never obeyed him. Emily had been something of an annoyance, really. They had been orphaned at a young age, and it had fallen to him to look after her through years of foster care. Between their schooling and the constant moves from one home to another, it had been his duty to make sure she was protected. It was the last promise he made to his parents. She was only nine when they passed. He remembered telling her the news, rather bluntly, and the awkward days that followed; she an inconsolable mess, and he the helpless older brother, clueless as to how to make his sister stop crying. She was sensitive—too sensitive, he thought. When she wasn't sobbing over their dead parents, she was trying to find ways to help the other kids in their foster homes—and worse, making *him* help too. Why should they care about kids they were never going to see again? Soon, they would be moved, and again, and again. They could never find foster parents who could handle both Emily's weakness and his strength. He thought of her as a burden and secretly wished that someone, somewhere, would finally release him of the thankless task of being the only guardian she could ever have.

The day Emily told him she was dying was also the day she finally thanked him, for everything he had ever done for her.

She had always been so different. Where he had excelled in his studies, she never seemed to have the focus required for anything academic. She followed her heart, flitting effortlessly from one endeavor to another, throwing herself into whatever cause, whatever fight against injustice struck her as earth-shattering that week. In that contest, Marcus supposed she was the leader, not him. She was always sure of herself, fully in the moment, and she propelled herself through life with sheer drive.

Until the day she just... stopped.

Perhaps he should have seen it coming, should have recognized the signs early. The blackouts, the sudden lethargic episodes—they should have been a warning of things to come. How had he not taken notice when a girl who never stopping talking, never stopped moving, suddenly resigned herself to sit quietly in the corner of his laboratory at midday, her head nodding off, fighting off inexplicable exhaustion? He didn't even have time to take her to the doctor; his experiments had to come first, of course. So when the diagnosis came in, anaplastic astrocytoma, a rare form of brain cancer, for the first time in his life Marcus had felt a wave of rage and a burning sense of injustice. It had slammed into him, a sucker punch to the gut, a roaring in his head, unlike anything that had come before. The bitter taste of every prior failure paled in comparison: when he had been passed over, repeatedly, for foster care, for scholarships, and even the lost feeling that seemed so overwhelming at the time when his parents had quietly passed away in their hospital beds... nothing could have prepared him for this.

She was just a young girl. A young, earnest girl who had fought for everyone else, every day of her life, despite having nothing herself. Not even, it seemed, an older brother who gave a damn about her. She had nothing to call her own, except her drive, her will to fight, and now even that was slipping away. After she had told him the news, it shocked him how weak she looked, how frail, almost translucent and ethereal. She was dying, and she could do little more than flash him a weak smile and tell him it was going to be all right, that maybe it was just her time. He remembered peering at her, wondering where his sister had gone. Where was the girl who had once rallied an entire school of self-absorbed high schoolers to action, setting up an impromptu blood drive in the wake of one of the worst hurricane disasters to hit the East Coast? Where was the strong, passionate voice that had once cried out against the rise of violence towards women on campus in her freshman year at college, leading a giant protest down Main Street and up the steps of Convocation Hall? She was nowhere to be seen. In her place was a ghost, a mere wisp of the vibrant soul that had given him the strength to go on, for all those years. She was dying. Where was the justice in *that?*

He remembered it so clearly. He remembered himself gasping as she thanked him for taking care of her, for looking out for her, ever since their parents had been taken from them. She was thanking him, when he should have been thanking her. What had he given her, really, that she had not returned tenfold? He remembered reaching out to do something he never remembered doing before. He drew her into his arms and held on for dear life. And he had never really let her go.

She gave him something else that day. A purpose. From that moment on, he had devoted his research to her. In retrospect, he realized he had made some startling advances in the field, but it wasn't enough. Of course it wasn't. There simply wasn't the time, and no one, no matter how brilliant or driven or lucky, could solve something so overwhelmingly complex in a few short years. She held on longer than anyone thought possible. It seemed there was still something of a fighter in her yet. Even now, years after she had slipped into perpetual sleep, Marcus was still looking for his answers.

So much time had passed, and still he was looking. And what was the cost? All that she had given him, was there anything left? His humanity. He had ignored it for so many years, only realizing its value when it was far too late. What little was left felt like it was slipping away. He almost laughed. He wanted to live. He *needed* to live. For her, for Emily. But to live, he had to do some terrible things. To live...

Marcus caught another glimpse of himself in the mirror. This time, he didn't look away. The hard lines that defined his lips, his chin, his cheekbones... they might have been considered handsome, but his eyes...

They held nothing.

They were his eyes, but not just his. He had seen them before, in another face. They were hollow. Dead. He blinked, and winced, watching Garvey's eyes blink back at him.

———————

"...BUT THE HORSES slipped on the glass mountain, and never reached the top," Ramon said, holding Virtue tenderly, as she held the bear. She sighed, and more tears escaped her. He paused in the story, for she usually hung rapt on his every word. "What is the matter, *mi corazón?*"

"I feel like that," she replied, as he gave her a tissue to blot her tears. "All the time. Like I'm on a glass mountain, and no matter what I try, I can never reach the top."

He fell silent, unable to think of anything to say to help her. He had no idea what it was they were trying to get her to do—and even if he knew, these special children, they could all do things that were like magic, and he felt as helpless in his ability to advise them as he was to save them. All he could do was hug her shoulders, wait to hear if she said anything else, and then continue the story. Maybe she would find some clue to help her in the tale. It was, after all, a story about how to do the impossible.

"And all the while this was going on, the king's son was wandering with his oxen..."

———•———

RAMON CLOSED THE door quietly and stowed the bear and tissues under the drape on his cleaning cart. He would have loved to leave both there, but he knew the consequences of doing so would be dire for both himself and the little *muchacha*. He did not mind punishment for himself... but it would be more than punishment for her. She would lose her only friend in this horrible place, *and* they would be even harder on her, if that was possible. They had not resorted to beating her—yet—but he had no doubt they would do so if they thought they would get better results.

The mere thought put him in a rage, a rage he quickly clamped down on. *Results!* Children were precious jewels, the hope of the future, and these men were treating them like... like cans of beans. *Worse.* Like helpless lambs in a slaughterhouse. He seethed, and was so preoccupied he didn't sense the presence behind him until he straightened up from the cart. And by then, of course, it was too late.

It was one of the *scientists.* They wore no nametags, of course. That way if "something happened" none of the underlings could identify them. And they all wore thick goggles that obscured the upper halves of their faces, which would make picking out pictures almost impossible. But Ramon had names for all of them. "The Boss." "The Sneer." "The Nervous One." To Ramon, they all were uncaring, brutal bastards, but this particular scientist chilled him to his core. He never seemed to betray anything about himself. Even his voice was hollow and monotonous. Ramon had named him "The Cold One."

He thought for a moment about greeting him as if nothing was going on, but that in itself might be a betrayal that something was going on. "The staff" were supposed to say nothing to the scientists. Like slaves of old, they were supposed to keep their eyes down and move aside. So that was what he did. He dropped his eyes and touched the cart to roll it to the side so the scientist could pass.

The Cold One didn't move. He stood in place, his hands clasped behind his back, his goggles fixed firmly in place on Ramon. He tilted his head, a curious gesture which Ramon took as quizzical. It was the first hint of emotion he had ever detected in this man.

"You are not allowed to disturb the test subjects," The Cold One said.

Ramon felt a chill. He had been seen. He had heard unsavory things happened to those who did not keep their heads down, to those who meandered from the razor's edge of their duties.

"I heard her weeping, *señor*." Ramon said. "I only went in to see if she was hurt."

The Cold One's head tilted further askew, and Ramon fought down a scream of terror when the man took a step forward, followed by another, and another, until his goggles were near enough Ramon could peer past the tinted glass to see the hard, unforgiving eyes beneath.

"You are not allowed to disturb the test subjects," The Cold One said again.

"*Por favor...*" He reminded himself that his father's father's father's father had fought the Spanish. That his father's father had fought the Nazis. That his own father had been a talented boxer. That he came from a line of fighters. It helped... a little, enough to keep from shaking in tooth-rattling terror of this creature that seemed more like a *thing* than a man. And to manage to choke out a few words, a quote he had heard... somewhere. "'No man stands taller than when he stoops to help a child in need.'"

The Cold One continued to stare at him. Ramon sniffed, stifling a sigh of relief when the goggles finally dropped, only to shudder in fear as The Cold One's gaze came to rest on Ramon's cart. Ramon watched, paralyzed, as a gloved hand reached out and pulled away the drape, revealing a box of tissues and Virtue's teddy bear.

The goggles rose, and Ramon saw the man's eyes again, boring into him.

"You've done this before," The Cold One murmured. "Tell me, Custodian Tomaso, just how tall do you need to be?"

The words came out of him before he could stop them. "As tall as the *muchacha* needs me to be." He gritted his teeth, but it was too late. The words of defiance were out, as was the secret.

"Ah, a man of compassion," The Cold One said. "You don't approve of what we do here, do you?"

"They are *children*—" Again, the words escaped him before he could stop them.

"It is not your *place* to approve or disapprove!" The Cold One barked. Ramon felt his resolve falter as he bent beneath the strength of that icy gaze. "It is not your *place* to do anything more than clean and maintain the infrastructure of these facilities! You are merely a tool—one that performs its duties, keeps its head down, and does not interfere with the delicate projects destined to shape the future of this nation! Is that understood?"

Later, Ramon wondered what had come over him in that instant. Perhaps it was hearing his *querida* referred to as a "delicate project." Perhaps it was time when a man was past all fear. Perhaps it was the spirits of his ancestors, deciding to step in and strengthen his backbone. Perhaps none of these, or all. But he suddenly straightened and said,

"You know *nothing* of children. You do not know that when you starve their hearts, you break them. You do not know that when you do not comfort them, you kill their spirits. And what you do not know is breaking *her*. Soon she will be useless to you. Is that what you want? Can you make a *delicate project* out of a thing that is broken?"

"As a matter of fact, I can. You assume we want them whole, with anything resembling spirit. Frankly, our job would be much easier with their backs broken. I can mold something soft and supple. I can..."

The Cold One took a step back from Ramon and rested his hands on his hips, his head down, as if struggling with indecision.

"*Señor...*"

"Shut up. Just shut up."

The Cold One stood still for a long time. Ramon struggled against his need to retort, that to break Virtue would be to shatter her like a delicate porcelain figure, and there would be nothing left but shards too small to piece together. Finally, the scientist relaxed, and turned to walk away.

"You should really be more careful when you make these visits," the scientist said. "There are eyes everywhere, you know."

"*Señor...*"

"Call me Marcus."

"That's... that is not allowed..."

"You're right, so try to do it only when we're alone, will you?"

The Cold One walked away. Ramon could only stare after him.

———•———

CRYSTAL CLEAR SURVEILLANCE footage played on the video monitor. Everything visible, from each stitch on Marcus's coat to the tiny beads of sweat on Ramon Tomaso's forehead. This was the third time Garvey had played the footage for Marcus, and he froze it as

Marcus walked off camera, the sharp patter of his footsteps growing faint in the distance.

"So. What am I supposed to make of this?" Garvey asked, rhetorically. "That you are encouraging insubordination in the help? Giving the nod to the contamination of my subjects? Is this why we're getting poor results from Sixty-seven?"

"I'm guessing you wouldn't have been so forgiving with him?" Marcus said.

"He's as good as dead," Garvey seethed. "Everyone here is easily expendable. Why do you think I go through the trouble of vetting everyone in this establishment? He's no one. At least, no one that will be missed."

"No one?" Marcus asked. "No family?"

"He did have a daughter, but she died a couple of years ago. He's taking a class or two but if he disappears the school will assume deportation. There's no one left to question his disappearance." Garvey's eyes narrowed. "Or yours, for that matter."

Marcus sighed, and shrugged in a helpless gesture. "I don't suppose you'd be willing to hear me out," he said.

Garvey was on him fast, faster than Marcus would have expected from a burn victim with a heavy metallic arm that swung him off-balance when he turned too quickly. In a flash, Marcus felt the powerful grip of steel fingers throttle him about the neck and heard the shrill whining of hydraulics as Garvey picked him up and slammed him back against the wall.

"You know," Garvey began, "I'm sure it has not escaped your notice that I am not a *patient* man. I have worked long and difficult hours to get where I am. I've sacrificed more than you can imagine to achieve what I have, of myself, and yes, of my *staff*. So don't think for a moment I have any reservation about simply turning you inside-out if I think it will help me in the slightest."

Marcus grunted in pain and tried to speak, but could only manage a hoarse cough.

"Oh dear," Garvey said, relaxing his grip. "I seem to have broken you. Pray, continue Dr. Dufresne. Please, convince me not to kill you, Subject 0067, and this meddlesome janitor right here, right now, and move on to the next subject."

"Y... y... you..."

"Really, man, you need to speak up," Garvey said. He released Marcus, who fell to the ground in a heap, breathing heavily and holding his throat in pain.

"You're..." Marcus wheezed. "You're missing an opportunity here."

"Oh, this should be *rich*," Garvey sighed. "You have thirty seconds. Convince me."

Marcus exhaled, drew a few deep breaths, and began.

"I've done a full analysis of her resting power. That's what we've been seeing, that mature, low-level resonance that's always in play when we record. We almost got the full read, once. It was coming back to rest after her last display, but we were too late to get a decent pattern. We need to have a recording *during* a full telekinetic flash. And the closest we've come since is when we threatened to throw Subject 0013 into the sensory deprivation tank for a week. The green one. The one the subjects call 'Gremlin.' She seemed to have some concern for the boy. What if we could use that? Run the scanners, get a full reading, *just one*, and I assure you everything you need to unlock her talents will be found there."

Garvey knelt down and pulled Marcus in close by his shirt.

"And how do you propose we do this?"

Marcus glared back at Garvey, and told him.

———

THE ATTENDANTS BROUGHT her in, dropping her unceremoniously in her chair. Test Subject 0067 slumped forward, face and body rigid with apprehension, her hair already clumping with nervous sweat. Without a word, Marcus stepped forward and attached the sensor to the base of her neck. There was a soft click, followed by a gentle hum as the device flared to life.

"There now," Marcus said, stepping back. He brought his tablet up and checked her vitals. All systems seemed normal, and the steady, resonant waves began to oscillate across his readouts, like clockwork. "I think we're just about ready to begin."

Test Subject 0067 stirred and gave him a furtive glance.

"No tests today?" she mumbled quietly.

"And why would you think that?" Marcus asked, his fingers tapping his tablet, queuing up the standard equilibrations and baseline monitors.

"Because…" The girl hesitated, and looked about, flinching as she caught her reflection in the one-way mirror. "Because you're in here, with me. Not in there." She pointed at the mirror. "You're safe in there. In here…"

"You think I'm in any danger?" Marcus asked. "Really, Sixty-seven, you've hardly done anything dangerous. Yet. I'm in here today to try and change that. I think we can give you a nice little boost and see what you're really made of. Would you like that?"

The girl didn't answer, at first. Finally, she nodded. Clearly she had learned it best to always agree.

"Very good," Marcus murmured. "If it helps, you might be happy to know that today we're not interested in hurting you at all."

Slowly, the girl raised her head. There were tears in her eyes, and a wild hope.

"R… really?" she said.

"Really," he answered.

"No shocks?"

"No shocks."

"No gas?"

"Not a bit."

She stumbled through a wavering sigh of relief and gingerly wiped away her tears.

"Thank you," she whispered. "Oh, thank you…"

"No, I thought we would do something a little different today, Sixty-seven." Marcus looked over at the mirror and nodded. "It seems you've made a friend here. I thought you could use some company right now. Would you like to see him?"

The girl looked simultaneously elated and terrified. "I don't have any friends! Don't hurt Gremlin! He doesn't even know who I am!"

"Oh no, no," Marcus said. "No, no, no, not Subject 0013. I don't think he'd provide the…" Marcus paused, scratching his head theatrically, "…the *depth* we would require for today's agenda."

The girl stared at him.

"I don't have any friends," she repeated. "The other kids don't talk to me, they…"

She paused as the door swung open, and a man strapped firmly down to a gurney was rolled in. He was frightened, shivering, his hands clenched into tight fists at his side. He turned to look at the girl and tried to give her a reassuring smile. Instead, he looked phrenetic and crazed.

The girl screamed. "Ramon!"

"Yes, Ramon," Marcus said, waving the attendants out of the room. He strolled over to the gurney, looking down at the struggling man with a curious tilt of his head. He glanced up, and the girl shrank from him, sobbing uncontrollably.

"P… please…" she stammered. "D… don't hurt him! Oh please, don't hurt…"

"Then show me!" Marcus barked. "Show me what you can do!"

"Yes! Please! I'll do anything you want me to! Just…"

"We're out of patience, Subject Sixty-seven! You have power! You've used it before! We want a full demonstration, *now*, or…"

Marcus paused, as Ramon stopped struggling and glared up at him.

"Her name is Virtue," Ramon hissed.

"I do beg your pardon?" Marcus said.

"Her name is Virtue," Ramon repeated. "She's not some number. She's a child, and she has a *name*!"

"Of course, she does," Marcus agreed. "Very well. Where was I? Ah. *Virtue*. We want a full demonstration, and right quick. If I have to ask you again, I don't think Ramon here is going to have a very good day."

Virtue's eyes overflowed with tears, which ran unheeded down her cheeks, dripping onto the front of her smock. She shook, her hands clenching and unclenching. The blood drained from her face until she was almost the same color as the smock itself. "I… I can try…"

Virtue braced herself, laying her hands flat on the table in front of her. Completely rigid, she stared at the foam ball on the table before her.

Nothing happened.

Marcus picked up the scalpel from the tray beside him and jammed it into Ramon's shoulder.

Ramon's whine of agony was drowned out by Virtue's scream. *"Stop it! Stop it! Leave him alone! I'm trying, can't you see I'm trying?"*

But the balls didn't move. Not even a fraction of an inch. Clearly this was going to require an extraordinary level of stimulation.

He twisted the scalpel, and with clinical precision, dissected out the brachial plexus, laying it bare to the air. Ramon's screams rang in his ears, and Virtue—*Sixty-seven's*—screams echoed them on a higher note. Marcus fought down an urge to join them. This was getting out of hand. For once, he was thankful for the goggles and the half-mask that Garvey made all the scientists and technicians wear. Keeping his hands steady from shaking was one thing, but if anyone could see his face they would know. They would see his doubt. He glanced at the mirror and could feel Garvey's cold eyes staring back at him. Marcus felt an odd tingle about his neck, where Garvey had so callously wrapped his metallic fingers around the day before.

He struggled with indecision, staring down at the screaming man, at the exposed nerve bundle glistening with a sheen of blood, and the blood dripping down the shoulder, onto the stainless steel of the gurney, and from there to the floor. This... this was wrong. People weren't... things, objects to be manipulated and broken. They weren't disposable. Were they? They weren't, surely. *Were they?*

It seemed an eternity, but then one, singular, sharp sound broke his concentration. A sharp rap on glass.

He looked up at the mirror. He felt Garvey's impatience. He felt what little tolerance Garvey had for him rapidly coming to an end. In a moment, Garvey would summon security, and he would die along with the janitor.

It was only a janitor. No one of importance. The man's last link to anything had died along with his daughter in a school bus crash. No one would care when he was gone—no one except the single person Marcus *needed* to goad into the full eruption of her potential.

Him, or me. Or him and *me.* It was no choice at all. He couldn't die. He had too much to do. For Emily.

With a single swift incision, he slit the carotid artery. Blood fountained over the edge of the gurney in a long arc. Marcus felt something snap inside of him. He had done it... dear lord, he had done it...

He glanced at Sixty-seven, bracing himself, expecting to see the horror of the moment consume everything else on that young frail face. She would likely be crying. Those who witnessed her last episode swore that her eyes had lit up in a brilliant silver flash, so he braced himself for that as well. Instead, he saw something else.

She wasn't Sixty-seven—*Virtue*—anymore. In her place, he saw another. He saw Emily's face.

And it was angry.

After that, there was nothing but incredible, excruciating pain as he smashed into the wall behind him. Then into the wall to the left. Then to the right. The ceiling, the floor, and the ceiling again. And now, barely conscious, he felt himself flung through the one-way glass, smashing it, to land in a shower of shards at Garvey's feet. His body was screaming, bent in odd angles. He was screaming as well. He heard himself stop, coughing, wheezing, and he stared, astonished, as a bloody froth erupted from his mouth.

Above him, Garvey peered over his tablet and flashed him a grin.

"Reading complete," Garvey said. "Well done, Dr. Dufresne."

Marcus stared back at him.

"You look dreadful," Garvey noted, sighing. "Those wounds are clearly... oh, what is the word... ah! Mortal. I doubt you would even last the trip to the infirmary. Still, you never know. We do perform miracles here, don't we?"

There are no miracles, Marcus thought, sinking into the black.

———

FAMILIAR SOUNDS PENETRATED the deep and formless blackness. The steady beep of a heart monitor. The whine of an overhead fluorescent light. Pings and clicks and hums of other medical equipment, all comforting in their familiarity. Cold comfort, but still, comfort,

Thoughts swam up, like curious fishes.

I'm not dead.

Where am I?

Why am I not dead?

A face appeared out of the shadows. Emily. Emily enraged, as he had last "seen" her. He cringed. And to avoid looking at that angry face any more, he opened his eyes.

And winced away from the light, that cold, pitiless fluorescence he had heard.

"Welcome back, Dr. Dufresne."

Marcus knew that voice. It filled him with an icy resolve. He let his eyes adjust to the light and looked around. There were the monitors, the IV drip, and next to his bed there was the man himself, Dr. Joseph Garvey.

"Where's Virtue?" Marcus said.

"I'm sorry, who?"

"Virtue," Marcus repeated. "Subject 0067."

"Oh, you need not worry about her anymore," Garvey said. "She's progressing nicely. No, Dr. Dufresne, I think our time would be better spent discussing *you*, and what a pleasant surprise you've turned out to be."

Marcus didn't respond, and instead tried to prop himself up on the bed. He felt some alarm as his arms refused to move. He strained to look down at himself, and snarled as something blocked his chin. Was he paralyzed? If this was paralysis, it wasn't like anything he would have imagined. For one thing, his senses seemed, if anything, ramped up. He could swear he felt slight eddies and shifts in the air around him. He thought he could taste a faint antiseptic perfume on

Garvey, almost masking the metallic, oily aroma wafting off Garvey's metallic arm. Marcus felt alert, energized, *alive*. He tried to lift his head again, and caught a disturbing sight before he let his head fall back down again.

His body was in a full metal restraining suit.

"What have you done?" Marcus demanded, glaring up at Garvey, who smirked in return.

"I saved your life, you ungrateful twit," Garvey muttered. "And more. You, Dr. Dufresne, are the first successful test subject of the next stage of the *Icarus Project*. I suppose I should thank you. It seems being so close to death was an unforeseen exploit for portions of the process. Pity, if only we had known that before. So many test subjects lost to pointless, stubborn attempts by my witless team. As for you, virtually every bone in your body was broken. You had multiple internal ruptures and bleeding, and severe head trauma. As I told you at the time, I frankly had no expectation you would make it as far as the infirmary. In any case, it would seem that congratulations are in order. Believe me when I say I am *very* intrigued by what you are now capable of. We'll let you rest for a spell, of course. You will be very weak for a while. We will need to monitor you quite closely while you recover."

Garvey rested his metal hand gently on Marcus's chest, and smiled.

"But when you're ready, oh my boy… you will be a wonder. The first of many. So believe me when I say, I *shiver* to think of the possibilities."

"You can't keep me here," Marcus seethed. "I did what you wanted. I got your results. A deal's a deal, Garvey."

"The situation has changed, dear boy," Garvey said. "You are now far more valuable to me than ever before. You can't think for a moment I would simply let my crowning achievement just… *leave*."

"You can't keep me here," Marcus repeated.

"Of course I can," Garvey scoffed. "Like all my employees and subjects, you were vetted. There's no one to miss you. There's no one to come looking for you. You are mine, Dufresne, and the sooner you accept that, the easier your life will be. You are alone. Best you accept that."

"I'm not alone," Marcus said, struggling within his iron prison. "I'm not! I..."

"You have no one," Garvey said. "You had... what... a sister? A sister who died years ago? I had you investigated quite thoroughly, you know. She was the only one, and from what I understand, you failed her. Spec-*tac*-ularly. You were supposedly a brilliant neurodegenerative specialist, Dufresne, but let's be blunt, hmmm? You were always a failure. And now, you are the first in a new, highly advanced line of prototypical meta-soldiers! You have me to thank for that."

Garvey leaned in closer and smiled again.

"Isn't it about time you did something *right*?"

Marcus didn't answer and continued to struggle against his restraints, for all the good it did him. He was stronger, much stronger, he could feel it, but it didn't seem to matter against the iron maiden that deadened any of his attempts to flex his muscles. He supposed he wasn't the first metahuman Garvey had to restrain. The suit would be reinforced, of course. It had to be. Metahumans, especially newly minted ones, had a tendency for rage. Aside from the moment Emily announced her diagnosis, Marcus could not remember a time he had ever felt rage. Some people just didn't have the temperament for it. Instead, he felt what he always felt when on the defensive—an icy resolve to turn the tide, to find a weakness to exploit, to *win*.

He buzzed with energy. It was a strange sensation and so surreal— to be so confined and helpless, yet suffused with so much vigor and life. And it was growing. He exhaled, a faint and cold mist trailing off his lips. It felt odd and out of place. Under the harsh lights and encapsulated in a heavy metal prison, the room had felt so warm...

"I asked you a question, Dufresne," Garvey said.

Marcus grunted, his breath steaming in the cold air.

"I asked you a question. Are you ready to finally do something *right*?"

Marcus glared at him and sneered.

Garvey sighed, and began to pull away. "A pity," he said. "Breaking your spirit will take time, and I was so hoping we could skip the dreary preliminaries and hit the ground running. Ah well. I suppose it was too much to ask for. I suppose it—" Garvey stopped, a puzzled expression on his face. He shook his arm, but it appeared to be stuck fast to the restraining suit, fused palm down to Marcus's chest.

"What in the—"

Garvey's eyes widened as wispy ropes of vapor flowed from his metallic hand and a frosty rime traveled up the arm. Garvey couldn't move; he was pinned in place, immobilized as a sudden chill had fused them together, a chill that intensified in waves from Marcus's suit, from Marcus himself...

Marcus felt the energy crescendo and let it flow over him, through him. In a sudden explosive burst he lashed out, shattering his now brittle prison into jagged pieces. Already he was moving, bounding from the confines of the bed, on his feet, his hand lashing out, gripping the astonished Garvey about the throat and ramming him back against the wall.

Garvey gurgled his surprise and tried to swing his arm. Nothing happened. The sound of the arm's hydraulics moaned and stopped. The arm shuddered in place and shattered, pieces falling to the floor, trailing wisps of vapor from the extreme cold, leaving nothing but a bloody stump that flailed wildly from his shoulder.

Marcus glanced at the stump, and back to Garvey.

"Oh dear," Marcus said. "I seem to have broken you."

He brought Garvey in close and scowled as he held the frightened man's eyes with his own.

"Now then. Where is *Virtue?*"

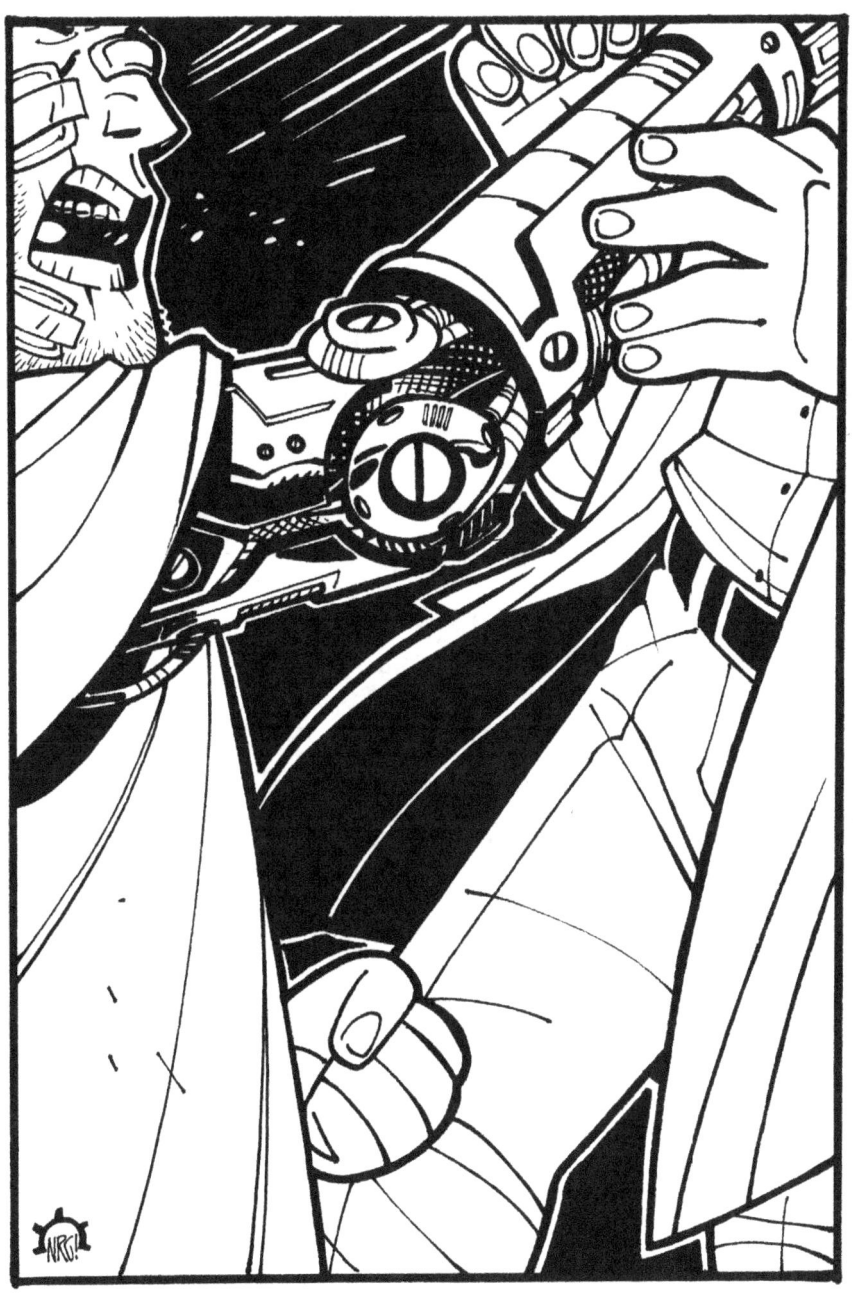

HUNGER IN
THE BONES

Anton Strout

THE STRANGER TRAVELED on, only glancing out through the hut's crooked doorway when he noticed the distant pinpoints of light becoming discernible flickering torches. Fire could go either way, he had learned, depending on the civil sophistication of those wielding it. After all, one was never sure how well a lurching hut propelled on giant chicken legs would be received by the locals.

He closed the massive tome spread open across his lap, lowered it into his satchel with care, and positioned his lanky body in the doorway as he warily surveyed the citizenry of the small Polish town he and his hut were entering. When the villagers and their torches stayed where they were and did not charge upon the stranger's arrival, he relaxed against the door's frame.

All across Europe, the names of the towns might be different, the architecture, too—certainly the languages—but here he saw what he'd hoped for on the faces of the villagers below—wide-eyed wonderment.

Good. Very good, in fact. It meant fewer complications from an ignorant populace and hopefully a quick retreat after the task at hand had been accomplished.

Not all the faces, however, expressed happiness with his appearance on the outskirts of their village. Many a wary and untrusting eye fixed on the gaunt outsider in the hut's doorway, his arms spread wide to resist the sway of the slapdash-looking building. Inevitably, their eyes shifted as if in unison down to the source of the hut's propulsion. Dull orange legs that ended in clawed toes edged forward though the parting crowd, and with a wave of a thin hand the stranger stopped the hut in its tracks.

Trampling the locals was bad for business, a lesson he had unfortunately learned the hard way over the last thirty years. And here especially he and his hut needed to tread with care.

Throwing his satchel across his body, the stranger lowered a rope ladder to the ground below and clambered down. Rather than greeting him, the villagers continued to stare while he pulled back his long black hair into a tight ponytail, adjusted his cravat and smoothed down the front of his suit.

"What?" he asked, unable to hide a bit of disdain in his voice. "You act like you've never seen a dwelling propelled by enormous chicken legs before…"

Some of the crowd flinched away visibly, while others threw their hands up in wards against evil, spitting on the ground where the giant chicken feet clawed and scratched. Other gazes, thankfully, still held that initial sense of wonderment.

"What is such a thing?" an older man in the crowd called out, staring wide-eyed up at the hut.

"Come come. Don't tell me you've never been tormented by the Yaga?" One of the stranger's hands reached into his satchel, pulled free a large leather volume, and began flipping through it. He consulted the pages within for a full minute before slamming it shut. "No, no, of course not. Never you mind."

As deftly as he had removed the book, the stranger slipped it back in his satchel.

A man dressed far too well for so late an hour—a gold-embroidered cape covering hints of a well-fitted coat, waistcoat and fine white linen shirt beneath—stepped forward from the crowd. Tufts of thin gray hair stuck out from beneath the *rogatywka* he wore, his forced smile not quite reaching his puffy eyes.

"Welcome to the village of Czermna," the man said and offered up his pudgy hand.

The stranger ignored the hand completely, and gave the man a cursory but disapproving look up and down. "I take it you are Mayor Wójcik?"

The man's smile faltered and he lowered his hand slowly. "You are indeed correct, sir," the mayor said. "How could you tell?"

The stranger gave a dismissive wave as he surveyed the crowd of villagers and their torches. "You're fatter than the rest. In my dealings, those who live highest on the hog tend to most resemble one."

"I beg your pardon?" the mayor said, shock and irritation full in his voice.

An older woman wrinkled by decades of life scrunched up her sour face at the stranger and moved closer. "*This* is the one, Wójcik?" Her thin boned hands plucked at the stranger's arms. "I thought the help you summoned would be more rugged. Like hunter."

Without hesitation, the stranger batted the old woman's hand away from his sleeve and sneered. "Have you ever heard the phrase do not judge a book by its cover?"

The old woman spit at the stranger's feet and made the sign of the cross. The mayor held a hand up as he eased the old woman back in to the crowd. He turned to the stranger, his face full of apology.

"Please, sir, our people cannot take this any longer. But my *obywatel* here brings up a valid point. Rumors that reached our village led me to believe you could help, but… please forgive me, you seem more scholar than fighter."

The stranger, however, paid him no mind, and having pulled his book back out of his satchel, he furiously scribbled in it, his quill scratching across its pages.

"Are… are you writing all this down?" the mayor asked. The stranger nodded, but didn't stop writing. "Why?"

"The devil is in the details," the stranger said, "or so my experience has led me to believe. If you must know, I am a collector of tales. We are, after all, the stories we tell."

The mayor's eyes narrowed with uncertainty. "And this will help our village how exactly?"

"That remains to be seen."

"And your price?" the mayor asked. If the man had looked any more sheepish, a wooly tail would have sprung from the seat of his pants.

"That remains to be seen as well," the stranger said. "I have yet to assess the threat to your village, but there *is* a threat here, yes?"

The mayor nodded. "Times have been hard on my people, as far as coin goes. Few visitors dare to venture to our humble hamlet. What I mean to say is that we don't have much."

The stranger smiled. "What price can one truly put on peace of mind?" The mayor's face went white, and the stranger could not help but chuckle. "Do not fret. My fee will be… reasonable. Now what seems to plague you and your people?"

"All we know," the mayor said, "is that people disappear from time to time, and they seldom come back."

The stranger looked closer at the village spread out before him. Even in the dim light of the gathered torches, he could see the cracks in the plaster of its buildings, the unkempt and muddy paths of cobblestones desperately in need of repair.

"Maybe those missing villagers have simply become disenchanted with so humble a place to dwell."

"Do not insult our village," the mayor said in anger, surprising the stranger by showing the first hint of a backbone. "We cannot help the state of our town when there are things that walk the night here driving others away."

The stranger held a hand up as an apology. "Do you wish my help or not?" he asked plainly.

The fire on the mayor's face died and his expression switched to something the stranger couldn't quite interpret. At a guess, the mayor looked both sad and full of regret, but for the moment, the village leader fell and remained silent.

"As I thought," the stranger said. "Now, what can you tell me about that which preys upon your village?"

"We aren't sure," the mayor said, "save for the yearly disappearances that occur within our village. They don't happen often, but our people know to board their homes securely at night, to shutter their windows, yet still whatever lurks in the darkness manages to find victims nonetheless. Tonight, however, there is one who has lived to tell from the latest attack. A girl. Jadwiga. The poor young thing was discovered earlier this evening cowering in the church yard, but she has fallen silent to our queries."

The stranger closed his book and slid it back into his satchel with a grim smile. "Rest assured, she will answer me."

The mayor blanched at the words and the severe tone with which the stranger dealt them.

"You're… you're not going to hurt her, are you?" the mayor asked.

The stranger sighed, then addressed not only the mayor but the assembled crowd of villagers behind him. "Fair citizens of Czermna, I apologize if I come off as harsh or insensitive. Long years of religious and arcane study have made me a bit unfit for human interaction, but make no mistake. Time is critical and the quicker I can assess your situation, the faster you can return to your miserable little lives." The stranger's eyes shifted back to the mayor, a wide but wholly insincere smile filling his face. "Now, if you would be so kind, please show me this girl."

The mayor gestured for the stranger to follow him through the village, which he did as a parade of townsfolk fell in behind them. The no doubt once beautiful town felt familiar to the stranger, but was perhaps so far from its former glory that all he could feel was a bittersweet sadness at the state of it.

At the far end of the village, placed far enough away to not be too much of a reminder of the fragility of life, stood Czermna's one church, and off to its left, a sprawling graveyard that rolled over hill and dale off into the darkness. Even the most recent grave markers were faded, chipped or slanting, and the oldest were worn with weather and age.

Several villagers stood crowded at the side of the church around a ramshackle wooden shed. Their ranks parted as the stranger approached, revealing a child who looked no more than ten curled up against the moss covered back wall of the shed. Her blond hair lay in braids over her shoulders, the only bright spot against the dirty farm girl clothes that she wore. Thin, clean trails ran from her eyes down through the grime on her cheeks.

"Hello there, my dear," he said. The stranger approached and extended one of his bony hands to her.

The frail thing recoiled, backing further against the back wall of the shed. If it were possible to burrow through the actual wall, there was little doubt she would do it.

The mayor stepped closer and grabbed the stranger's wrist, drawing the man's hand away. "Can't you tell she's terrified?"

The stranger's eyes fell to his wrist and sneered at the hand holding it, driving the mayor back from him as he pulled free.

"Is she?" he asked as he considered it. "I never know how to read children."

"Jadwiga hasn't spoken since one of the women found her cowering here in the church yard."

The stranger examined the girl's dirty, frightened face. "But something you've seen put such fear in you, didn't it, Jadwiga?" The girl's name hung on his lips with an almost familiar taste, and he watched as she nodded in response.

Kneeling, but keeping his distance, the stranger spoke in a soft tone. "My dear child, can you tell me what put you to such a fright?"

Jadwiga thought for a moment, then gave a barely perceptible shake of her head.

"I told you," the mayor said with irritation as he repeated himself. "She won't speak."

"Nonsense," the stranger said. "Of course she will. Look at the face of this poor frightened child. In my humble experience, that is the face of someone who has a terribly interesting tale to unfold, wouldn't you say?"

"She hasn't spoken to any of us," the mayor said, but the stranger silenced him with a withering look before turning with a sweet smile back to the girl.

"There is no need for this foolish fear, my dear," he said, then lowered his voice to a whisper only the girl could hear. "I can make the bad things go away."

Hope crept into the still skeptical look on the girl's face, and her lips parted.

"H-h-how?" her thin, cracked voice managed to croak out.

The stranger's eyes lit up. "Ah, so you are capable of speech!" He reached into his satchel and produced the book once more, drumming his fingers down the spine of the great tome. "With this."

The girl's nose scrunched up, and her face fell in disappointment. "A book?"

The man nodded. "This is no ordinary tome, though. These pages help me take away the bad things, but in order to do so, I will have to know *your* tale."

The girl's eyes lit up with hope. "That will make the white cave go away?"

The spine of the book creaked as the man opened the tome and pulled the quill out of its special inkwell and casing hidden inside the spine. "Tell me about this white cave."

The girl's eyes searched the faces of her fellow villagers who stood both inside and outside of the shed while she struggled to find the words. When they did not come to her, the man closed his tome and rose. Once again, he extended his hand out to her.

"Come," he said in a pleasant, even tone. "Show me this cave of yours."

After a bit more coaxing and hand holding from the stranger, the reluctant Jadwiga started off back into the furthest reaches of the graveyard. Judging by the worn and often rudimentary headstones, the stranger assessed their trek would lead them to one of its oldest sections. When they finally stopped, most of the crowd of villagers had petered off as the girl pointed off into the darkness.

"This must be the place," the stranger said. The girl's hand trembled in his.

"*Potwór*," she said.

Even with the lanterns and torches of the remaining crowd it was hard for the stranger to see where exactly the girl was directing him, but after a few minutes in the darkness his eyes adjusted. Before them, a barrow rose between two headstones which then sloped down into the ground.

"*Potwór*," the girl repeated.

"Monster," the stranger said, and the girl nodded.

The stranger turned to the mayor and what little of the crowd remained. "Has not one of you in this village found the bravery to venture forth? None of you?"

Eyes shifted away from his gaze as the stranger tried to meet theirs with his, but only the mayor would look at him.

"I'm afraid there are none who would have discovered such a place," the mayor said. "This part of the cemetery has not been cared for in decades."

While the stranger heard the mayor's words, his eyes never left the crowd. "Shame on you," he said. "Shame on all of you."

The silence that answered him was deafening. Rather than waste his time, the stranger stepped towards the barrow. If he bent over, he could fit his lanky form into the entrance to shine his light, but even with the lantern the darkness from within was almost palpable.

He turned and looked to the girl still holding his hand. "*White cave?* Are you sure?"

The girl nodded, but made no effort to move closer, her hand locked with the stranger's own. "You'll see."

The stranger gave her hand a reassuring squeeze. "No harm will come to you while you are under my protection," he said. "This I promise."

"Who's going to protect *you*?" scoffed the mayor.

The stranger whirled around to face him. "Certainly not the likes of you." Silence. "Any further comments from you, or anyone else in this miserable little town?" Silence. "I thought not. Now be still and let me help this poor girl, and for that matter, the rest of your pathetic lot."

The stranger proceeded forward towards the opening in the ground, but the girl stood stone still. He turned to her and spoke in a soft gentle tone.

"You don't have to go first, Jadwiga, but you will have to be terribly brave and come with me. As I said, no harm will come to you." The stranger patted his satchel with reassurance and when he smiled at the girl, she met his with a nervous one of her own.

"Very well," she said.

"Godspeed," the mayor muttered and crossed himself.

The stranger shook his head. "I do not think God cares much for these types of goings-on. Rest assured, I will get to the bottom of this. If, however, for some reason we do not return, be sure to feed my traveling hut. As of late, it has had a peculiar craving for rabbit. I'm not quite sure why."

Lantern in one hand and the girl in his other, the stranger ducked into the barrow. The steep downward slope and twisted turns meant every step was a fight to keep both he and the girl from tumbling forward, but soon the ground evened out into a more open cavern somewhere beneath the cemetery.

"So this is what you do?" the little girl asked. "Travel from village to village collecting such stories?"

"More or less," the stranger said.

"That book you write in is quite thick," she said.

"That's because I've heard quite a lot of stories," he said. "No two the same, mind you, but all unique and quite special in their own way."

As the stranger pressed forward, the light of the lantern began to penetrate the darkness more and more. After a few moments, the reason—along with the meaning of *white cave*—became clear. Light reflected off the white of the walls deep down in the burrow where piles of neatly stacked bones and skulls lined the space from floor to ceiling. Whole and identifiable pieces—leg bones, arms, ribcages, full skulls—stretched off into the far distance of the barrow as far as the stranger could make out.

"I see I'm not the first to come this way," he said. "And I think your village's problem may be even older than the rumor that led me here."

"I thought our mayor summoned you?" the girl asked.

"He did," the stranger said as he moved down the line of bones, "but I've been following certain types of rumors throughout Europe since I was a boy."

"Oh?" Jadwiga said. "Where were you raised?"

"That part's never been quite clear to me," the stranger said. "I'm afraid those memories have all been repressed. Lost as the result of a traumatic childhood, I suspect."

"Something more traumatic than *this*?" the girl asked.

"No," he said, running his hands over a perfectly clean set of ribs on the wall. "As exactly traumatic as this, now that I think of it."

The girl's hand fell from the stranger's as she backed away.

"What sort of rumor brought you here?" she asked.

"There was a tale of a village," the stranger said, flipping through his book until he found the pages he was looking for. "A tale older that most of those still living amongst us. One of a great darkness that must be fed. For centuries the citizens of this one village used to disappear, all throughout the year, and no one knew why or to where. Grief and sorrow filled this town. Its prosperity faltered and its numbers dwindled. Late every evening, their people would whisper dark tales by candlelight while they latched their windows shut and barred their doors. Terrible tales, really. Parents warned their children, as all parents do, about the dangers out there in the world, but, being children, all did not listen. The version of the tale that made its way to me spoke of two young friends—the 'bestest' of friends, it was said—who disappeared together nearly a quarter century ago."

"That's a long time ago," the young girl said.

"Yes," the stranger agreed. "Too many lives have passed since last I was here."

Jadwiga cocked her head at him. "You've been here before?"

The stranger nodded. "As a boy, yes. That's the problem with rumors, with stories, if you don't write them down. People get the details wrong. Talk of the two missing children spoke of those 'poor girls,' and while it's true that those children were best of friends, not both were girls, no. One was a boy. A young boy who fled when he first saw the horrors down here. A boy who has had to live to adulthood carrying the tremendous guilt of running away, of leaving his friend behind. A boy who has spent a lifetime trying to alleviate that guilt and find a way to combat such evil so he could atone for abandoning his friend. He's grown older, become a man…" The stranger stopped, lost in contemplative thought, then turned with a cold eyed stare to face the little girl. "But you, Jadwiga, haven't aged a day in the past twenty-five years since I saw you last, have you?"

The little girl's smile grew into a wicked grin that threatened to crack her face in two. "I thought your bones smelled familiar," she said.

The smile on the girl's face continued to grow to an impossible width, to the point where her skin tore open and the top half of her head fell back. Her hands clawed at the sides of her head, taking purchase on the loose flesh there and peeling it down her body, a creature with more bones than could possibly fit inside the skin crawling free of the girl's form. When it was done, the creature held up the husk of the girl, examining it as one might a fancy suit they considered buying.

"Oh, I remember your girl," the creature whispered growled in a deeper, different voice from that of Jadwiga. "I've killed thousands in my time, but I do remember. She has, after all, served me well these many years since you left her here. She died in agony, you know. In confusion, with one pathetic thought in her foolish little head—*why had her friend abandoned her?*" The creature turned the girl's torn apart face to the stranger. "How could he leave her to die so?"

"Enough!" shouted the stranger, readying his book. "There is no trickery of words you can twist that can cause me more pain than I have caused myself."

"We'll see about pain," the creature said, dropping the empty husk of the girl to the floor of the cave, "when I rend your flesh from your bones. Then I'll add what's left of you to my collection."

The creature stretched its form to its full extent, arms wide and claws open. Dust fell from the ceiling as the walls of the burrow shook and the bones comprising them came free as they moved to join the creature's body. Like the heavy armor of a knight, they amassed on the figure until the creature rose to twice the height of the stranger. "Fear not. You and your precious Jadwiga will be reunited."

"I don't think so," the stranger said as he pulled the quill from the book's spine with the hand that held the lantern. "Yours is not the first tale to be recorded in my book. The stories we tell about ourselves are true, binding. Judging from these walls, all the years and sorrows, I am sure there is indeed a much longer tale that wound be both horrific and delicious to unfold, but for my needs, what I have should suffice for my purposes."

One of the creature's bone covered arms lashed out at the stranger, who moved, but not quite fast enough. The jagged claws caught on the lantern, pulling it free of his hand and sending it crashing off against the side of the barrow. The flame quickly sputtered and died, submerging the space into sheer darkness.

The stranger backed away from where the creature had stood, then stopped.

The quill. Where was the damned quill?

It had been in the same hand that held the lantern, but now it was gone. Without hesitation the stranger dropped to his knees and began feeling around the dirt floor of the barrow.

Somewhere in the darkness, a young girl's giggle filled the air and the voice of Jadwiga called out. "You wouldn't hurt the little girl you abandoned down here so many years ago, now would you?"

Despite the words sending a cold knife into the core of his heart, the stranger continued his search unabated. "If I thought any true part of her remained, no. But it will soothe my soul some simply to lay what's left of that girl to rest here today."

"But the mayor and I have come to such a beautiful arrangement," the creature's true voice growled out. "I spare his precious people and once a year he quells my hunger by bringing unsuspecting fools to this wretched little town for me to feast upon."

Bones clacked in the darkness, closer than the stranger wanted, but he didn't dare stray from the site he desperately searched.

"Your failure of that little girl will be your eulogy," the creature called out as if to taunt him.

"That failure is one I've lived with for far too long," the stranger said and let out a sigh of relief as his hand fell upon the feathery part of the quill. He quickly snapped it up into his hand. "Now it's time to write a different ending, one where I don't back down. We are, after all, the stories we tell. This time there will be no running away."

Even in complete darkness, the stranger could easily set quill to page, and almost as easily, spell out one simple word.

Lamp.

A glow erupted from the pages in the stranger's hand and he reached for them—through them, into them—pulling up until the named object rose from the book and hung from his hand.

The bone creature stood poised far too close to his left side, ready to leap, but it paused as it saw the stranger's feat. "What sorcery is this?" it hissed out.

"I've dedicated my life to stopping that which threatens humanity just so I could return here, learning all in the arcane world that I could. The Yaga, Barbagazi, Melusine, even banshees. All in preparation for a return to this cathedral of bones, all to vanquish you." Setting the lamp down, he pressed the tip of his quill to the tome's page.

The words came fast and furious, flying from the stranger's quill to the pages of the book. In response, the creature cried out in agony, huge piles of bones sloughing off its form and scattering to the dirt floor of the barrow.

"In these pages, your story ends," he said.

Despite the panic on the bone creature's face, it was the sweet girl's voice that spoke sadly and softly from it. "You would not harm so youthful and innocent a creature such as I. You promised no harm would come to me, remember?"

"No harm *will* come to you," the stranger said, his quill unwavering. "Or to this village for that matter. I'll give you the safety I promised. You'll be perfectly preserved, immortal, forever in the tale within the pages of this book. With every retelling you'll live on and on and on."

"Trickster," the creature growled, as what remained of its form tensed to pounce.

"No, but I've fought my fair share of them in my journey back to this village, and if I've gleaned a thing or two from them along the way, so be it."

The desperate creature leapt at the stranger, but with a final swirl of his quill on the page, he dropped the tome to the ground. The book hit the dirt, and form of the creature hit the book. Its bones bent, twisted, and cracked like firewood as its stretched form seemed to vanish into the very pages themselves. Its howls filled the barrow, echoing over and over until the creature's form disappeared entirely into the tome as it slammed shut, leaving the barrow once more in dead silence.

Skirting the formless husk of the girl, the stranger composed himself and gathered up the book, checking to make sure the pages within were just that: pages. Much to his relief, they were nothing more, so with the last of his lamp's oil, he put Jadwiga's remains to rest and worked his way back to the surface of the barrow, where he found a shocked mayor and an assembly of curious-faced villagers waiting.

"You seem surprised to see me, mayor," the stranger said, dusting off his book.

The mayor craned his neck to look past him into the burrow, anxious. "Where is the girl?" he asked.

"You needn't worry about her or the threat to your village anymore," the stranger said, and closed his book before lowering it back into his satchel.

Some of the villagers grew agitated and the old woman who had pecked at the stranger earlier shouted out to him. "What have you done to the girl?"

The stranger reached out a bony hand to the mayor and lifted the man's chin until their eyes met. "They don't know, do they?" he whispered to him. "Do you wish to tell them or shall I?"

The mayor's eyes filled with fright. "Please, no," he pleaded, then lowered his voice to a whisper. "I had no choice. I sent innocent people—strangers—to their deaths. Yes, I may have saved my own townsfolk by doing so, but those deaths sit with me all the harder. Please, don't hurt me."

"Hurt you?" the stranger repeated. "My dear mayor, do not worry. I do not think I could inflict on you a greater pain than the one you have no doubt inflicted on yourself. Believe me, I know a thing or two about regret. If I have to live with my pain, then so will you yours."

The stranger pushed past the mayor and started back through the graveyard, but the confused and oblivious villagers crowded around him, blocking his way.

One eyebrow rose on the stranger's face. "Really?" the stranger asked. "Tell me, do any of you truly find it wise to tangle with the person who just took on a centuries old threat to your village and lived to tell the tale?"

After a quick moment of group contemplation, the crowd fell back as one, allowing the stranger a clear path on his journey out of the cemetery to his hut on the far side of the village.

"So what now?" the mayor called as he chased after him, desperate to keep up.

"Your village is safe," the stranger said. "Isn't that what matters most?"

"Yes, but your price. What about your price?"

"I do not require coin or riches," the stranger said. "No. There is payment enough in what I did for myself here tonight. As far as what my services have cost you, I've recorded the events of this forgettable little town of yours in my book of marvelous tales. In doing so, the story, your legend—or curse, if you will—becomes *mine*."

"But how is that possible?" the mayor asked.

"Did I not arrive in a shack propelled by the legs of a gigantic chicken?" the stranger said before shaking his head as he ascended the rope ladder back up to his hut. "Yet you ask me about my book instead? Never you mind, Mister Mayor, but trust me when I tell you that with time the tale will fade from *all* of your memories. Every grandmother who whispered it to their child in bed to scare them into obedience, every over-concerned mother or father who wished to frighten their spawn into compliant obedience… all of it will fade and become mine for all time, recorded here in my book alone. The truth will fade, as will, I hope, the guilt you feel for sending so many to that horrible fate below."

"Will you forget, too?" the mayor called up to him.

The stranger gave a sad shake of his head. "It is my burden to remember," he said, "but for my part in this tale, there is hope both vengeance and redemption will help quell what drove me here."

"What will you do now?"

The stranger gave a grim smile. "I do not know," he said, "but there are still many a blank page in my tome, and perhaps I will find solace—or at the very least, distraction—in the challenge of filling them. As for your village, I should think a chapel of skulls would be quite a draw to outsiders, now that there's nothing in it to devour them. Call it an ossuary like the dozen or so scattered throughout Europe."

The mayor's face was a mask of confusion. "Ossuary?"

"A shrine," the stranger said. "Cover up what really happened here the old way, the way they've done for thousands of years: blame the church. Say it's a mass grave of those who have passed, be it the Thirty Year's War or cholera, plague, syphilis… what have you."

The stranger turned, and the hut on legs turned with him, striding out of town.

"And if they don't believe me?" the mayor called out after him, but already the hut was a good field length away from Czermna.

"Tell them to seek out the man with the chicken-legged hut," the stranger called back, patting the satchel at his side. "Will I have a story for them."

ALL THE BRIDGES BURNED

Clay Sanger

NOTHING ILLUSTRATED A thief's predicament quite like watching his partner get fed to dogs. All to the tune of the laughter of the gangsters they'd robbed, whose senses of humor proved fouler than the rotten slaughterhouse stink in the air.

Josiah Starling licked his lips and tried not to vomit.

Thomas, his friend and partner, a big brawler of a man, kicked and screamed profanities as a man called Skoren carved tender bits off for the hounds. Thomas dangled by his wrists from chains thrown through a rafter overhead, his toes brushing the hay strewn floor of the rundown cattle pen. Powerless to escape, but lively enough to make the whole affair entertaining.

Skoren. That was a problem—a deadly one. Handsome, easy-going, good-natured. And because of that, people underestimated the mad fucker all the time. If you didn't know he was a murderous devil, you'd never have guessed it over evening ale. Starling had himself misjudged that one. To disastrous effect.

Skoren had one question. And even in the asking, it seemed rhetorical. "Where's my gold, Starling?"

Every carefully prepared lie evaporated in the face of those four words, taking with them Starling's hope in kind. No tiptoeing around it then. No doubt why they were here.

There was a reason the question sounded rhetorical. He didn't have the money and he had no idea where to get it. He knew this, and the murderous gangster with the bloody knife knew it. All the chuckling scoundrels in the room seemed to know it too. Everyone except for Thomas, that was. That poor bastard knew just enough to get fed to the dogs. Sure, he had plenty of his own sins to answer for, but this wasn't one of them.

Skoren's wicked little knife flicked and sliced Thomas's nostril like splitting an orange peel.

The man jerked and sputtered. "Give him the fucking coin, Starling!" Thomas's chest heaved, and his eyes went wide and wild like a terrified horse.

"Oh, he can't," Skoren said, poking butcher-like fingertips along Thomas's bare skin looking for what he might slice off next. "Tell him why you can't, Starling."

The thief gave a nervous laugh taking in the dilapidated room. There were eight of them. Eight gangsters he'd robbed, one by one, now accompanied by their favorite goons. The only door, guarded. Skoren, with his smile and his knife, made nine. "I wish I knew what was going on here. But, I don't."

Skoren tapped the back of the little blade against the single gold ring on his index finger in a thoughtful tempo. *Tink, tink, tink.* Then he nodded, straightening his bloody apron. "All right then. Here. I'll help." He snicked the blade through the middle of Thomas's nipple and the man screamed in fresh agony. The gangster waited for his convulsion of pain to calm before he continued. "Do you remember a raven-haired beauty, a singer and dancer come to us from the deserts of Valasega? Your partner had such a shine for her."

The simmering hate rising in Thomas's eyes said that he did. Her name came out a growl. "Sadene."

"I lost no less than nine thousand kingsmark to Sadene and Starling here," Skoren said, prodding a spot he considered for dog fodder before deciding to move on to some other target. "How did I lose all that money, Starling?" He looked over his shoulder at the nervous thief. "How did *you* lose all that money?"

"I wish I could tell you," Starling replied, cold dread tightening his voice. Skoren knew. The bastard *knew*.

The gangster turned back to his work. "See, I actually believe that. You have no fucking idea where my gold is. You have no fucking idea where Sadene is."

"I don't," Starling admitted. Even then, in the face of a far worse fate than a broken heart, his stomach knotted at the thought of her.

Skoren looked up at his current victim as if sharing a companionly understanding. "This is what happens when you try to run a con above your weight. The conman gets conned."

Thomas glared at his partner. "Did your cock get us killed?" he snarled, spittle flying from his bloody lips.

Chuckles, hoots, and jeers circled the gathering of gangsters. Starling felt every insult, every barb, every mocking chuckle like a jab to somewhere tender. That place where he stored what little remained of his pride now bled out like a slit pig in the stockyard mud. "Not exactly," he replied.

Skoren perked up, a man eager to contradict. "Oh. Yes. That's exactly what got you killed, actually."

"You little cunt!" Thomas growled bucking against his bonds.

The fit made the rafter overhead creak and groan, bringing with it a wretched shower of grime and old rat shit. The sweet stink of it filled the stale air. Starling could taste it.

Skoren whistled a happy tune and sliced off Thomas's left ear with the knife, sending the man into a fresh fit of screaming. He tossed the severed bit to the slavering dogs at his back, and they snarled and fought over it in a clatter of rusty chains.

Skoren gave the poor bastard a moment to regain his composure and turned to Starling, wiping the bloody blade clean on his apron hem. "Let's make an accounting, shall we?"

Starling shrugged, then nodded helplessly. He was in no position to argue.

Skoren gestured around the dank pit of the abandoned slaughterhouse. "Everyone in this room is out coin to you and Sadene. Only one of you is here to answer for it."

Starling took in the gathered cabal, eight notorious gangsters from the city's underbelly. Eight horrible ways to die, plus whatever Skoren might have in store for him once he was done carving up poor Thomas.

"Who started your little shell game?" Skoren asked. "Was it you? Or was it Sadene?" Starling was slow to respond, so Skoren answered for him. "It was Sadene, wasn't it? Because no offense, Starling, you're not that clever."

Starling raised his hands in surrender. "Is there anything I can do to make this right?"

"Do you have my money?"

"I don't." And he didn't. Sadene had robbed him as blind as they together had robbed everyone else.

"Then, no." Skoren motioned to one of his goons lurking in the corner, and the man came forward with a familiar set of saddle bags. Starling's saddle bags. "Pour it out," he ordered.

The thug turned the bags out onto the filthy floor and came up with a collection of coin purses. Nothing else. None of Starling's other belongings. Just six bags of coins, ones he thought he'd had carefully stashed in six secret locations. Apparently not so secret after all.

Skoren came over and squatted over the pile of purses and saddle bags. Then, picking up each one, he nicked them open with his knife and let the coins spill out into the pile. Gold kingsmarks, silver drakes, bent pennies, and tineyes clinked and clattered to the floor in a spreading pool.

"Two hundred forty-seven kingsmarks, seven drakes, thirty-one shill," Skoren declared, waving his hand over the pile like a presenter at a carnival. "I believe this is every penny left to your name."

Starling nodded. No sense in denying it. "Yessir."

Skoren picked through the coins with the point of his knife. "That's a lot less than what you owe us."

Again, there was no sense in denying it. "Yessir."

"But, not an inconsiderable sum. Enough for a man to drink and whore for a year. If his tastes aren't too refined, anyway." Smiling, the gangster looked around the room at his associates. "Does anyone so owed wish to make a claim on good Starling's last fortune?"

Chuckles of amusement. Little more.

Starling felt his heart sinking, and he fought to keep it from turning to piss running down his leg.

But Skoren shrugged. "Well. Good fortune for *you* then, Starling."

The thief blinked in confusion. "Beg pardon?"

"You can keep it."

Starling didn't know how to respond. So, he held his tongue.

"You have five gates and two harbors to choose from. If you can get out of Peregos alive, this is yours to keep." Skoren smiled. Like a friend. Like a man who wasn't kneeling there with a wicked knife and bloody hands. He picked through the pile of coins and took up nine kingsmarks. He tossed one to each of his conspirators and tucked the last one into the pocket of his apron. Then he winked. "There. If there was any question, now we're all cashed out. The remainder is yours."

Again, snickers from the gaggle of gangsters.

Starling swallowed the lump bobbing up and down in his throat. "If I can get out of Peregos alive?"

"Yes."

"And how am I supposed to do that?" Starling wondered aloud before he could stop himself. He couldn't help it. He didn't know what the game was, but he couldn't believe these esteemed murderers would let him out of the *room* alive, let alone the city.

"By whatever means suits you," Skoren replied. "Donkey cart. Row boat. Boot leather. Whatever carries you away from here."

The fear, the rioting paranoia, it got the better of him. "But?" Starling asked, a pained hitch in his voice.

Skoren's smile turned unfriendly, altogether sinister. "*But.*" He rose and walked his knife through bloody fingers with the deft touch of a bard at his lute. "How long since my men scooped you up? Half an hour or so?"

Starling nodded.

"Well, then that means every cutthroat in the city has a half hour lead on tracking you down." The glittering knife stopped, and Skoren used it to point to the pile of coins. "And *there* is the bounty on your head. The sum welcome to be kept by whoever puts a miserable end to you. Or the prize you win for surviving. Whichever comes first."

Starling's heart skipped and skittered in his chest. His mind raced, events moving too fast and chaotically to snatch hold of, like trying to catch sparrows in an attic.

"Fly fast, Starling," Skoren said, turning his attention back to his work on poor Thomas. "The word on the bounty has been out for a while now. Time isn't waiting for you." The hungry dogs began to whimper and growl in anticipation as their master moved back toward the meat.

Hands trembling, stomach clenching, Josiah Starling scooped the coins out of the grimy rushes and ran for his life, while Thomas's screams, the baying of hounds, and the laughter of killers echoed after him.

———•———

THINGS HAD NOT always been so desperate. Not so long ago, Starling was up and coming in the underworld of Peregos. He had built his own crew, surrounded himself with real talent. Inside a year they went from small time to taking real scores. People who mattered were beginning to take notice. Admittedly, Starling had always been more of an *idea* man. Much of the heavy lifting, the day to day, he'd left to Thomas, who was now feeding the dogs, and to Maeda, who was running the crew in his increasing absence.

Now, he was cowering in the ass-end of a rundown stable not a block from where Skoren's men had turned him out onto the street. Wondering if he'd live to see the next block over.

You can't just sit here and die, he thought, his belly full of quivering worms. *Get yourself together.* One thing at a time. Take it all one thing at a time. What did he need first? What did he need most? What would keep him alive for the next ten minutes?

Curling up in a ball right here until I die of thirst, he thought. But that wouldn't do. Though the idea wasn't entirely without merit. He wouldn't actually die of thirst. There was a moldering rain barrel just outside the alley door. He'd shit himself to death from drinking putrid water before he died of thirst.

Starling couldn't help it. He giggled. A madman's chuckle. Since he couldn't stop it, he indulged himself and let it happen as nature willed it. Then, when the giggling fit dried up, he tried to carry on, head pounding, eyes hot with tears.

What did he need? And what did he have? He needed a lot. Other than the clothes on his back and the damnable coins in the saddle bags, he *had* nothing. There would be no going back to his apartments. Same for any safehouse he knew. He had cached a few essentials here and there throughout the city, for emergencies, but retrieving them would require him to expose himself.

You're going to have to do that, no matter what, he thought, swallowing the lump of dread that came with it. A thief could disappear from the Law, from the Kingsmen easily enough. But the scoundrels of Peregos would be hunting him on the rooftops, the thieves' highway, the sewers, in every alley and flophouse. His head was worth a year of drunken fuckery. And word would be spreading like wild fire. Anywhere he might hide from decent folk would put him right in his hunters' laps. And anywhere he could hide from his hunters was no place to hide at all.

A disguise. What he needed first was a disguise.

He ransacked the stable, looking for anything he might use to make him look less like himself. A ratty red horse blanket thrown about his shoulders was worth a try. That lasted five seconds before he decided all it accomplished was making him look like Josiah Starling gone mad, running through the streets in a ratty red horse blanket.

Come on, you idiot, do better. What would have served best was a dress and a bonnet. Starling knew from experience he made a fine looking woman—bristly scruff of a beard aside. He checked the corners of the barn and peeked into the alleyway, seeking clotheslines laden with any suitable fare. He found almost nothing to pick from. *Is it not washday on Ashby Street, you miserable bastards?*

He hovered over the rain barrel, staring down into his own murky reflection, trying to come up with something near at hand that would hide him from prying eyes. The man looking back at him seemed to have aged a decade in a day. His eyes were wild and hollow. His cheeks sunken. The gray spreading at his temples and creeping into his short beard made him look like an old man.

I can look like an old man, he thought then he laughed at his own reflection. *How the fuck does that help you? You* are *an old man.* Good God. Running for your life was a young man's game. He could feel that in every unsteady breath he took. He didn't have the nerve for this anymore. Maybe once, when he was still too young to know better. But not now. Ten minutes on the run and his nerves were already shot.

You don't need a disguise, he thought, flicking his fingertips against the glassy surface of the black water. *What you need is a way out of this city.* He spat in the barrel and slunk back into the stables. Of course he needed a way out of the fucking city. He had to survive long enough to do that. Every crooked guardsman would be watching the gates for him. Every harbor rat on alert. Maybe he was getting the cart before the horse. He didn't need a way out of the city. Not yet. He needed a way out of the neighborhood.

He stared a thousand-yard hole through the stable wall until dusk fell, reciting the same question over and over again in his mind.

How? Where? Who? He came back to the same answer every time.

Maeda. The lady rogue who had helped him keep the crew running and in the good graces of everyone he hadn't outright insulted along the way. And with less and less of his participation since Sadene had come along. The lady rogue who had kept all the daggers juggling while he'd played at being a gentleman thief and falling in love like a schoolboy. Maeda, who he'd overlooked, abandoned, and betrayed in every way short of taking a knife to her.

If Maeda couldn't get him out of the neighborhood and out of the city, no one could.

And she had no reason to help him at all. But he didn't think she'd knife him either, just for the coins in his bag and the favor of Skoren. At least, he very much hoped not.

With no better plan than that, Josiah Starling pulled his hood low over his head and made out into the streets, ducking and weaving along a mad random path like a man who'd lost his mind *and* sense of direction on the same day.

To be fair, he had.

———————

"NO," MAEDA SAID. She was standing over her fishbowl in her worn apartment, crumbling a dried cricket over the surface of the water for a school of tiny blue darters with feathery fan tails.

It was the answer Starling most expected. "Hear me out, please."

"Let me try this another way," Maeda said, "Fuck off." She smiled as the little blue streaks pecked and nipped at the brown flakes floating on the surface of their bowl. She touched the tip of her finger to a larger piece of cricket wing lingering on the surface and skimmed it around in a slow figure eight, prodding the hungry little fish to chase after it.

"I will, Maeda. I promise. Once I'm out of the city, you'll never have to hear from me again." He thunked the coin laden saddle bags down onto the thick slab of a table. "And all of this is yours."

Maeda finally turned away from her fish, scowling at the saddle bags. "I don't want Skoren's money. Not without your head to go along with it. That *is* the gist of the arrangement everyone's chattering about."

"Who would know? If I was gone and you kept the money?"

"Whatever bastard you blabber to when someone *does* catch up to you and finds you without it, that's who. Besides, whether you believe it or not, Skoren just *knows* things. *Sees* things. No one even asks what sort of evil he does in the back rooms of his gambling halls. How do you think he caught onto *you*?" Maeda crossed her arms and shook her head. "I don't want the money, Starling."

Fighting down the panic, Starling changed tack. "A favor then. Just your help, this once, and I'll be on my way. Out of your life, out of your affairs forever. The crew, all its business. It's yours. Like I never existed at all."

Maeda cocked a slender eyebrow. "I seem to recall asking Josiah Starling for *his* help and favors no less than three times in as many months. And receiving no answer at all, because he was too busy with his newest distraction to be bothered. How is Sadene, by the way?"

Starling took the knife twist to the gut in stride. "Gone."

Maeda gave a chuckle. "I told you. Didn't I?"

Starling nodded, the well of shame and regret rolling in his belly threatening to show itself in a display of dry heaving. "You did, Maeda. For what it's worth I'm sorry."

"Well, at least I gave you a 'no.' That's more than I've heard from you in months." She shrugged. "There's your favor. I said no. Now you don't have to wonder if I'm ever going to show up and do my part."

"I know," Starling conceded. "I… bobbled everything. Left you cleaning up my messes. Left you holding the bag."

"Yes. You did," Maeda said. "But this one, this one is all yours. And I can't help you clean it up."

"Please. Maeda. I just need a little help. That's all. A single, tiny favor. A hand out of the city. It'll cost you nothing."

"Being in business with you has cost me plenty," Maeda said, her expression darkening. "Sums owed add up. You already can't pay me what you owe me. And Skoren's gold doesn't count."

Starling opened his mouth to protest but found no words.

"Look around you, Starling. See all that smoke and fire? That's all the bridges you've burned. Catching flame all at once. I wash my hands of you. As far as I can tell, our business ended when you got your cock knotted up in Sadene. And good riddance to you at that."

Starling wilted, throwing up his hands in resignation. "Is there nothing at all then? After all we've been through together in this city?"

"Sure," Maeda said, and the dagger at her belt came free of its sheath.

Starling jumped, expecting violence. He was still woefully unarmed, and even if he hadn't been, he didn't think he could take her in something approaching a fair fight. But rather than come at him with the blade, she stabbed it into the table beside his saddle bags and left it there quivering.

"There you go, Starling," she said with sneer. "A fighting chance for you, between here and wherever you wind up next."

The startled breath Starling had been holding exploded out, and with a grateful nod, he plucked the dagger from the table. At least he had that much. He fished into his saddle bags for a token gesture, a kingsmark or two for the dagger if nothing else.

"Not a chance," Maeda said. "Don't you leave a single penny of Skoren's money here."

Starling retreated without another word, his head hung low, shame and regret taking their toll as he fled into the deepening night.

ALL OTHER DOORS closed, all other bridges burned, Starling knew he only had two *real* choices. Run or hide. He knew you couldn't do either one forever, but the farther he ran from the city, from Peregos, the more likely it was his pursuers would give up the chase. Miles and days would peel the hounds away one by one until the doubt of catching him and the return on chasing him combined to discourage the effort. If he stayed, if he tried to hide, it would only be a matter of time. He'd be caught. He'd be found. And it would end badly.

If he ran, every day would increase his odds of survival. If he stayed, each passing day would make them worse.

So, there wasn't really any choice at all.

Every minute you wait makes getting out harder. One more run across the city, he told himself. *One more artful dodge. By the time the sun comes up in the morning, you'll be a free man.* The dagger up his sleeve and the bag of gold dangling from his shoulder did very little to help him believe it.

Summoning up his courage for the last time, Starling ran.

For a man of four decades, he was still light and fast on his feet. And the newly fallen night had come on blessedly dark. He dashed pasted tradesmen closing up shop for the night. Past tavern-goers mobbing the street in search of a mug. Between carriages as they carted the well-to-do off to supper or an evening at the theater. He skated over the narrow bridges that spanned Peregos' winding canals, down the twisting streets in the lamplight evening murk. Had anyone seen him call on Maeda and then slink out again? Of course they had. If so, were they somewhere back there in the dark, giving pursuit? Most assuredly.

He kept out of the alleys and side streets and stuck to the main avenues. He was much less likely to find himself murdered on some wide-open public street at a busy tavern hour than in some back alley. He wasn't *hidden* in plain sight. Not by a long shot. But it might keep him alive for a while until he came up with something better.

Of course, it didn't take long, darting down the street like that, for a curious watchman to wonder what he was up to.

"Oy!" a yellow bearded watchman called out. "Hold there. What are you about?"

Running for my life, Starling thought. But instead he slowed to a trot and answered, "I'm going to be a father!" He capped it off with a happy hoot and a cheerful wave. And with no one calling out alarms in his wake, the guard lost interest and let him pass unmolested.

The tide would be right soon. Ships would be putting out that evening. If he could make Bell Harbor in two hours, he could throw a sack of gold at a captain or sailor and maybe get himself hauled aboard with few questions asked. To where didn't matter. Anywhere was better than Peregos Failing that, maybe he could stowaway or ride out of port in some ship's quarter netting before being found out. He had enough gold to spread around that it might make him a captain's favorite unexpected passenger.

All was going according to plan until he turned toward the harbor down Pale Moon Avenue and soon found the street ahead all but deserted. Gods be damned. The whole block was cordoned off for a wedding celebration. Someone with more money than sense no doubt. And other than the block where revelers were hours into their cups, celebrating some idiot couple's nuptials, the street was empty. With no traffic coming and going it left a hollow hole in the heart of the city's nighttime activity.

By the time he'd realized his mistake and turned back, three hooded horsemen had arrived on the street behind him. They didn't look like they were on their way to a Pale Moon Avenue wedding reception.

Starling didn't wait to test their intentions. He was up the nearest drain pipe and onto the rooftops, the thieves' highway, as fast as he could scramble. Just as he pulled himself up over the gutter onto the third story roof, a crossbow quarrel hissed past his ear, ricocheting off the slate roof and into the night. A frantic glance back toward the street revealed one of the hooded riders leveling a crossbow at him while the other cocked and reloaded. Starling rolled onto the roof and tucked up tight behind a chimney as a second bolt sliced past.

Pulse hammering in his ears, he dashed out from behind the chimney and took off at a run, angling up a slope of the roof, dislodging tiles behind him. They clattered and clinked on their way down, pinging off the gutters to shatter in the street below. A third bolt chased him, sailing just over his head as he crested the peak of the roof and slid down the opposite side in a shower of tiles.

He caught the gutter with his boot heel and, very much in the image of the young sneak thief he'd once been, he was up and loping down the roof edge like a billy goat on a mountain ledge. He hopped that gutter to the next and went up and over that roof top as well, leaving less of a mess in his wake as his steps became more sure and steady. He crossed three blocks down, bounding over rooftops before dropping back into the street.

He landed in a back alley behind the Salty Dog Tavern and, without missing a beat, cut through the building by way of the kitchens. A startled barmaid gave a shout, but he was already gone and out the opposite alley before anyone could mount a response.

The chase was exhilarating. For a brief moment, he forgot the cares of the larger matter and focused on the escape itself. The wild flight of a sneak thief caught with his hand in the till. Darting and dashing one step ahead of those who meant to string him up. He couldn't help but grin, a manic thing, he was sure, all teeth and wild eyes.

He got his bearings, crossed fast and light-footed over a canal on Westerly Way, and broke out onto Asher Street, a lamp lit main avenue that could carry him all the way to Bell Harbor. His wild grin became a genuine smile. Hope. A glimmer of it, that he just might make it. If anyone wanted to take him and the prize he carried now, they'd have to do it right in the middle of a gods damned public street.

With carriages and theatre goers and evening revelers all in plain sight, and city guardsmen a shout away.

Which is exactly what that great big bastard with the sneering hair lip and the two-handed cudgel meant to do, it seemed.

Starling caught the man out of the corner of his eye just as he exploded from the darkness of a shuttered-up bakery's doorway. The big cudgel led the way, whistling as the thug took a skull-shattering swing for Starling's head.

Starling ducked with an inch to spare and backpedaled frantically.

"Thand thill, you little bathturd," the big man snarled with a nasal lisp, bringing the cudgel around for another swing.

"Chaipps!" Starling called out in surprise. "Right here in the fucking street? Stupid as ever, man." His gaze darted left and right, equal parts trying to pick a vector for escape while feinting the big club-swinging lunatic with his eyes. If he dodged when he should have dashed, Chaipps would smash him to pieces.

A woman loading up on a nearby carriage gasped in shock at the scene of sudden violence.

"What goes there?" the driver shouted as the two men spilled into the streets, Starling dodging another pair of swings from the big brute.

"Mind your own thucking bithness," Chaipps snarled back, sparing a half a glance in the direction of the carriage driver.

That was all the distraction Starling needed. He picked Chaipps' off-hand side and bolted. By the time the big man spun back to face him, he was out of swinging range of that nasty club. The big, neckless thug would never catch him in a foot race.

Out of swinging distance, yes. Out of throwing distance, no.

Starling made it five fleeting steps before the flying cudgel caught him in the shoulder blade, heaving him from his feet with a stunning impact. He wheeled and found himself on the cobbles, gasping for breath, stars darting and flickering across his field of view. The saddle bag of coins came crashing down alongside him with a metallic jingle.

Chaipps was coming, fast, a big knife clutched in his even bigger fist.

Still trying to sort out up from down, Starling shook Maeda's dagger from his sleeve and gave it a desperate sidearm fling from flat on his back. The blade gave a single turn, slicing across the dark, before burying with a satisfying *chunk* into Chaipps' thigh.

The big man howled and hobbled.

It bought Startling the second he needed to shove drunkenly to his feet, scoop up the saddle bag, and take off in a weaving, weak-kneed run. Chaipps hurled his own knife in return, but his throw was artless, and the knife clattered off down the street, wide of its mark.

"You're a dead man, Tharling!" Chaipps shouted, clutching at his wounded thigh. "I'm gonna be wearing your ballth round my neck come daybreak! You hear me?"

Starling heard him, and he believed him. So he kept running.

Somewhere behind him the carriage driver was calling out for the guard. That was bad, especially with Chaipps back there howling and causing a ruckus. No way he'd slip past alerted guardsmen now with a sly distraction or excuse. They'd stop him on principle, being the man running away from a knifing and all.

Shit, shit, shit he thought desperately, his momentary good humor at the thrill of the chase gone. Dried up. Evaporated. Starling heard the clatter of approaching hooves and imagined either angry guardsmen or the hooded crossbowmen who'd tried to perforate him earlier.

Sheer desperation drove him down the nearest alley, his plan for safety in plain sight gone to hell.

He yelped and nearly struck a boy when the little waif child caught hold of his sleeve. "Hands off, lad!" His heartbeat clicked in his clenching throat in time to the pounding pain his shoulder.

The little boy stared up at him with a narrow, dirty face, apparently unconcerned by his gasp of alarm. He held out a single red poppy with a nod back down the alley. "The lady says that way."

A red poppy. Sadene tossed red poppies to the lust-struck boys and girls in the crowd when she danced. He'd introduced himself to her by returning one she'd tossed his way. Once upon a summer eve in what felt like a forgotten dream.

Starling blinked and tried to imagine every possible scenario compressed in the time between two startled breaths. Then he snatched the flower from the little boy's hand and took off down the alley.

"Josiah," a woman's lyrical voice whispered from a darkened doorway ahead.

He saw her then, leaning into the alley, waving him on.

Sadene.

He didn't hesitate, didn't question his good fortune. He dashed for the door and hurried inside as she shoved it closed behind them.

And there she was, her face alight with a relieved smile, a lover's joy. Beautiful as ever with pair of red poppies clutched in her hand. She tossed the remaining flowers aside and buried him in a joyful kiss.

"I thought you disappeared," Starling whispered against her lips. "I thought you were gone."

Sadene pulled away, a wounded look in her eye. "You think I would abandon you?"

He swallowed the lump in his throat, unsure what to say.

"Skoren has us," she said. "And your name and my name are on the lips of every killer in the city. We have to go, Josiah. We have to go now."

"I know," Starling replied. "But how will we—"

"I have a boat for us," Sadene said. "We must go. Now."

"How did you find me?" Starling asked.

Sadene pulled at his hand and led him toward a cellar door. "I'll explain once we're safe. Come on. Let's go."

For a moment he hesitated, his old rogue's instincts crying a warning. But, as with every warning related to Sadene, he ignored them, and as he'd done since the day they'd met, he followed her off into the dark.

———•———

THEY WAITED FOR the tide in a sewer junction-made-safehouse under Chandler Street near Bell Harbor. Shady men he didn't know came and went in the dank, candlelit gloom, apparently in service to Sadene. He had a thousand questions and chose to save most of them for the boat. There'd be time for that, he figured. Now, he was simply grateful to be alive. Grateful to be on his way out of the damnable city.

And grateful to be with Sadene.

He bristled at the way she touched one of the men's arms, a handsome dark-skinned rogue she called Daeglin. Something in that single touch lit a fire under his jealousy. Daeglin's knowing grin at having spotted his unease stoked the flames. That was the smirk of a man who had a certain knowledge of a woman. Something else Starling set aside for the time being with plans to settle on the boat.

Daeglin left them with a half empty bottle of wine and a couple of dented tin cups. "A quarter hour," the man said, setting the bottle down on the ledge beside Sadene. "Then we sail." He departed down the grimy passage into dark.

"I take it he's coming with us when we sail out of here?" Starling asked.

"He is," Sadene said as she uncorked the bottle of wine and poured them each a cup.

"What's he to you?" Starling asked.

"Loyal," Sadene replied, handing him a cup. Then she smiled, nodding toward the wine. "A Glossler Fina."

Starling laughed. The very same fine wine he'd offered her on the night they met, pilfered from the personal stock of a fur and timber baron no less. He wondered where she'd stolen this bottle from. He raised his dented tin cup with a conciliatory nod and took a long swallow.

"Where are we sailing to, Sadene?" he asked. The wine's finery had dulled to a sour undertone, clearly having sat open too long. There was a petty part of him that wondered if Sadene and that smirking bastard Daeglin had been the ones to polish off the first half.

"Does it matter?"

"I suppose it doesn't." Starling licked his lips, the tart, dry wine tingling in his throat. "We both know I'm going to ask, so I might as well ask now. Where's money?"

"I've got it," Sadene assured him with a pretty smile. Then she tapped the pointed toe of her shoe against the saddle bags under his boot. "Well, almost all of it anyway. I assume that's Skoren's prize, then?"

Starling nodded. His lips had gone numb.

"All of it?" Sadene asked.

Again, Starling nodded. Cottony confusion began to set in. The first cramp knotted up in the bottom of his stomach. He touched fingers to his numb lips and stared back at her in mute shock. By the time he realized Sadene had never touched her own cup, the edges of the room were already growing dark.

He dropped the dagger from his sleeve with a snarl, but his wooden fingers fumbled it and it clattered to the grimy stone underfoot.

"Oh, I'm afraid that won't do you any good," Sadene said, rising from her seat on the ledge and wiping her hands clean on the hem of her vest.

Another wave of gut cramps sent Starling to the floor beside his dagger.

"What are you doing?" he gasped as the tunnel began to spin in the pale candlelight.

"What I do best, Josiah," Sadene replied. "How did you really think this was going to end?"

With the two of them sailing away to somewhere better than this to spend their ill-gotten gains, naked and drowning in wine. That's what he'd thought. "Why?" Starling gasped, the scent of blood and bile and rotten stomach filling his nose.

"Loose ends," Sadene explained. "Ill fortune just flocks to you, Josiah Starling. Like crows to carrion. You told me that yourself. The curse of your whole life. I have enough luggage, love, without taking you on."

Starling choked and sputtered and reached out for her foot, his fingertips brushing her shoe. But she paid him no more mind. She stepped past where he lay and retrieved the saddle bag of coins. Then she turned and started off down the tunnel the way Daeglin had gone.

He croaked, groping for words, and none came. What was he going to do? Gasp out about love? About betrayal? That's all he and Sadene really were. Betrayal of one flavor or another. Means to different ends, and she was taking what she wanted most. How *had* he thought all this would end?

In the painful dark, creeping like thorny vines into the edges of his mind, Josiah Starling remembered Maeda's words. *I don't want Skoren's money. Skoren just knows things. Sees things. No one even asks what sort of evil he does in the back rooms of his gambling halls. How do you think he caught onto you? Don't you leave a single penny of Skoren's money here.*

Starling gurgled, a ragged bloody chuckle that stopped Sadene in her tracks.

She turned back and glared down at him where he lay curled up around his rotting belly, dying. "What could you possibly be laughing at, you simple bastard?"

Don't you leave a single penny of Skoren's money here. Skoren just knows *things.* Sees *things.*

Starling had no doubt, as candlelit vision faded to black and everything became pain, that Skoren would find his lost gold. Every last penny.

See you in hell, love, he thought. *We'll square up there.*

Sadene stalked away then, leaving Josiah Starling alone in the dark. Choking on his own blood. Spending his last few agonizing breaths on drowning, hopeless laughter.

CAT SECRET
WEAPON #1

Walidah Imarisha

T HERE ARE EVIL scientists, and then there are evil scientists.
And this kid just isn't going to cut it. I've sat in the laps of
some of the evilest of them all, so I know.

Do you ever wonder what happens to the cat when the villain dies?
Probably not. Humans are usually so busy rooting for the "good guy,"
they forget about the little ball of fuzz the villain pets while revealing
their nefarious plans.

Well, once our villain expires, we get shipped back to the pound.
I've been in and out so many times, I've lost track. Invariably I always
get adopted by the same kind of person: namely, someone bent on
world domination and/or destruction. Perhaps it's my flat face and
unblinking eyes—I mean, most cats have them, but I've been told I
look exceptionally superior and disdainful, even to other cats. Not that
I've spent much time speaking with other cats; they're all beneath me.

How is it possible the only people who adopt me are evil, you
ask? First, you'd find yourself quite surprised what percentage of the

population has devised plans to take over the world.

But second, there is an animal shelter right across the street from the headquarters of the Organization of Evil Villains (yes, the redundancy is annoying, but no one ever listens to the quadruped). OEV is *the* association for villains—in fact, to put a diabolical plan into action, you have to be sanctioned by OEV. If not, their retrieval teams come to… retrieve you. You do not want to be retrieved by OEV.

So usually my new owner is an established villain who has already gotten approval for their next plan to bring the world to its knees. Often, their last feline died in a freak nuclear explosion (cats are curious creatures—if you leave the door open to an atomic reactor, you have to expect that will happen now and again). They come into the shelter to pick up a new fuzzy lap accessory before their ultimatum call to the UN.

You may ask, why do so many villains have a cat? I mean cats can be somewhat selfish and other things (I've never listened beyond the first adjective), but they are still adorable fluffy balls of fur (at least before the claws extend). Wouldn't a Doberman or a Rottweiler complete the tableau more menacingly?

Ah, but you forget about ironic juxtaposition. What is more jarring than holding the button to blow up the entire world in one hand, and petting a purring cat with the other? Clearly, if this scoundrel can be so cavalier while controlling the future of the human species, they did not come to play. Even if there is a ball of yarn in the corner.

Hence, the need for a cat. In fact, Regulation 14A.5, set forth by OEV, states you must have a cat in all videos, broadcasts, photographs, video conferencing, oil paintings (don't ask) and any other forms of visual communication when you issue your ultimatum.

But even beyond the bureaucratic requirements, having a cat is more important to a villain than having nuclear weapons. The evil scientist would be nothing without the cat. In fact, you know the first villain's laugh? That cackle they always do in the middle of sharing their evil plans with the world, usually followed by some evil finger motions? Villain cat lore tells us that the first one was nothing of the kind. It was a villain covering a scream of pain as cat claws punctured flesh, conveying (quite effectively) that said cat was hungry.

In summary, having the right cat is vital.

There are typically two kinds of evildoers who come into the shelter—the seasoned villain with years of diabolical scheming under his belt, and the plucky upstart trying to prove himself to the world. As they bring me out this morning to the adoption area, it only takes a moment to deduce I am staring at the second.

A young Black teen stands awkwardly. He is tall and gangly in that way teenage humans have, seeming to have more limbs with many more joints than anatomically possible. He paces the small space back and forth in high top sneakers. Every few minutes he pats his high top fade, which stands like an impressive hair monument eight inches off his head.

Usually this kind doesn't gravitate to me. As I said, I am not your average villain's cat, and they usually know they can't handle the massive malevolence I bring to the table. These upstarts prefer to go with a younger short hair for their first regulation cat. I, in contrast, am infinitely more distinguished, with a luscious coat of jet black fur. Technically, they created a new category for me: "overlong long hair." I have piercing yellow eyes. I have the second longest stare in cat history (the scientists, when not planning world domination, have created a *Guinness Book of Evil World Records*), and certifiably the loudest hiss of any cat alive (page 827 of section 2, the 14th edition).

What I'm saying is, the very look of me convinces most of these newbies they couldn't handle me. If one does get delusions of grandeur,

I usually just have to issue a low growl and start the second longest stare, and they remember their place.

This upstart, though, is completely clueless. My growl and stare produce no quantifiable results. I escalate to the fully extended claw swipe, and finally I break out Cat Secret Weapon #2, that record-setting hiss. This kid just throws back his head, crowned by its eight-inch-high curly Tower of Pisa that leans as he laughs. "Yeah, now I know for sure that's the one I want!"

Today definitely is not going as planned.

Most times when I am chosen, my villain is ready for me. He often still has the accouterments from his late cat, so I ride home in a gold flecked carrier with caviar and bottled spring water, until I get to his lair and can retire to my cat house, usually multi-level with a modest two or three diamond encrusted food bowls throughout.

Can you imagine, then, how humiliating it is being grabbed unceremoniously and thrown in a surplus cardboard box for god's sake, with the logo "save one cat, save them all" printed on the side? Being shoved into the back seat of a faded brown '98 Honda Civic, which I later learned was his *mother's*? And then, how horrifying it is to arrive at his room in said mother's basement, to be shown a pile of old and clearly unclean t-shirts as he says, "make yourself at home"? He then plops down at what I assumed was a desk underneath the mountains of gears, soldering tools, bits of wire, and other miscellaneous choking hazards, and promptly ignores me.

Well, what would you do? The same thing I am, I'm sure—pee all over the t-shirt pile while staring at the kid. Cat Secret Weapon #3. While it mostly likely won't be enough on its own to get me a return to the shelter, I'm sure it will result in screaming at the very least, if my past experience with villains is any indication. This will be the first link in the chain of destruction I forge around this impertinent boy.

He doesn't even notice.

How is that possible? I stare at him for five straight minutes. He never even lifts his head.

My tail thrashes furiously (kicking up dust as it does—when was the last time this kid vacuumed?). Momentarily at a loss, I watch him. When I first saw him, I was struck by his awkwardness, yet he is clearly in his element here. He even moves with a sort of grace, for a biped. His hands are little brown sparrows, their movements both purposeful and natural. I want to swat at them, for a number of different reasons.

He works intently, oblivious of how dangerously close his towering hair is to the Bunsen burner's open flame.

As I turn my attention to the bed, contemplating if I have a second liquid assault in me, the door bursts open. A whirlwind in the shape of a ten- or eleven-year-old Black girl with massive afro puffs enters the room. She wears a black leotard with a gold tutu that battles with her afro puffs for circumference supremacy. She's paired scuffed combat boots and an oversized ragged leather jacket to complete the outfit.

"Are you ready to do the demand video now, Khalil?" she asks, as she begins immediately touching and moving almost everything on the overcrowded table, revealing additional layers of gadgetry, like excavating an archeological dig.

"Stop touching that, and you know we're not making the video until I complete the first phase of construction." Khalil catches a falling box of broken light bulbs right before it hits the ground and shatters. Well, shatters more.

The girl stomps a foot. "I know that! I just thought we could do a practice video, so we could review it and make sure everything is perfect for the real one. I even got dressed up for it!"

"Yeah, um, about that. What exactly is it that you're wearing, Mini?" he asks.

She looks down at her outfit proudly. "This is my evil-scientist-demands-video outfit, duh! You have to wear something that's super scary, but still shows you have style." She twirls to emphasize the latter part.

As she comes out of the spin into a surprisingly good plié (one of my villains loved the ballet so much, he kidnapped a national troupe to force them to perform for him, so I've seen my fair share of quality pliés), her eyes fall on me.

"Oh my god, oh my god, oh my god, you got the cat!" The bouncing and handclapping look both more ridiculous and more adorable given her current attire. That's not me being sentimental in any way. Just an impartial observation.

"When did you get it? What's its name? Is it a boy or a girl? Can it sleep in my room? Can I pick it up?"

The barrage of questions distracts me from the fact that the last is actually rhetorical, as she swoops me into her arms. Typically, I have all kinds of defenses against this, as I have detailed previously (see: my record-winning hiss), but she moves so quickly, like, well, like a cat. Certainly that is not to say I don't have a veritable arsenal to deploy on the rare occasions I am cathandled against my consent. The few who have previously been so brave or so foolish as to attempt this carry literal and figurative scars to remind them of their folly.

But none had the evil genius of this oddly dressed girl, who uses her nefarious Spidey senses to suss out my only vulnerability. My Achilles paw, if you will. Part of being a villain's cat is being impervious to normal petting. Where as a normal civilian cat would purr at an under-the-chin scratch or a base-of-the-tail pat, I feel nothing. It's like my nerve endings have all been severed. But every stone has a crack. She scoops me up, her hand sliding to scratch just inside my upper left leg (the paw pit as we cats call it), while simultaneously rubbing behind my right ear in counter clock motions.

How could she possibly have known? My entire body goes limp as I lean against her chest, powerless.

Khalil answers her earlier barrage of questions sequentially. "I picked the cat up this morning since I had to go to OEV headquarters to get my ID picture taken."

He pulls out his official OEV member license, wearing the same proud grin he has in the photo, which is missing the top four inches of his high top.

"The cat doesn't have a name yet," he continues, putting his worn wallet away. "I honestly didn't ask about the gender—I mean does it really matter? It's a cat that's been fixed."

My eyes widen a little in surprise. Khalil has seemed fairly oblivious to everything happening around him up to this point. I would not have thought him capable of understanding that cats transcend such petty human constrictions as gender binary.

"Also it's a cat; it'll sleep wherever it wants. And clearly you answered your last question yourself, Mini." He nods to me in her arms. Appalled at the indignity of my position, I will myself to fight. But my body, overwhelmed with pleasure, just won't respond.

"I guess you're right about the gender," the girl muses. "But it does need a name. Like now.

"And speaking of names," her attention zeroes in on Khalil, "stop calling me Mini. That's a baby name. I haven't used that name in like, forever."

Khalil rolled his eyes. "Right, how could I forget. Sorry, Amina, Oh Grown One."

But Amina seems to have her sarcasm forcefield set to maximum, because she just nods like a benevolent monarch. She turns her attention to me, nary a break in the dual petting.

"Now what should we call you?' she wonders. She is contemplative for a few minutes.

Then her eyes brighten and she shouts, "Wuzzie McCuddlekins!"

She must be having a stroke. She's shouting gibberish. Her brother should call the paramedics. Any second now her limbs will seize up and she'll drop me, and I can make my escape.

But Khalil's high top bows solemnly as he nods. "You know, I never would have thought of that, but it does seem to fit the cat perfectly."

I cannot believe my ears, and as you know, cats have excellent hearing. I have been part of—nay integral to—dozens of plots to destabilize, control, and/or destroy the majority of the globe, and the name they want to give me sounds like a knock off Care Bears line?

"That settles it," Amina rubs her chin on the top of my head. "Welcome home, Wuzzie!"

Typically, I would flatten my ears in anger, but that would interrupt Amina's scratching of the right one. So I content myself with a terrifying eye narrowing.

It occurs to me that I've belonged to so many villains, but I've never actually been given a name before, atrocious as this one is. Once the transmission demands were done, I was typically plopped unceremoniously onto the ground and left to my own devices, ignored until the next worldwide appearance.

Something unfamiliar flutters inside me. Obviously a reaction to the generic cat food brand at the shelter—my constitution is not suited to such plebian cuisines.

Amina leans over Khalil's shoulder. "So when is it going to be ready?"

Khalil sighs and pushes back from the desk. "Well, as you know, the prototype is complete and fully operational…"

"Like the Death Star!" Amina giggles.

Khalil smiles, clearly proud of his little sister's nerd reference. "Yeah, just like the Death Star. But now I'm waiting to hear back from OEV about financial support to complete the full scale version. I had to turn in like eighteen forms in triplicate."

"And the real one is going to be big enough to affect the whole world?" Amina asks.

"Yeah, but not the whole world at once. Since it will be in orbit and accessing a network of satellites the OEV has hacked into, it will only affect the parts of the planet within its range. But I'll program it with the earth's rotation so that it will eventually get everyone. I decided to start with this hemisphere though, just in case it gets deactivated by some 'hero' before it's completed a round. I figure the U.S. is the country that needs it most right now."

I look back and forth between them, my curiosity almost unbearable. What is this new weapon that has the potential to affect the entire earth? What are their ultimate fiendish plans? I have to know.

And don't do the curiosity and the cat thing. Just don't.

"Oh," Amina says, as if reading my mind. "But Wuzzie doesn't know what we're talking about! We should show them the pro-type and how it works!"

"Prototype," Khalil corrects. "And I'm not sure it would even work on an animal," he adds skeptically.

Amina rolls her eyes. "I know the word, but I like calling it a pro-type, cause that means you're a pro! You're official now, with your OEV membership and everything."

Khalil ducks his head and grins. "Thanks, sis."

He pulls her in for a hug. Which means, since she is still holding me, I get sandwiched between them. Normally, I would make them pay for that, but it catches me off guard again. I also realize Amina stopped petting me in my spots a while ago, and yet I feel no compunction to get down from her arms. Clearly I am more fatigued by this whole affair than I thought.

Khalil digs around in a chaotic drawer of papers until he pulls out a messy roll of blueprints. He lays them on top of the desk (and everything covering it, so it looks more like a 3D relief map).

From here I can see plans for a giant globe with protrusions and an opening. Two extended knobbed rods are labeled as "sensory inputs," and the curved narrow opening, "beam port." Apparently it is curved so as to provide better coverage in connection with the curvature of the earth. At least, that's what I read on Khalil's blueprints. And of course cats can read.

He also pulls out what looks like a laughably small super soaker water cannon that has been spray-painted silver then dropped into a vat of glitter. Pride fills Amina's eyes, and I am fairly certain who is responsible for the exterior design.

Khalil points the tiny glittered barrel at Amina, which is also at me. I start to squirm and claw. I am not sure what exactly is going to happen, but I have been the subject of other "tests" by my villains. I still have a bald patch I have to lick the fur over to cover. I am never doing that again.

Amina holds me up gently. "I understand why you're scared, Wuzzie, but you don't have to worry about anything. Khalil's already used it on me and on himself, with nothing bad happening. My brother would never do anything that might hurt me. And also he is an amazing scientist, like the best! Like the very, very best!"

Khalil subconsciously runs his hands up the sides of his high top, smoothing any errant hairs and ensuring it stands tall and proud.

I typically never trust anything humans say. Primarily because every single one I have met lies to everyone all the time. And I'm not just talking about the villains; that's a given. Heroes have lied to me, too. I remember the first hero I met, who "rescued" me. It had been an exceptionally bad defeat for my villain. The secret lair caught on fire when the doomsday device blew up. Flames burned everywhere. I cowered underneath the desk, terrified, smoke clogging my lungs and blurring my vision. I'm not ashamed to admit I've never been more terrified in my life. I was barely out of being a kitten, and none of the other cats at the shelter had prepared me for this possibility.

The hero barged in to grab the jewels my villain had stolen. I raced forward, so relieved that help had come. I climbed the hero's trouser leg. He screamed and swore, shaking his leg. But I clung to my only chance at salvation like a burr in my overlong long fur. Finally the hero promised to adopt me if I let go. Said it in such a sweet calming voice. Said we would live together, that I'd have the biggest cat tree and all the treats I wanted. I was so happy, I released my claws and curled up in his arms, purring in between coughs from smoke inhalation. But of course he lied. He took me straight to the shelter, threw me down and didn't glance back once, no matter how loudly I cried for him to come back, my dreams fading like smoke.

So no, I never trust anything a human says.

But as I stare into Amina's earnest eyes, I don't know why exactly, I stop fighting.

"Good Wuzzie," Amina murmurs as she scratches under my chin.

She nods at Khalil. He suddenly turns around and holds out the gun, now pointed towards all three of us. He backs towards us, until we are all lightly touching.

"It's easier this way," Khalil says, I guess for my benefit since Amina clearly understands.

"It's like a science selfie! Smile, Wuzzie!" Amina presses her cheek into mine as Khalil pulls the trigger.

A beam of blindingly bright light shoots out of the barrel and bathes us all.

It takes minutes for my vision to clear. As it does, I feel a sudden wave of nervousness. My tail twitches furiously. *Did it work? I want it to work. I'm pretty sure it worked. But what if it didn't? Does that mean I'm a failure?*

Confusion fills me. Why am I so anxious? I am not at all invested in this gadget functioning properly. I don't even know what functioning properly means in relationship to it. I know all of this, and yet I feel like it's my entire life's work on the line.

As I focus on the feelings, I realize something strange. The feelings have a direction—like they are pouring into me from a point of origin. My eyes flick towards Khalil. He smiles, relieved, and the nervousness recedes. I am overcome by a new wave of excitement and pride. I don't remember the last time I felt either. It's not unpleasant, I suppose.

"Mini, it works! I can feel impressions from Wuzzie! Not as strong as with you. More just vague feelings. But I sensed Wuzzie was confused, then I sensed understanding, and maybe a little awe trickling through now?" Khalil looks at me.

I turn my gaze away and flick my tail. Now that's taking it too far. I am intrigued, perhaps, but what cat wouldn't be? However, no legitimate cat would ever be in awe of a human being. Unless said human was made of cat treats.

Khalil laughs and pets my head a couple times. "Ok, I must have been mistaken, not awe."

Feelings of amusement flow from Amina. "Yeah, you must have been wrong, bro. And also, I said don't call me Mini!" She glares at Khalil, who throws his hands up defensively.

"It's so funny," she continues, after confirming Khalil is properly chastised. "Like you said, I get senses of Wuzzie's feelings, but they feel blurry, like they are wrapped in a blanket. With another human, it's so clear and sharp. Sometimes it's overwhelming, getting flooded with all their feelings, and sometimes even their exact thoughts if they are super strong."

"It's like you're Deanna Troi, not Luwaxana," Khalil quips.

Both Amina and I just stare at him, unblinking.

"You know, from *Star Trek*? *The Next Generation*? Cause she's half Betazoid? She's an empath? But can only sense vague and mostly useless things that are pretty obvious? Like when someone's shooting at the ship and she's all like, 'Captain, I sense hostility?' Hello, anyone?"

A very long moment of silence breaks when Khalil mutters, "Whatever."

"But anyway," Amina continues, drawing out the end of the word, "It's nice, to feel your feelings, Wuz Wuz, even a little bit. I'm glad you aren't scared to be here anymore."

Again I flick my tail. I wouldn't say I was ever scared per se…

Amina laughs. "Ok, Wuzzers."

This is going to take some getting used to.

"And I got to name the invention too," Amina says, satisfaction flowing from her.

Khalil rolls his eyes in annoyance, but I feel his real emotions of affection. "Yeah, I'm really looking forward to going on the transmission and saying, 'Prepare yourself, world, for the power of … The Friendanator!'"

Amina claps her hands excitedly.

I turn back to the blueprints. If you look at it a certain way, the two knobbed black probes do resemble eyes, and the very narrow opening for the beam does curve upwards on both sides. It actually does look like a giant smiley face, if one is inclined to see it. I have no doubt Amina is very much inclined, especially now that I can sense her feelings.

Unfortunate emoji design notwithstanding, this is quite the grandiose plan right out the gate for a first-time evildoer.

Khalil nods. "Yeah, I know, it's a lot. But hey, go big or go home, right?"

More seriously, he says, "I just didn't know what else to do. How to fix things. I know other people change laws, or even start revolutions, which is awesome. But that's not me. This is what I do. I've always been good at science."

"Good?" Amina interjects. "He's a genius. They said so at school like a million times, and skipped him like fifty grades," Pride and love dance off her. Unrelated, I feel a strong urge to settle deeper into her arms. Which I of course resist.

Khalil shrugs. "Whatever that means. But yeah I have always been good at making things. When I see a problem, I just start thinking up a solution. Whether I want to or not, I just start seeing what could help and how to build it."

"I remember you made that car where you pressed the button and it folded down into the size of an Xbox. That was so cool," Amina says. "Oh, and the portable swimming pool that did the same. That one was less cool in real life."

"Yeah I forgot to take into account where the water would go," Khalil chuckles. "Hey, I was only seven when I made it. But yeah, as I stopped being a kid and got older, I started being aware of what's happening in this world. And what's happening to people who look like me. How much we are at risk. In the crosshairs.

"I took Mini to a #BlackLivesMatter protest for a young Black teen—she went to the high school not that far from mine. She was just two years older than me. She was killed by police for nothing. They said they thought she had a gun. It was her history textbook." His tone, full of pain, doesn't begin to encompass his radiating emotions.

Khalil's eyes drift away. "I had to do something. So I said I was going to this demonstration, and Mini insisted on going with me. And then at the protest, the police came out looking like storm troopers. They attacked us all, even though we were peaceful."

"It was so scary," Amina says wide-eyed, and I feel her remembered fear. But I also get blurry mental images—maybe because they are both remembering the same incident. It is hazy, and skips back and forth between their perspectives, like a stuttering old movie projector.

"They started shooting tear gas, and Khalil pulled his beanie off and made me put it over my mouth and my nose." Amina's confusion and fear. Khalil's terror as he realized what was happening, not for himself, but for his sister.

"Luckily we were at the back so it wasn't as bad there. We could get away. Khalil snatched me up and ran like four blocks, coughing the whole time." Playing split screen, Khalil coughing violently leaning against a wall, tears streaming down his eyes. The other screen, Amina staring up, concern all over her young face. But the feeling from Khalil, despite his wretched condition, is just joy as he looked down at his sister. And I notice in both memories, their hands clutched together tightly.

The visual images fade as their thoughts diverge from the shared trauma.

This room is so dusty, I think irritably as I blink rapidly.

"My bro is like a real-life superhero." Amina smiles.

Khalil pats his high top again, radiating self-conscious embarrassment. "Yeah I don't know about that.

"But that's when I realized that this was all happening because there are lives that just don't matter in this world. Because of who they are. The color of their skin. Where they are from. The police saw that Black woman as less than human, and that's why they could murder her and say it was justified." His conviction burns so brightly off him, I can almost feel the warmth.

"And the more I thought about it, the more an invention began to take shape in my mind. It really came together when I remembered what my mom would say whenever Amina and I fight—I mean, when we used to fight, because obviously I'm too old to fight with her now. And I saw you roll your eyes, you're not slick," he directs the last toward his sister, who good naturedly sticks out her tongue. "Anyway, yeah, so after mom broke up a fight, she'd always say we should try to put ourselves in other person's shoes, try to see through their eyes. Feel what they feel.

"That's when it hit me—if everyone felt what everyone else felt, they couldn't say we aren't human. I mean, I know it's not going to solve everything," Khalil continues, and the brightness tempers slightly. "I know from studying history that this brutality isn't just caused by people not understanding one another, or needing to learn to 'tolerate' each other. There's a whole system in place that keeps it all going. People often are part of it without even being conscious of it. Also there are lots of folks who know exactly what they are doing, and still do really horrific things. For money. For power. I know this won't stop that."

I feel hope pouring off him. "But maybe it will help wake up those white people who don't know, who didn't understand their role. Maybe they can then join with the Black people, the Brown people, who have been living through this every day for years, for decades, for centuries. And then maybe all together, they will decide that this system has to change completely. I don't want to be in charge of that. It's not my place to say how things should change. I just know they should." Khalil's certainty is so unshakable, so solid, it fills me as well, and nests in me.

"It also doesn't last that long," Amina adds. "For us, it's like a day that we can feel and hear each other's thoughts, then it fades away."

"Yeah, and I posit less time if you're not in a controlled environment, and instead integrating with the feelings of multiple people—well, creatures. Beings. Actually, I hadn't considered before now the implications for life forms other than human," Khalil muses, slipping into scientist mode. "I'll have to do more field tests with the prototype and see how far these results extend."

He starts to reach for his laptop, his gaze already far away.

"Ok, but do that later!" Amina says. "Finish telling Wuzzie—can't you feel how curious he is? It's almost overwhelming."

I blink up at her, surprised. No human has ever understood how it feels to be a cat before. They make jokes and think they do. But then they yell at us for climbing on things, for exploring everywhere we can. If they actually understood us, they would know it wasn't a choice, but a biological compunction.

Amina gives me a little squeeze.

Khalil laughs. "Ok, ok. The rest is simple. When I realized how much money it would take to construct the Friendanator, I knew I'd need way more resources than I could ever scavenge and adapt, which is how I make most of my inventions. So I joined OEV."

I feel disgust, but I can't tell which of us three it's coming from. "I mean, I don't like OEV, but at least they are honest about what they are doing. OEV is funded by the same places that fund pretty much everything—oil, weapons manufacturing, wealth from centuries of taking money from every day working people, stealing labor from Black people, stealing land from indigenous people. They try to pretend that they are in opposition to those forces, and then the world governments act like they are working to stop them. But really it's just two sides of the same coin. Symbiotic. They need each other."

My whiskers shiver. I am a little ashamed to say I've never

wondered about the funding for my villains. I mean, of course, I know about the OEV, and it fills all the villain cats I've met with trepidation. But I never considered before where they get their seemingly endless stream of money.

"To get them to fund the Friendanator, I fudged the blueprints a little. Ok, a lot. I told them it will control the minds of people globally, and we could use it to get everyone to transfer all money and nuclear codes and everything to OEV."

Khalil does a good beginner evil villain laugh as the mischievous delight pours off him. "And I told them it would work on everyone unless you are wearing one of these on your heads." Khalil pulls out what looks like a colander with springs haphazardly glued to it.

"So extra bonus that the day of, all these uber rich evil dudes are gonna be walking around looking ridiculous. It might actually help us to see who is in cahoots with them—probably gonna be a lot of these up in the White House that day."

Amina laughs so hard she snorts. Having observed a number of the OEV leaders at various functions, I definitely appreciate that trick being played on them—it's the very least they deserve. But I still have a question, which Khalil senses.

"If you're wondering what protection there is from the Friendanator," Khalil says, "there isn't one."

My surprise encourages him to explain. "All of us humans, and I guess now animals too, and who knows, maybe plants, we are all going to be affected. Mini—Amina," he corrects himself quickly as Amina makes a face and starts to open her mouth, "Amina and I are going to be part of that, just like everyone and everything else on this planet. We're all in this together." Again that blazing certainty.

Amina twirls around with me in her arms. "Yeah, it's evil do or die. Evil-do or do not, there is no evil-try!" she says in a singsong voice.

As Amina spins closer to the pile of clothes I had... christened upon my arrival, she starts sniffing. She kneels down and sniffs more, then looks at Khalil, clearly communicating without words. I feel nothing from either of them—apparently you can not only transmit feelings, you can direct them. And whatever they are both thinking and feeling, they don't want me to know any part of it.

Real fear claws at my throat in that moment, and I know it is all mine this time. I had quickly learned to sparingly deploy Cat Secret Weapon #3, as it makes humans incredibly angry. In fact, my bald patch is a direct consequence of the utilization of Cat Secret Weapon #3.

Somehow, though, my biggest fear this time is not physical reprisal. I have already experienced so much of that from humans. I know how to elude and, if cornered, how to give as well as I get. But surprisingly, what I most fear now is feeling (literally in this situation) Khalil and Amina's anger, their disappointment, their disgust. I feel like I am that barely-grown kitten all over again, meowing piteously as the only human to show me any kindness abandons me.

I have to get out now. Leave on my own, while it's still my choice to make. I twist and kick, trying to get Amina to drop me without hurting her.

"Hey," Khalil steps forward and gently takes me from Amina's arms. "It's cool, Wuz. I get it. Change is hard. Those were my old scavenging clothes anyway. They should have been thrown out a long time ago. I was kidding when I said that was your bed, but of course, you couldn't have known that then. Your real bed is in Amina's room—she insisted on it." Khalil strokes from the top of my head to the end of my tail, and I feel the tension leave my body. Because he has opened his feelings back up to me, and all I feel is warmth and care and... I'm not quite sure what else, but it makes me feel like a bowl of warm milk does.

"Well, I just knew Wuzzie would want to sleep with me rather than you! I mean, part of why I didn't notice the pee smell earlier is because your whole room is funkety funky anyway!"

Khalil makes a mock grotesque face and she giggles.

Amina takes me back, settles on the bed, and pets my head. "Wuzzy Buzzy doesn't have to worry, does he, Khalil?"

"Naw," Khalil pets the secret tail spot that more unsophisticated cats love. I will say I don't find it completely awful. "Wuzzie's home now."

The purring emanating from me is, I assure you, strictly a ploy to lure them into a false sense of security, so they will be caught completely off guard by my next ambush.

As I think this, Khalil and Amina look at each other, and burst out laughing.

My tail twitches furiously. This is going to be awful. I mean, if a cat doesn't have their inscrutability, what do they have?

THE BLOODLETTER'S PRAYER

Cullen Bunn

THE LAND, THE Bloodletter remembered, was once fertile and rich, an expanse of lush fields and thick forests.

Now, though...

He crouched, running the fingers of his gloved hand over the dry, cracked earth. The movement stirred whispers of dust drifting across the ground. What was once abundant soil had shriveled to a barren, fractured shell where nothing could grow. One might think this place had never seen a drop of rain.

The Bloodletter rubbed his fingers together, letting the dust fall through the still air. He stood, looking into the distance, across the badlands. Desolation where there had been trees and crops, grass and streams of clear water.

And cities.

He had visited the great cities of old. He had studied within them when he was but an acolyte. He had studied in the spired libraries of Cereakis. He had been cut and beaten and trained in the art of the sword in the halls of Rellisar. He had been tortured in the scream-haunted dungeons of Sendarken. Even now, decades later, he still bore the scars of his studies—across his back, his shoulders, his chest, his knuckles, and his face. An ache in his left wrist. A hitch in his right knee. His flesh, his muscles, his bones traced a history of grueling training and brutal ministries. The scars remained but Creakis, Rellisar, and Sendarken had all crumbled.

No rain, he mused, but blood in great supply. And blood did not yield crops or feed cities.

Ghosts, but no crops.

Once, before the gods went to war, he had been one of a thousand missionaries sent out with scriptures and blade to guide, to comfort, to protect, and to punish. Now, though, the mantle and robe of his order were threadbare and worn, his leathers scuffed and gouged. His chain of holy symbols and reliquaries had been cast into the dust years ago.

He no longer resembled a priest.

The blade at his side, though, still marked him as a Bloodletter.

He had wielded the sword while discharging his sacred duties. The blade was still sharp, honed in battle during his travels through the war-ravaged wastes, etched with the words of sacred texts. But while the sword served the same purpose as it had in the name of the gods above and below, it could not be described as the same weapon. Something had changed in the years after the Godwar. The Bloodletter had plunged the blade into the heart of the Mad Bishop, and the metal had been tainted by the slaying. Now, if one examined the symbols closely, they might see the etched letters moving slowly, crawling around the blade, the words changing in blasphemous ways. If one listened closely, they might hear a chilling whisper, low and steady, as if the sword had forbidden secrets to share.

The Bloodletter had listened to these whispers and lamented.

These void-borne whispers had brought him to this wasteland, lured him with horrible promises.

The gods, the Whispering Blade vowed, have not abandoned the Cathedral of Vanris.

It spoke other promises, too.

But the Bloodletter knew it did not tell him everything.

The Bloodletter did not trust the sword. The Whispering Blade had saved his life more times than he could count, yes, but it also lied, hissed untruths with the same ease it spilled entrails and blood.

From a hiding place among standing stones, he watched the road to Vanris for hours. He grew more impatient—more certain that he wasted his time—with every passing minute. Soon, though, he saw a group of men marching along the path. They were monks, dressed in the dark robes of their order, heads shaved, skin tattooed with holy symbols. Chains marked with the symbols of a dozen gods—some of whom had loathed each other—were draped across their shoulders. Their feet were bare, kicking up little puffs of dust as they walked along. Swords hung at their sides.

A young boy—maybe eleven years of age—accompanied them. He wore the white robes of an acolyte who had not chosen his god. The monks surrounded him, protecting him as they continued on their pilgrimage.

The Bloodletter counted nine monks.

Nine men who would die.

They don't matter to their own gods, the Bloodletter thought. Why should they matter to me?

Only the boy was of consequence.

Sword in hand but held behind his back, the Bloodletter rose from his hiding spot and stepped out into the road. Holding his weapon as he did, he looked almost as if he was presenting himself formally and politely at the royal courts of old. These men might be approaching their own demise, but there was no need to be rude. The monks staggered to a stop when they saw him, and they drew their own swords, held them—uncivilly—at the ready. The boy's expression was blank. He did not acknowledge the Bloodletter.

"The boy," the Bloodletter said. "Leave him to me, and you can go."

His voice, once so soothing and clear, was now a dry and quiet. It sounded strange to him. He had not spoken to anyone—not even himself—in many weeks. He sounded, he thought grimly, not unlike the whispering of his sword.

"Your heavens and your hells are overcrowded enough as it is," he continued, "and they are left untended. I can't imagine they are nice places to visit. So why be in a hurry to do so?"

Five of the monks stepped forward, their eyes narrowed, their lips curled in sneers.

"Heretic!" one of the monks hissed.

"Sin-spawn!" rasped another.

"Infidel!" cried a third.

The Bloodletter had been called these names before, more often than not by men who would soon die upon his hissing, sigil-marked blade, men who would scream the names of vestigial gods as they fell screaming into the void, men who had served so devoutly in order to secure their place in the afterlife but who—upon death—find nothingness waiting for them.

Behind the Bloodletter's back, his hand tightened upon the hilt of his sword.

His muscles tensed.

He prepared to spring from his formal stance and into a death-dealing position.

With wickedly hooked and permanently blood-marked short

swords, the monks came at the Bloodletter. He knew they had wielded these blades in countless butcher-orgies to honor gods that represented lust as much as slaughter. They had sliced the throats of innocents in their beds to pay homage to the god of dreams and nightmares. They had disemboweled shackled unbelievers in the name of hungry, feeder gods. The stained swords were implements both holy and unholy, symbols of awful times when the great and terrible lords above and below had roamed freely.

Devotion and sacrifice bought each of the monks a half-dozen steps. As they charged, the Bloodletter welcomed them with vicious slashes and stabs, gutting them, opening their throats, piercing their chests. Their ceremonial blades fell to the dirt along with their spilled blood. Their faith did not save them.

The Bloodletter murdered without malice—murdered, even though he struck in defense of his own life, because he had come to kill these men. He had lain in wait for them. In his planning, he had killed each of them a dozen times already. His work was clean and efficient. In a matter of seconds, five men lay dead at his feet.

His sword whispered in delight.

Four monks remained. They had not thrown themselves at the Bloodletter as the others had. This, the Bloodletter thought, showed them to be the most dangerous of their ilk. They would not fall so easily. Three took up defensive positions before the fourth, who stood behind the boy. The fourth monk held the boy's arm tightly, yanking him back. He placed his hooked sword across the boy's neck and sneered.

"I'll kill him!" the fourth monk said. "Stand down or I'll open his throat! I know what you want, but you'll never have it! He'll not pray for you!"

The hissing blade urged the Bloodletter to strike.

The Bloodletter watched the monks. They were unafraid. They were bolstered by their faith, though it might be unrewarded. They were prepared to die for their beliefs, and they had been preparing to meet this destiny for years.

"Stand down!" the monk ordered once more.

The blade scratched at the boy's skin. A trickle of blood ran down his neck. He did not react in any way.

"You're bluffing." The Bloodletter took a step toward them. "If you kill him, you won't be able to use his gifts, either."

"Stay back!" the fourth monk commanded, panic in his voice.

The other monks clenched their weapons tightly. They braced themselves for the fight to come.

"There's no need for you to die," the Bloodletter said.

The hissing blade rasped in disagreement.

"Give the boy to me," the Bloodletter said, "and be on your way."

"Not another step!" The fourth monk cried. He shook the boy by the arm. He held his blade in a white-knuckled grasp. He was sweating and trembling.

He might just do it, the Bloodletter thought. He might slay the boy to prevent any prayer other than his own from being heard. He might actually be a believer.

A subtle shifting of his left foot through the dirt, and now the Bloodletter was in striking distance. Now he was poised to attack. He had already decided who would die first. The monk on the far right held his own blade in such a way that he'd be unable to parry an upward stroke coming in from the low left. The other two monks, scrambling in their surprise, would stumble into each other and be unprepared when the Bloodletter's sigil- and blood-covered blade changed direction and came for them in two inelegant but effective hacking strokes. With any luck, the Bloodletter would be done with them in such brutal speed that the fourth monk would be too stunned to carry out a murderous slash across the boy's throat.

But the monk on the left—the man who was the Bloodletter's intended third victim—cocked his head, taking notice of the hissing blade, and he gasped in fear.

"His sword! It's—"

The Bloodletter drove his blade through the man's throat before he could finish speaking.

Now, though, he had opened himself up to attack, and he could not pivot in time to avoid the slashing blades of the other monks. A hooked and blood-flecked sword bit into his right side. If it had not scraped against his ribs, it might have killed him. He growled in pain, drew his arm back sharply as he yanked the hissing blade from the dead man's throat. His elbow smashed one of the remaining monks in the nose, staggering him back, giving the Bloodletter some breathing room.

Ignoring the pain from the wound in his side, the Bloodletter whirled, and he claimed another life—and a pair of eyes—with a vicious, backhand slash.

The third monk drove his blade forward. Metal screeched against metal as the Bloodletter parried the attack, knocking the monk's sword aside, then riposted stabbing his enemy through the heart.

Before the third man fell, the Bloodletter sprang at the fourth. The remaining monk wore an expression of fright and confusion. He was alone now, and his conviction to kill the boy faltered. Before he could regain his senses, the Bloodletter sank the hissing sword right through the man's mouth, silencing his useless invocations forever.

The hissing blade lapped up the blood.

To the Bloodletter, the whisper sounded a bit like, "Gooooood boy!"

Panting and sweating, the Bloodletter stood among the child and dead men. He put a hand over the wound at his side. His clothing was sodden with blood, but he did not think the wound would do him in. It was more painful than deep. It could be tended later. He did not bother wiping the gore from his sword. He knew from experience that the blade would be clean within the hour, the blood seeping into the sword's slowly moving sigils. He looked toward the boy, who stood unafraid before him. He held his own pale hand to his throat where the monk's sword had scratched at him.

"Don't worry," the Bloodletter said. "You'll live."

"I... I'll live," the boy said.

"What is your name, boy?" asked the Bloodletter.

"Name?" the boy repeated.

The Bloodletter busied himself checking the bodies of the monks. He did not like looting the dead, but even Bloodletters had to eat, and times had been lean since the Godwar ended. He found only a few coins secreted away in the monks' robes. He found a small supply of Communion Dust, too, and he took that as well. He had no use for the hallucinogenic properties of the Dust, but some addicts he might encounter in his travels would pay a handsome price for it.

All the while, the boy stood nearby, waiting.

Waiting for guidance.

"Do you know where they were taking you?" the Bloodletter asked.

"Taking me?" the boy parroted.

"Never mind." The Bloodletter threw the last few baubles, coins, and a bit of food in his bag. He sat upon a stump and tended his bleeding cut, stitching it as best he could and placing a simple poultice—the last of his medicine—over the wound. Then, he motioned for the boy to join him. "Come on. We have a long road ahead of us."

Without argument, the boy followed.

———

THE GODS WERE not dead, though it wasn't for a lack of trying.

Long ago, they had flooded greedily into the world. They came by the hundreds, gods both great and small. They represented love or beauty, hate or murder. They boasted dominion over the sun, over the air, over the water, and over the earth itself. They were the gods of the harvest, of the hunt, of festivals. They were the lords of the wild places as well as the cities.

There were some that mused that every blade of grass had a deity associated with it.

Perhaps that had been true.

But all of the gods hated one another. They killed one another to claim spheres of influence the way some killers collected trophies from their victims. The god of cities became the god of cities and forests, though she knew not what to do with the latter. The god of the sun took the moon as his prize. The twin gods of disease became the gods of disease and feasts and of waterfowl.

Soon, their hate and rage and jealousy erupted into war.

The gods were all but wiped out. They died. They fled to hidden places. They vanished.

And they almost took the world with them.

Still, there were those who rejoiced at the thought that the gods yet lived. They uttered modest prayers. They scraped together meager offerings. They sacrificed livestock and let the carcasses rot while they themselves starved. One day, the monks and priests promised, the gods would return, and they would have learned humility, and they would rain miracles down upon the world that had suffered so at their hands. Mankind only needed prove that they had not forgotten the gods.

"Bullshit," the Bloodletter spat.

He did not swear often. Such utterances had been forbidden by his order and now, when he was free to say whatever he pleased, there was rarely anyone to listen.

"B-Bullshit," the boy said.

The Bloodletter and the boy had traveled the rest of the day, not stopping until well after dark. The wound on the Bloodletter's side throbbed painfully with every step. His companion, however, had complained about nothing, and so the Bloodletter had kept his own grousing to himself.

Now, they sat by a small campfire, huddled close to the crackling flames as the cold crept in all around them. The boy stared into the flickering glow. The Bloodletter watched the boy for a while.

"What shall I call you?" The Bloodletter asked, talking more to himself than to the boy.

As much as the man was known for his profession—bloodletting—the boy was known for his lot in life. It was possible he had a name once. His parents might have named him when he was born, before they recognized him for what he was. His parents were likely long dead, and the name they had given the boy had died with him. He was a Prayer Vessel. His mind was empty, and his soul was pure. The purity might attract the attention of those gods who remembered the value of such things. The purity might also draw the baleful gaze of those who wanted to feed upon such a delicacy. Either way, when the boy spoke, the gods above and below—forgotten though they may be—were likely to listen. The boy's emptiness meant that holy... or unholy... men might guide his words. They would speak their prayers to him, and he would parrot them to the gods, asking for blessings and miracles on behalf of someone else.

Maybe, the Bloodletter thought, that's why the gods listen to the Prayer Vessels, because they never want anything for themselves.

"I had a brother once," the Bloodletter said. "His name was Errol.

He was an annoying little shit, always running his mouth when he should have been listening. That's what got him killed, I imagine. I always wanted him to be more like you. I wanted him to be quiet. I think I'll call you Errol, if it's all the same to you."

"Errol," the boy said.

Satisfied, the Bloodletter nodded, settled his back against the trunk of a tree and closed his eyes.

SOMETIME LATER, THE sound of singing woke him.

His hand went to the hilt of the Hissing Blade. He jumped to his feet.

The Bloodletter knew many tales of ghosts and night-sirens and goblins that lured travelers with sweet songs. Such creatures were the messengers of the gods, and now that the gods had all but vanished, their emissaries grew confused and frightened and angry. They would fall upon hapless victims, torment and kill them, without cause and without mercy.

In that way, they were not unlike priests.

Or Bloodletters.

But there were no goblins, no apparitions or phantoms. Instead, Errol sat quietly, staring into the embers of the dying fire, singing softly and sweetly. The Bloodletter listened to the boy's soothing lullaby for several minutes. His fingers relaxed on the hilt of the Hissing Blade. The tension in his shoulders eased. The tune made the Bloodletter think about simpler, happier times, before he had been laden with the duty of slaying or cursed with the burden of the Hissing Sword.

He could not help but wonder, though, who the boy—the Prayer Vessel—was listening to as he sang.

Thus, even the thought of happier times filled the Bloodletter with unease.

———•———

ANOTHER TWO DAYS of travel, and they reached the Temple of Vanris.

In the distance, a tall but crumbling temple rose from a barren wasteland of slate. The structure stood miles away, black against an angry red sky. A line of people—men and women, young and old, priests and penitents alike—stretched into the distance. These hopeful worshippers shuffled forward—slowly, slowly—moving toward the temple step by step. Some carried valuables. Some brought chickens or kittens or small dogs in wooden cages. Others brought dried flowers or foodstuffs. A few bore hand-carved idols of warrior gods with multiple, sharp-toothed mouths. All carried prayers on their lips and in their hearts. All hoped the gods would hear their pleas.

Even as the Bloodletter and Errol approached the meandering line, more worshippers approached to join the procession. Still others could be seen in the distance. The line would continue on forever, especially considering that those who had already visited the far-off temple would often march back to the end of the line, joining the group once again in hopes of getting their message to the god. At other temple sites, it was not unheard of for penitents to fall dead from exhaustion or malnourishment or exposure. When that happened, one of the people in line behind them would gather up the body as an offering to the deity that awaited them.

The Bloodletter did not join the procession. It moved too slowly for his tastes. He took Errol by the wrist and together they skirted along the line, passing the slow-moving penitents and the prayer-uttering holy men. The Bloodletter kept his eyes down, hoping that if he ignored the people in the line, they would in turn ignore him. It took maybe a dozen steps before this plan fell apart.

"You there!" A man called from the line. "Where do you think you're going?"

The Bloodletter paid him no mind. Clutching Errol's wrist tightly, he moved a little more quickly.

"Wait," another voice called. "Wait!"

Another yelled, "You can't just walked to the head of the line!"

"Stop, you!" cried another.

"Your prayers are no more important than mine!" said another.

Soon, the entirety of the line called out to him, a cacophonous riot of angry voices. Anger, the Bloodletter could contend with. He did not stop. But then he heard the exclamation he had been dreading.

"The boy! The boy's a Prayer Vessel!"

He quickened his pace, but it did little good. The temple was still quite a way off. He and Errol would pass hundreds of desperate, pleading men and women. They no longer called for the Bloodletter and his companion to stop. Instead, they clutched at the boy, begging him to pass on their prayers.

"Tell him," an old man said, "that I served him well on the battlefields! Tell him I deserve my place in his Feast Hall!"

"Ask if my brother is by his side," pleaded a red-eyed woman.

"My child," cried a desperate mother, "is so ill. I know he will not heal her, but perhaps he'll ask one of his brethren."

"I'm sorry for what I've done," whimpered another man. "You'll let him know I'm sorry, won't you?"

The Bloodletter moved along, dragging Errol step by step, ever closer to the massive temple. All along, the people standing in line grabbed at Errol, begging him to pass on their messages. The boy's lips moved as he spoke to himself, reciting to nothingness the hundreds of prayers that were passed on to him. The Bloodletter payed them as little mind as he was able. He did not want to hear their prayers. He did not want to know what they needed. He knew that the boy would not help them—far from it—and he didn't want to understand just how terribly they would be let down.

The worshippers nearly cheered as the Bloodletter and the Prayer Vessel reached the steps to the temple.

Fools, the Bloodletter thought. Poor fools.

He climbed the steps toward the enormous entrance to the temple. Once, the titanic metal doors had been sealed. Now, they stood open. The metal was dented as if the doors had been battered open by giant fists.

Within was a great hall, impossibly long, with a ceiling rising high above, held aloft by massive columns.

The real miracle, the Bloodletter thought, is that this place did not fall in the war.

He led Errol along the hall. The place was unlit, save for the light streaming in from beyond the great, battered doors. What awaited them at the far end of the temple was shrouded in darkness.

But it smelled of decay.

This was a tomb.

As the Bloodletter and the Prayer Vessel moved through the temple, a great silence rushed in around them. Even the boy, who had been echoing the desperate prayers he had heard outside, fell silent.

Before them rose the throne of a giant. The seat looked to have been carved from the floor itself, and it stood at least thirty feet high. Around the base of the throne were wilted flowers and moldy bread, rotted meat and gold coins, sacrificed livestock and pets, dried blood and even a severed finger or two—offerings to the thing that sat upon the throne.

The seated god was a skeletal horror, a withered behemoth that might once have been godly but was now horrendous. Withered flesh sloughed off thick bones and tusks. The thing slouched in the chair, its massive skull lolling to the side.

What god this was, the Bloodletter did not know, nor did he care.

He placed a hand on Errol's shoulder, guiding the boy to stand before him.

Errol gazed at the dead god.

"It's time," the Bloodletter said.

He drew the Whispering Blade.

"And I'm sorry."

The Bloodletter held his hissing sword next to the boy's ear. The runes crawled across the metal, the movement of the etched letters creaking, forming whispers.

The boy listened.

The boy spoke.

The Bloodletter squeezed his eyes shut. He tried to think of anything other than the words coming out of the boy's mouth. This was the Vile Tongue, a profane language of blasphemy and curses, of hatred and terror.

Tears rolled down Errol's face as he repeated what the sword told him.

He went on and on, and—listening, though he tried not to—the Bloodletter thought he might go mad. He wanted the boy to stop speaking. He wanted the sword to cease its ghastly whispering. He thought if it did not stop soon he might use the blade to hack the boy's head from his shoulders, though he wondered if even that might bring silence.

And then—just like that—the boy closed his mouth and lowered his head.

"Amen," Errol said.

All was quiet again, but only for a moment.

The dead god upon the throne drew a ragged and rattling breath. Its bones creaked as it shifted his enormous bulk. It slowly, painfully, gripped the arms of the chair and pushed itself to its feet. Dust fell from its body, hissing against the stone floor like rain.

The dead god did not acknowledge the Bloodletter or Errol as it stepped past. Its gait was unsure and unsteady as it lumbered toward the light at the end of the hall.

Errol moved to follow, but the Bloodletter held him back.

"You've done enough, boy. Neither one of us wants to see what comes next."

The dead god staggered through the open door to the temple. A great cry of wonder and adulation rose from the gathering of worshippers outside.

Soon enough, those cries turned to screams.

The Bloodletter watched Errol. The boy's eyes were wide with wonder as he listened to the shrieks coming from outside.

When he grew sick of the screams, the Bloodletter busied himself gathering coins from around the base of the throne. After all, the dead god had little interest in them.

Once the screaming stopped, the Bloodletter and the boy walked slowly to the door and exited the cathedral.

The dead god was gone, but he had left a trail of mutilated bodies in his wake. They had been torn apart, crushed underfoot, tossed around and broken. Every person in the procession lay dead, an awful pilgrimage of corpses stretching as far as the eye could see.

The Whispering Blade rasped in delight as the Bloodletter sheathed it once more.

Errol stared out across the bodies.

"We did this," the Bloodletter said.

"We did this," Errol repeated.

"And, no doubt, we'll do it again."

He took the boy's hand—gently—and together they walked along the trail of dead bodies. The Bloodletter could not help but notice that some of the men and women had died with expressions of happiness and love upon their faces. Soon, he turned away from the corpses and walked south, unsure of his destination other than—

Somewhere else.

"Sing us a song," the Bloodletter said to the boy.

To his surprise, the boy did.

THE SECOND SIEGE OF TELEA

Anna Smith Spark

This story is set in the world of Irlast, but can be read
without prior knowledge of the Empires of Dust *series,*
of which it is a brief and peripheral part.

S O THIS IS me. Tobias. And here we are. Roaring fire, mugs
of beer, complimentary bar snacks. Pork scratchings—love 'em.
And you want me to tell you a story about myself.

Why?

I'm a squad commander in, clears throat, The Free Company of
the Sword. I tramp around much more rarely than you'd think killing
people. Mostly I really don't kill people. It's not as dangerous as people
think, being a sellsword. Honestly. Walk around. Cook meals. Yell at
people. Hold a sword in a vaguely threatening way. Most exciting job
of the last week was giving my kit a full clean and polish. Most exciting
event of the last month was a woman selling meat pies at a knock-off.

You're assuming I'm going to say something to the effect that the meat pies turned out to be rank, aren't you? Second most exciting event of the month was us all needing the urgent shits?

Second most exciting event of the month was the meat pies being fine and healthsome. Which does go to show exactly how dull the last month was, I'll give you that.

No, you just thought I meant something else by 'meat pies'? Gods, you're filthy-minded, you are. Now shut up.

Okay, right. Anyway. Tries to get that thought out of his mind. Nice fat juicy meat pie, hot and dripping... gods, thanks, that's put me off them for life.

Anyway. Right. Ahem. A story. For some unknown reason. About me, Tobias, being a squad commander in a company of sellswords. Not an exciting life, most of the time. Walking, drilling blokes into some attempt to at least pretend to do what I tell them, bollocking them, bollocking them again. Sleeping out in the open, which is miserable, or in a stinking tent with a bloke who's not washed for a week and had beans for supper and likes to relieve the pressure we all sometimes feel at night while lying two feet from my head. The free life of the glorious killer! I'm not even thirty and my knees bloody crack like my grandma's, and my fingers ache all the time and I get a pain something chronic in my right shoulder when the wind blows from the east.

"Lighten up?" Fuck off. Life's pain etc.

But I can give you a story. Oh yes.

You ready? Got a beer? Pork scratchings? Sick bowl?

Then I'll begin.

THE SECOND SIEGE of Telae. Heard that tale yet?

No?

What do you mean, "No"?

And there was me thinking what we did there was something famous.

I'm joking. Like I was about the meat pies. Don't sweat yourself. It's not like I'm a hard bastard sellsword with a fuck-off big sword I killed a bloke to get hold of, is it? You don't need to look so nervous around me.

Bloody nice sword too. Got a real ruby in the hilt and all.

Yes, it's a real friggin' ruby. Oh ye of little faith. I'm not stupid. Checked with the bloke before I finished him.

Anyway. The Second Siege of Telea. Here we go:

Telea, rich in men and horses! Telea, whose walls are made of gold! An oasis of civilization on the wild border between Immish and Cen Andae. Sits on a bend of the fast-flowing river Enias, that runs down from the Mountains of the Heart to the Bitter Sea bringing timber and furs and iron and precious gems. Sits on a bridge over the fast-flowing river Enias, that carries the trade road from the old wealth of Ith and Immier down to the new wealth of Immish and the ancient wealth of the Asekemlene Empire of the Eternal Golden City of Sorlost. You might, if you're feeling particularly acute today, notice a few hints there to the idea of "rich." "Very rich." "Stinking rich." "Unbelievably chuffin' rich." Thus much fought over by Immish and Cen Andae and almost anyone.

During the Salavene Wars, the Queen of Telea fought in single combat with the Godking and almost defeated Him: "You are invincible!" He cried to her, and granted her that her city would be left untouched by the demons of war. And to this day, the walls of the city are impregnable, cannot be damaged by iron or bronze or wood or stone.

During the conquests of Amrath, the Teleans decided to fuck it, who needs impregnable walls, marched out at meet the Army of Amrath in battle. Didn't do too well. Swore never to march out again.

Might even be some good in having impregnable walls.

During the Seven Years War between Immish and Chathe, the Teleans allied themselves with Chathe and the White Isles. Didn't march out. Sat tight. The Immish besieged them and tried to starve them out. Nearly succeeded, the walls not being impregnable to hunger and disease and boredom. Until the White Isles sent a general to aid them, Prince Tiovyn Altrersyr, the second son of Fylinn Dragonlord, who was smuggled into the city disguised as a beggar in rags. Tiovyn ordered the Teleans to demonstrate their resolve by throwing their children headfirst from the city walls. "Look!" he shouted to the Immish. "We have plenty of fresh meat!" Tiovyn changed sides a week later, opened the gates to the Immish army. Charged his fee twice as a part of the city's sack. Once to the Teleans, once to the Immish.

Telea! City of horses! May the stories told of her never cease! Pig-ugly city, actually. Her walls aren't made of gold at all, just grey stone covered in yellow paint. They can still show you the house where Tiovyn stayed, though. And the bloodstains on the rocks where the children hit the ground.

Ruled over by a prince of the House of Selba, who could trace his ancestry back at least ten years. Knew the name of both his parents, and even one of his grandparents too. But, gods, his people loved him. Merciful to the poor, firm to the powerful, fair to the innocent. Firm but fair to the very large army he was building up.

That's the background, that you probably already knew. Who hasn't heard the name of the city of Telea?

Oh, shut up.

THE COMPANY WAS sitting around on its collective scrawny arse in the shit-hole that's the town of Reneneth. I won't waste time describing

Reneneth to you, seeing as it's one of the top five most depressing places I've ever been to. Falling down buildings, piles of rubbish in the streets, the houses are made of white stone going green with mold. The air in the place stinks. The people in the place stink. Poor and grumpy, the people of Reneneth. Getting poorer and grumpier as every day goes on. Living in the rubble of your great-great-great-great grandparents' boundless riches maybe does that to people. Turns you to drink and letting your dogs crap in the middle of the street. Not a place I'd choose to visit, or ever intend to go back to. But our last job had been as caravan guards down in Maun; Reneneth, being a depressing shit-hole, was a cheap convenient place to sit around and wait for the next job to turn up.

"Good news, Tobias," Skie said to me one morning. "We've got the next job."

"About time. Thank all gods and demons."

Skie gave me a cold look.

Skie. Our commander-in-chief, leader of the Free Company. And you should be nervous around him, oh yeah. See his left hand, do you? That area of empty space where his left hand used to be?

You should see what the other guy looked like.

Skie said, "Telea, rich in gold and horses. Telea, whose walls are—" what I just said, only in a grey dull monotone voice. He got out the company's map, pointed. Greasy-looking, the bit of the map showing Telea and Cen Andae and Immish. Generations of commanders-in-chief of, clears throat, The Free Company of the Sword had poked and prodded and stared and traced route marches and sneezed bits of bacon on that bit of the map. Shame, cause it's a nice map, nicely drawn, with little decorative pictures that are a smart touch. I'm told it once had gold leaf on the edges, before some previous commander-in-chief of the Free Company picked the gold leaf very carefully off. Skie said, "Telea is proud of its independence. Fifty years, its independence goes back. Imagine. Chucked out the Immish while the Immish were preoccupied hammering Cen Andae. Fifty years later, the Immish want control of Telea back."

As I just said, greasy-looking, that bit of the map. Like the blood's soaked in to it, I'd say, if I was a superstitious man.

Skie said, "Telea fell to the Immish three weeks ago, following a short, sharp siege and a very large bag of gold."

Pretty standard.

Skie said, "The Teleans butchered the Immish troops in the city two weeks ago. The siege has resumed. The Teleans are proving rather more resistant this time around."

Pretty standard again.

Skie moved his finger up to the city of Raen to the north. "Cen Andae is sending troops to relieve Telea. We've been hired to go into Telea in advance. Confirm it. Prepare them."

Sneak into a city during a siege. Joy overflowing filled my heart. Although, actually, this kind of thing is what the Company does best. And pays bloody well, which is the main thing. And a good chance of killing, as well as of getting killed.

"I'll get the lads ready, then," I told Skie.

As I said, being a sellsword is mostly not an exciting life.

———•———

WE MARCHED OUT at dawn the next morning, noble men with hard faces and harder weapons, slaughter and glory and lust for coin singing in our hard hard hearts. The whole Free Company of the Sword, an old and illustrious company. Bright our swords and bright our legend, we did not fear to march out. Let the earth shake! Let women tremble! Let men cower before us in the dust! All ten of us. Boom boom.

We're a bigger company now, yeah. Very astute of you to notice that. Been on a recruitment drive.

Not that that makes me think of it or anything, but you want another beer at all? Sure?

Marched north with a brisk wind in our faces. Grey desert harsh with dust. Grey rock that rang with our footsteps. Only the shriek of carrion birds overhead to accompany us. Their shadows fell on the dust before us. Ill-omened, that. The desert opened into grassland, silvery, dry, coarse grass that cut at your legs. Fewer crows. More insects. Wild horses, sometimes, at a distance, running, the ones the Teleans caught and broke to make themselves rich. Clear skies every night. Bright stars. The red star of the Dragon's Mouth. Skie made us go as fast as possible. Jog along, all ten of us. Get the blood going, stretch the limbs out, wear off the rot of Reneneth, all the rank wine and rank meat and rank pastries a man could eat. Hurry up there, lads. Get going. No sloggers on the job. It's kind of urgent.

"What happens if the city falls before we get there?" Alxine asked me. Sitting by the fire one evening, we had maybe six days to go still till we got there. There were Immish soldiers now occasionally, moving around on the roads. Five of us, me, Alxine, Piyrce, Mela, Jag the slowcoach, and another five under the command of Skie somewhere else nearby in the darkness. Half a night's walk off, maybe. Meet up with them again in the city, on the chance both lots of us made it in. I remember really clearly that night turning, looking away into the dark, thinking about them somewhere out there, the rest of the Company, might be alive, might have been captured and killed by the Immish, might have been eaten by a bloody wolf. Might never know what the fuck happened to them. Never stops being a strange thing, thinking about that, not knowing if your comrades are alive or dead. Strange generally, this time before something happens. Like you're not really alive right then. Run forward a few days and you could be dead. They're dead, your comrades, far as you know. I'm dead. Skie's dead. Alxine's dead.

Morbid fuck, ain't I? Sorry. Honest, it's not so bad really, just me being a grouch. Too cynical for me own good. Ignore me.

Sure you don't want another beer there?

"What happens if the city falls before we get there?" asked Alxine.

"If the city's already fallen, there's still an army on the march from Cen Andae."

You've met Alxine, haven't you? My second-in-command, really, now. Back then he was the new boy, green, wet behind the ears, those kind of things.

"The city hasn't fallen, anyway." That was Piyrce. Been with us five years. Knew what's what.

You haven't met Piyrce, no.

Alxine said, "How do you know that?"

"Wind's blowing from the north. Take a sniff."

Alxine took a sniff. Looked puzzled. Gods, it's funny, thinking of Alxine all wet and green like that back then.

"What can you smell, then?"

"Dunno. Woodsmoke. Us lot. Dinner cooking. Someone farted."

Piyrce said, "That's life you can smell, Alxine. You can't yet smell death."

———

COULD SMELL THE siege, the next evening. Ten thousand men, the Immish had, ringed all round Telea. Came on a burned village that must have done something stupid like ask the Immish for payment when they gutted it. Bodies in the village, stretched out, painful-looking. Two of them had bound hands. One of them was wearing armor. The Immish went in, took prisoners, then something happened and they ended up killing everyone.

"Check for anything left." Wouldn't be, place would have been gutted, but a smashed-up abandoned village is always worth a quick look. Might be few sausages or a keg left lying around. Call it the eternal optimism of the sellsword in the face of despair: they died for no reason, slaughterhouse, this place is, these poor blokes, some fucker killed a fucking baby here, and these two could have been me and my mum—but I've got a string of sausages out of it.

Stripped. Nothing. Professional soldiers done a damn fine professional job.

"Tobias!" Alxine calling. I strolled over. An old woman, lying on her back hunched up, soaked in blood. Clothes torn to ribbons. Face black and blue. Wrists black and blue.

Rasping breath. Very loud. It sounded like the wind in bare trees. Sounded like a spinning wheel turning. Click click click. Made me itch.

I looked at her and I looked at Alxine.

Alxine got his water bottle out. Tipped a bit of water over her mouth. She licked her lips. Her tongue was black and it left bloody slime round her lips.

He did it. Well and smooth, no flailing around, one stroke of the knife.

"You didn't need to call me over and show me, lad."

He looked proud, you know?

———•———

WENT ON FOR a few more days. Tramp tramp jog jog. Keep going. Got a deadline here. March, you fuckers. March. Quick! And then one afternoon we reached the top on a ridge, in a thicket of trees, and Telea was there on the other side before us, ringed round with ten thousand Immish soldiers in leather and bronze and boars' tusk helmets, strong and healthy on looted food.

"Told you it hadn't fallen," said Piyrce.

"Just about, it hasn't," said Mela. "Clinging on by its fingernails." The Immish had brought five siege engines up. Trying out the old story, to see if the magic had worn off them painted walls as much as the paint had. Gold walls? Don't make me laugh. Chipped paint. Plus, whatever magic there might be round those walls, no one ever said the houses inside them couldn't be ground down to powder if you hit them enough. That old Queen of Telea, she nearly defeated the Godking.

A stirring down there in the Immish camp. General moving and swirling around, flashes of sunlight on armor, distant noise. Like a ripple in deep water, someone throwing a stone into a pond.

One of the siege engines went into action. A yelling followed by crash. Lots of people moving. The whole damn machine shaking after it went off. Don't often see that, a siege engine losing. Fuck, is all I can say, really. Fucking fuck. A rock big enough we could see it, streaking through the air, watch it, watch it… Hit the city walls, and I swear all five of us closed our eyes and jumped and felt the earth shake.

Big cloud of dust.

Cheers.

Big cloud of dust clearing.

The wall was entirely unharmed.

The rock was… a cloud of dust.

Cheers from inside the city.

Groans from the Immish camp.

"City hasn't fallen," said Piyrce.

———•———

WE MADE CAMP in the trees back down the other side of the ridge. Felt better not seeing all those Immish campfires that we'd have to get through to get in. The Immish didn't seem entirely perturbed by the walls being impregnable. Dull regular crashing noises of rocks being thrown against the walls and pulverized, people shouting—swear we could hear the people of Telea jeering and shouting insults back. Late afternoon, now, and they'd built up to all five engines going. Crash smash snigger crash smash snigger crash. Pity the poor blokes who had to haul the pointless useless massive lumps of rock.

"Maybe the Immish plan is to build up so much dust against the walls it forms a ramp?"

"Or choke the Teleans to death?"

"Mercy, mercy, I surrender, I've got too much dust in my hair to go on! My coat's dirty! Such cruelty of war!"

But the noise and the dust and the Teleans all looking at the engines pointing and laughing... chaos and confusion... and if we stay here, behind the Immish lines, a scouting party or a foraging party or two blokes looking for a private spot for a quicky—someone'll be bound to turn up and fall over us with a sword drawn. So...

"Get some dinner and a few hours rest, lads," I told the squad. "Once it gets dark... we'll go in. Get it over with."

And it's that weird bit again, when you're sitting eating a bit of stale bread and a hunk of dried meat, trying to get some sleep, knowing you'll probably be dead by morning. Look at the meat you're eating, think about how that'll probably be you in a few hours' time.

Your face, there... I'm joking. It's fine. Exciting. Like that wait while the desire of your heart debates whether to get their kit off, that's all.

Pass the pork scratchings there. Damn fine beer, this, don't you think?

Piyrce woke me with the twilight coming. Long summer evening, red fire on the western horizon, in the east the stars were showing and the sky was dark like silk. Warm still. Birds singing for the sunset. Swirling in to roost for the night, black against the sun.

Strong smell of smoke. Greasy, acrid, nasty smoke.

"What's happening?"

"Come and have a look." Me and Piyrce scrambled to the top of ridge again, peered down at the Immish camp and the city. Thousand, thousand, thousand fires. The Immish were hurling barrels of burning oil at the walls. Red fire, red as the sunset. Thick black smoke. The walls stained black with soot. A barrel shot up like a shooting star. Everyone there, me, Piyrce, the Immish, the Teleans, all of us watching it and, gods, honestly, it was beautiful. Red like the sunset. Trailing sparks and fire, dripping fire as it went. Flying. And it hit the walls of Telea, those famous legendary walls glowing yellow in the twilight. And it didn't break them down, no, because they were impervious to stone and bronze and iron and wood. But the oil broke over them. And the oil burned. And the magic wall began to burn.

Another barrel went higher. Over the walls and gone.

I swear, even from that distance, I heard someone scream as the oil hit them.

"Fuck me," said Alxine. He was crouching beside me, his eyes wide.

"Fuck off back to the others, I didn't tell you to follow me." And I said to Piyrce, "Perfect. Chaos, bloodshed, murder, firelight to guide us. We're going in."

We went over the ridge all together, crouching low. Organized chaos down there. Ten thousand men and horses, and the siege engines going, and a ram moving towards the gates. The walls of the city on fire. Dark, clouds coming over, and no moon tonight.

You'd almost think we'd judged it exactly, getting there to go in on a moonless night during an assault. Wouldn't you?

Trumpets. Drum beating. Ten thousand pairs of feet on the march. The Immish were also going in.

I WISH I could describe it. That moment, going down into a war. I've only done it once or twice, thank and curse the gods. The air smells of it; you can see the death in the air above the soldiers as they're waiting, like heat haze. You can see it on their breath. Dark, and the light from their torches, and the light from the walls where they were burning, and the city was lit up too, blazing lights on the walls and in every tower, because they knew the Immish were coming, and they wanted to kill and die in the light. And the siege engines still going, throwing fire. Arcs of fire in the air. The Immish soldiers marched beneath them, with the fire dripping down on them; in the fire their armor looked red and black.

And the tramp of their feet, and the crash of the war engines—I said waiting to go in feels like the wait while the desire of your heart gets their kit off, yeah? Well, going in, going in the midst of a battle— that's like... gods, it's like... I can't put it in words. I wish I could tell you what it's like. It's like that moment when they hold out their arms to you, your first time... only... only... more. Like that... only... everything.

One of the siege engines failed. Something snapped or bent wrong. A barrel of burning oil came down on a troop of Immish soldiers marching forward with ladders. Screams. Squeals. The Immish troops behind flowed round them, marched on, tramping on the flames.

A ram up now. Battering at the main gates.

What? No. No, we weren't in there. Nowhere near it. We were round the back, of course. "Sounds like I was part of it?" Sorry, maybe it does. Too excited, thinking about it. Gods, I can see it still, that night. Biggest battle I've ever been in. But we were round the back of the lines, creeping, crawling in place like bloody lizards, angling our way round. Skie's directions were that there was a postern gate, round to the east of the walls, sheltered by tower buttresses, and we'd try to get in there.

Yes, I can see what you're about to ask. Hang on. One step at a time, right?

The Immish were nearly at the walls now. A ladder being maneuvered up. The siege engines loosed and trumpets sounded. The ram was pounding. We kept moving round eastwards—thank all the gods the Immish attack was focused on the main gate and the wall just to the west of it. Very, very few people looking anywhere near us. And there's the tower, massive thing, sticking out of the city wall like a wart. You know those things trees get, when they have those big lumps on their trunks, itchy looking things? Galls? Really? Okay, I'll take your word for it. So the tower looked kind of like that. You could see why the Immish weren't trying anything right there. And why someone decided it would be the best place for us to go in.

Right. Now or never. Mad dash across no-man's land and pray and pray and fucking pray we make it.

A blast of white light. Gold sparks, like someone kicking a bonfire. A scream. A thousand fucking screams. The trumpets and the singing stopped very sudden. White light again, and white heat, and my eyes hurt. Lying on the ground in the mud gasping for breath, the air ringing, that silence after a thunderclap that's louder than the noise itself.

And this screaming started. Shrieking. Like a man whose bones are being ripped out.

"What the fuck was that?" said Alxine, when any of us could speak.

"That was a mage," said Mela.

A mage.

Yes, a mage.

M A G E. Mage.

Gods, you had a sheltered life or what? Shut your mouth, you'll get flies in your throat; or the wind'll change and you'll be stuck like that. Actually, okay, look, cards on the table and all, seeing as I like you—no, I haven't seen that many of them myself. This might possibly have been the first time I'd seen one fight. Hopefully the last time, too. But I at least managed to keep my mouth from dropping open quite that much.

Alxine had pissed himself, I'll grant you. And Piyrce looked like he was going to puke.

There was a smell in the air, like hot metal, and the air was thick with oily smoke.

There's bits of people, there in that smoke.

Everyone and everything was very still. Like the Immish were sitting thinking, "Fuuuuck" and the Teleans were sitting thinking, "It worked. Whoa." Then a trumpet sounded, and a voice shouted, and the siege engines loosed, and there was another flash of mage light from the walls, and more screams. And the assault was on again, Immish soldiers running and shouting and dying, and I could see a ladder almost at the burning bloody walls when it went up in flames.

"Run!" I screamed at the lads. "Fucking run!"

In the firelight and the magelight, the smoke and the darkness… gods, it was like there were so many of us, so many and so few of the Immish soldiers, of the defenders on the walls. Ghosts and spirits running everywhere, an Immishman came running towards us and past us screaming, all over blood, and then a whole troop of them, blood on their spears, their eyes rolling in their heads, we were up so close to them when they appeared out of the smoke and the dark they almost fell over us, but whatever they thought we were, if they even noticed us in their terror... they just ran past us and ran on. Like ghosts. Us and them.

"Fucking run! We're nearly there."

And we were. We were. There's the tower, and the wall in its shadow, and there's the postern gate. We were up against it, hands on the wooden gate and the stone wall. Rough. Dry. Real. Small. The tower was between us and the fighting. Peaceful, suddenly. Just strange distant noises, a glow and stink in the darkness. But the stones of the wall felt warm, from where the walls were burning. The walls trembled occasionally, when a stone from the siege engines struck them. Made the walls feel like they were alive.

This small locked door.

"So..."

"So," Piyrce said, more nervous than I've ever heard him: "We just... knock?"

"We..."

You're not stupid. You can see where this is going, can't you?

Never make complicated plans. Complicated plans just go to shit.

Not making complicated plans goes to shit too, but in a less disappointing way.

"We...?"

And then there was a squad of Immish soldiers on us with swords, yelling for us to identify ourselves.

We...?

Fuckers ran Piyrce through.

See where this is going. Oh yeah.

A sword in my face. Nicked me, I could feel it. Hit back at them, four against four; they were good, these boys, good tough soldiers, holding us, battering us; wet crash and Mela went down. Fuckers.

I got mine down.

Rolling about. His helmet rolled off. Nice hair. Make that boys and girls.

Sword back in my face, jabbing. Lashed back, kicked at the fucker, hammered at him. Her. Whatever. Never found out, with this one. Actually, thinking about it, more likely to have been a bloke, when I kicked him in the nads and he screamed. Got me back, made my left shoulder scream.

Jag went down.

Me and Alxine left. Alxine was bloody bleeding. I was bloody bleeding. Bloody blood all over me. Three of them, looking well and truly pissed at us. Our backs really quite fucking literally up against a fucking wall.

Alxine was a crap swordsman. Only still alive cause his bloke was already hurt.

Two of them ran at me. A sword in my right shoulder. Balanced the wounds. A sword in my face. Alxine up against me. Getting in my bloody way. New boy, and green. Green and red and brown bloody striped, right now, was Alxine.

 Pauses for appreciative laugher and none comes. What do you mean, you don't bloody get it? Green and red and—never mind. Never mind. This was a remarkably crap way to die, is all.

Get it now?

Still no? What do they teach young people nowadays?

Anyway. I'm rambling again, aren't I? Remind me where we were again?

Oh yeah: dying.

Dying. Fucking fucking useless fucking fuck.

The postern gate smashed open and ten massive blokes in armor charged out. One of the Immish yelled "Kill!" and threw herself at them. One of the Immish yelled "Shit!" and legged it. One of the Immish yelled something unintelligible and died.

Me and Alxine. Standing there. Green and red and brown stripes, the both of us. So, uh… this could go one of two ways.

"There's an army coming from Cen Andae to relieve you!" I screamed at them. "Can't be more than a few days march. Honest. Honest!"

Sword in my face again. Voice barked, "March."

The postern gate smashed shut.

We'd made it in.

———•———

THE CITY WAS in a remarkably good state.

Okay, skeptic-face, hands on the table, no, I haven't seen that many sieges. Who has? Mostly dead blokes. But I'll bet you another beer I've seen more sieges than you have, and, with the caveat that I'm talking from fairly limited experience here, the city wasn't really that badly knocked about. Considering. I've mentioned the magic walls: obviously, they were basically fine; most of the major buildings still seemed to be standing, everyone about still looked like they'd had something to eat in the last month. A crow flew down with a lump of someone in its beak, and no one rushed at it salivating.

Immish weren't going to break this place, with the caveat, etc. Not before the guys from Cen Andae got there.

Oh, that made me feel good. It's a nice feeling, when you know your job is really going to be of use, that you're properly adding value.

"Talk," the guy who'd just saved us barked at me. I talked. Not much to say: Cen Andae, being super nice and caring, is sending some troops to relieve you, champing at the bit to kick the Immish in the nads, just hang on and hang on and they'll come, I'm telling the truth I'm telling the truth, I'm about to pass out from blood loss, no, I'm lying, I just decided sneaking through enemy lines during an assault and counter-assault to lie to you would be a right laugh, gods, look, half my company's been slaughtered, I really am about to pass out from—

One of them gave me bit of dirty cloth to bandage my shoulders with. A drink of water from his waterskin. The filthy state we were in, we were dragged off up to the citadel to tell the high-up high up there everything. Confirm it, rather: the guy I was speaking to seemed to know something about it, nodded, smiled, "Thank the gods, praise the good people of Cen Andae" and that, proper pleased.

Relieved, even.

Looks relieved himself that you've got that one.

You have got that one, right?

General bustling around, shouting, people yelling heroic stuff like "redouble the defense of the main gate." Eventually they remembered about me and Alxine standing there bloody and stinking, gave us a meal and a drink. The sweet, sweet taste of cheap, cheap beer. A loaf of stale bread, even a scrap of salt meat. Then we sat for a while, looking at the floor, thinking of Mela and Jag and Piyrce being dead.

"Wonder where Skie is?" said Alxine. "If they got in?"

"Yeah."

"They can't have got in," said Alxine then. "The Teleans would already know the troops were coming, wouldn't they, if Skie had got in?"

"Yeah. They would."

"Assault's ended. The siege engines aren't going any more. The Teleans must have beaten them off."

"Yeah. Must have done."

Alxine finally shut up.

"I'm going to get some sleep," I said. "You get some sleep, Alxine. We got things to do tomorrow. You need some rest."

———•———

WE HAD A sleep. I did, anyway. Woken up some time the next morning by the Immish redoubling the assault. All the siege engines, the ram, blokes with ladders, the whole shebang. The Teleans shooting back fire arrows, getting a machine on the walls going, the Telean mage blowing off. It began to pour with rain, too. Dark sky, high wind. Me and Alxine sat and cowered. A massive crash and the building we were in shook like a child, a load of dust came down over Alxine's head.

The building shook like all siege engines had loosed at once. I got up, went over to the door.

"Come on, then."

"Come on?"

"Yeah. Come on."

There was a bloke guarding the door, cause the Teleans weren't stupid.

I called him over.

I killed him.

Alxine looked at me. "Uh…?"

"We need to go and open the postern gate," I said Alxine.

"Uh…?"

"The gate. The one we came in through. We need to go and open it."

He gave me this look, really puzzled, like I might have to knife him for being dumb. Then he smiled as it clicked in him.

"That makes more sense," he said. "Yeah. A lot of sense." And in that instant he stopped being new and green.

I said, "Come on, then. They're all waiting on us."

———

YOU PROBABLY KNOW the story from here, yeah? Or can guess it: you're smart, I can tell. The army from Cen Andae was still two days' march off when Telea fell to the Immish. The army from Cen Andae turned back round, marched home again with sad bowed heads. The Immish flattened Telea to rubble. Half its people died in the sack. The Immish hanged the king and the mage bloke from the gates of the citadel. Tore the famous magic walls down with their soldiers' bare hands. The walls not being impregnable to flesh and skin. Built some new one in grey stone without the yellow paint-job. It's part of Immish, now, Telea. Timber and furs and iron and precious gems come down the fast-flowing river Enias, travel straight on to the Immish capital of Alborn.

Makes me proud, thinking I did all that. Damned fine job.

—•—

AND THAT'S A story about me. Enjoyed it, I hope? Yeah? I killed someone for this sword I'm wearing, I'll just casually mention. Apropos of nothing.

ASSASSIN OR THIEF
·A STORY OF TABAT·

Cat Rambo

H AVING BEEN ONE of—" the Dark said, stressing "one of" just enough to show her polite self-effacement by its inclusion, "—the finest assassins in the multiverse," (she had learned the word from her husband only last week during his pontification about the extra-dimensional nature of the city in which they dwelt, and took a certain delight in displaying it now), "I feel it essential to establish the distinction between assassin and thief."

The conversation, taking place in the crowded, jostling noodle shop and bar around the corner from the small garden apartment the Dark and Tericatus had chosen as their living quarters, was yet another of the interminable bar discussions that often take place in the city of Serendib. Situated and composed as it is of a multitude of realities, its citizens approach philosophical issues from a variety of viewpoints.

This time the participants were the Dark; her husband, the sorcerer Tericatus, her oldest friend and enemy, Chig the Rat God; and an unnamed woman who none of them knew, who had wandered over from another, presumably less entertaining conversation, and was listening in without introducing herself. Such behavior was a little rude, but not outside the bounds of Serendib courtesy, where often the silent have a reason to be so.

"If there is a distinction—and I am not agreeing one exists—it is surely only a matter of degree," Chig said. "Thieves steal from people, and what is taking a life but a form of that?"

"You are trying to annoy me," said the Dark. She suspected he'd introduced the topic on purpose to that end, and opted to use unexpected directness to throw him off guard.

But Chig was not to be diverted. "That is an interesting way to deflect my question," he said.

Tericatus cleared his throat. "I have found two things," he interjected. "One is that such things are often a question of how a person thinks of themself. The actions of a thief in a situation may be very different from those of someone styling themself an assassin." He took a sip of ale.

"And the second?" the Dark prompted.

Chig interrupted before Tericatus could reply. "Then we should be able to put someone into a situation and determine whether they are thief or assassin by how they act."

Tericatus opened his mouth anew, but this time the nameless woman interjected. "You are saying that whether I am thief or assassin predicts what I will do? That seems easy enough to put to the test."

The Dark peered at the woman with interest. "Are you one or the other?" she asked.

"I am," said the woman, "but I will not tell you which, in the interest of science."

The Dark's eyes narrowed, but she nodded.

Tericatus said, "But if you know it is a test, you might change your answer."

"Now you are growing overly complicated," Chig said. "Let us think of our test situation before we concern ourselves with that."

"What do you propose?"

Chig stroked his whiskers with a thoughtful paw. "We certainly have the Dark as our baseline, for who is a better example of an assassin?" He gave the Dark an oily smile that she did not return. She was feeling a trickle of unease deep inside. Chig was very fond of long-hidden machinations, and the Dark was reasonably sure that the woman was his catspaw, so to speak. She looked over at Tericatus in one of those moments of unspoken marital telepathy that they shared from time and time. He shrugged at her, meaning, *Wait and see.*

"It could be a situation that calls for an assassination or a theft, but that would seem a heavy-handed choice," Chig mused. "Therefore, something outside either realm and yet still a trifle unsavory and outside the law." He stroked his whiskers lovingly once again, setting them in perfect order.

The Dark decided that supplying her own factor into the situation would surely change it up enough to disturb Chig's plans. She did not wish to be predictable, and she and Chig had known each other a very long time indeed, so she discarded the first notion that came to her, and then the second, and then even the third as a precautionary move (she congratulated herself on the acumen displayed therein), and said, "Gambling, in the form of the beetle bets." She was pleased to see what she interpreted as a flicker of annoyance crossing over Chig's face (although rats are notoriously difficult to read in their expressions) and that he took care not to look at the woman.

"That seems fair enough," Tericatus supplied.

"Very well," Chig said in a sullen tone. The woman nodded, and they paid their tab in order to exit.

"What is your name?" the Dark murmured to the woman as they made their way toward the door.

"Victoria," the woman said, giving her a little smile, flirtatious as a wink, charming the Dark despite herself. She was a very pretty woman, when one looked at her, with long, black hair as lustrous as though it had just been brushed out, and eyes the same shade, made even darker by the lashes surrounding them, reflecting slivers of light from the colored sign pulsing behind the bar.

Tericatus laid his hand on the Dark's elbow, steering her ahead of him. She leaned to murmur in his ear, "Does she have charms laid upon her?" He shook his head, and she frowned, but kept moving nonetheless.

The beetle races are illegal in Tabat because they alter the laws of chance itself, and that is a very risky thing, because so many things there depend on those laws.

Such events are held near the great coffee roastery that usually (but not always) sits on Serendib's southern side. The aromas wafting from that establishment—and all the consequent nearby coffee shops— hide the acrid smell from the race/battles that would otherwise force Serendib's law enforcers to notice their presence on occasions other than the pre-scheduled monthly raids.

The world of the coffee roastery is assuredly a pleasant one. The trees around it, tall and leafy, are laden with lemons almost as fragrant as the factory's product. In their highest boughs, owlkits nest, the progeny of parents in the nearby brewery, whose line will spread even further with passing generations.

But go farther up the street and the puddles grow oily from a constant, acidic mist, shifting to cobblestones slippery underfoot. The buildings change to fungal, pallid, and flabby structures that must be grown anew every few months.

The coliseum that holds the beetle races is an immense puffball, its massive, warty outer walls sprayed with fixative to hold them in place, flammable as fireworks if not for the constant rain on the other side. Stands held the watchers now, and in the middle an immense round of violet and green marble, perhaps ten yards in width, spun like an enormous turntable on which the beetles crawled, and in its center was a black sphere, filled with stars.

Despite the number of people there—at least a hundred gathered into the wooden stands—silence held. The only sounds were breathing and the ticking of the legs of the great hand-sized beetles crawling over the round.

Each beetle wore around its neck a tiny basket woven of silver wire. Surrounding the round were the beetle-brats, who constantly removed or slipped tiny glass beads into the baskets of passing beetles, marking the bets, while their juniors ran back and forth between them and the crowd in response to wordless hand signals.

Tericatus breathed in the Dark's ear, "You know it is possible here to lose one's luck entirely, and that is not something I can cure easily with magic."

Her only response was a sideways flick of her ebon eyes and a quirked lip that told him that, although he had no clue what it was, she held some plan.

Victoria stooped to a vat by the entrance and took a handful of beads, as did the Dark and Chig. Tericatus refrained, although he gave the vat an uneasy glance as they passed on their way to the stand, noting the thousand colors of beads that seemed to roil of their own volition under his gaze, as though urging themselves toward him.

They began to bet.

The beetles crawled and clacked on the marble round, sometimes meeting to mesh mandibles and attempt to push each other into the great black central round. Two perished in this fashion, the loser pulling the victor in after it, and several faces in the crowd paled or flushed, or looked about for ways of escape before a beetle-brat came to show them towards a booth in the back.

They all gave their beads to a single beetle-brat.

"That means we all win or lose together, you know," Chig said in question to the Dark.

"I am familiar with the rules, yes," she said. He shrugged, and they turned their attention back to the game.

How many hours passed, while they watched the beetles?

How many beads went from one basket to another, then another, or went spilling down the void in the center?

How many times were the guttering lamps near the doorways replenished? Dawn was tentatively touching the doorway's edge by the time they stood, a beetle brat filling each's hand with a clump of beads much smaller than originally, and moved to the booth to cash out, the only way to know who had won or lost.

"I am not sure what any of this has proved," Tericatus muttered. He had grown to the age where a sleepless night was not as effortless as it once was, and tiredness gnawed redly at the corners of his eyes and etched lines around his mouth.

The Dark, untouched by the rigors of the night, shrugged.

They stepped into the reckoning booth.

"It appears we have lost our luck!" Chig said in pretend shock.

"Indeed," said the Dark. "And yet I was prepared and brought my own to substitute, so I have lost luck pre-purchased in the market."

"Ah," said Chig. "Then it will be sad to tell you that this was all a trap, and I swapped out ownership of the markers through certain arcane preparations, and you have been saddled with twice the loss, and both of us with half." He bared his teeth in a grin.

"Ah," said the Dark. "That would be sad, had I not refrained from doing the same and also performing certain sleights with ownership."

Chig started to say something, then stopped. "What?"

"You were about to tell me you had anticipated that move, were you not?"

The rat god frowned and nodded. Victoria's brows furrowed slightly.

"Anticipated. And since your co-conspirator did not do the same..." She shrugged. "She is a thief, and not the same as an assassin, and hence I have won the argument as well. An entertaining evening, for which I thank you." She bowed to Victoria and Chig with elegant satisfaction, and took her husband's arm, smiling.

As they walked home, past the trees where owlkits stirred, chirping out a morning sound, she said, "When all of this started, you said you had found two things, but you only told us the one."

"That is true," Tericatus said, yawning.

"And the other?" she pressed, after a few more steps.

He tilted his head to examine her. "I am not really sure you wish me to say."

She frowned. "Out with it."

"As I said, one is that such things are often a question of how a person thinks of themself. The second thing I have found," Tericatus said, rubbing his nose, "is that such things usually matter only to oneself, and realizing that may save one some sleep."

And after that, the Dark was silent all the way home.

THE WEIGHT OF SHADES AND SHADOWS

Shanna Germain

K ANSA, BONE-ACHED AND barefoot, walked the narrow wheel track road into town alone. She was red-on-red. Sunscorched, blood-washed. Her clothes, once blues and yellows, were now darkened by dirt and death. Even her pale hair was twisted and tangled with the reckonings of the ages prior.

The sun dragged itself to midday as she crossed beneath the town's arched pillar post, and her bloodied shadow grew smaller with each step. Overhead a silver sign swung in no wind, promising a kind of town and whatever else someone might read into the name of Last Hope. Perched atop the pillar post, the devil's piebald magpies regarded her with a single eye each. She raised her left hand, palm open to show the silvered whirls upon it, and called, "Be your mourning ending as soon as it's begun." The final word sent her coughing up dust and sand. She couldn't remember the last time she'd spoken.

The birds had no response for her. Under the weight of their silence, she entered the town where she'd been born and raised. The place she'd once thought of as home, but which she now hoped would be her end. Come one way or another.

Her bare feet left crimson tracks in the hard dirt. She vaguely remembered when she'd said goodbye to her boots. First one had gone south on her, heel sprung to nails that bit the ball of her foot with each step. She'd stuffed it with moss and leaves, and then a crumple of her dress. Learned to live with another pain. The other boot gave up the ghost somewhere in there, and one morning she couldn't bear to put them back on. She reached for the memory in more detail—had it been before or after the Crim? Was Haile still with her then?—and found she couldn't quite grasp it. No matter. She wasn't here for that.

She was Kansa, Devil's Only (née Eldest) Daughter, and she was here to ruin her father, or die trying. Once and for true.

Sixteen years she'd spent doing his bidding. Then sixteen more rejecting that call to hone her skills, narrow her path, see clear and true. These last sixteen, then, for pain and blood, her heart cut to tiny ribbons and flown for all to see.

She was *this* close. She thought she'd feel fear now. Or maybe dismay. Remorse. Apprehension. Any of those, maybe all. She felt nothing but gritted determination. It sang through her teeth, through her bones and blood, urged her forward like a war cry.

Kansa focused on this step and then this step, her gaze never leaving the brown building that sat at the street's end. Unobtrusive. Nothing to think twice about. You might notice the metalwork hound asleep on the porch or the bit of wood that read "Road's End" in painted white letters, but a watchdog and a saloon sign were not uncommon in this end of the world. And you'd not notice the elaborate metalwork beneath the eaves or the protective insignias upon the door if you didn't already know to look. She knew where to look. It was her blessing, and her curse. One of many.

A figure in gold and green slid into the road and lowered itself in front of her. Far enough away that Kansa didn't have to make an instant decision, close enough that she would have to make one soon. For now, she kept walking. This step. The next.

The robes, the hood, the woven green-gold details of the fabric—it all ticked something in Kansa's brain that she couldn't quite pattern out.

Before she could, a visage unfolded itself from beneath the layered hoods. One eye sewed to a permanent wink, lips rouged red, an intricate weave of gold and rubies inlaid in her face.

Kansa held her breath against the swear that rose. When she swallowed it away, she felt the word's edges sharp against her throat.

A Lady of the Deck. Here, in Last Hope. Kneeling in the street before her.

The best sign or the worst one. A complication, either way. Kansa had tangled with Ladies of the Deck before and had no desire to do so again. But then, she had no desire to be here either, walking down this street, bloodied hands and heart, toward the end of this long road. Yet here she was. Desire and determination—long ago, she'd thought them the same thing, or close enough. Now she knew better.

She thought of the magpies' answering silence as she'd walked beneath the gate. The crimson footprints that followed behind her. Perhaps she should have turned away at their silence, gone back. But gone back to what? There was nothing left for her out there. She'd used the world all up and spit it out, just to walk here now.

Kansa made her decision. "Lady," she said. Her voice had returned, and she felt the road in it, gravel and steel. Not a quaver. She hoped she wasn't using up all her iron on this; she was going to need every bit of strength she had later. Her father was no dealer to shrift on.

"Lady," A little softer. "I've no bones with you. I urge you, take none with me." Neither threat nor plea. Something in between.

Kansa didn't truck with wire-builts or metalwork. She left that to others. Guns made her hands sweat and swords were cumbersome to carry. But she had the etchings of the dust devils on her skin, the talisman of Sardeon around her neck, and—if those didn't do their job—a pair of heftwood blades stowed at her hips. The Lady would know that. There was no need to show them.

The Lady rose to her full height, which was a good head shorter than Kansa but somehow felt much taller. It was the way her shadow stretched and danced, covering Kansa in dark chill. The way her sewn-shut eye measured Kansa without seeing her.

The Lady reached into one of the metal slots in her neck and pulled out a card, sweat-bent and edges worn. Then another. Their backs were all-black.

Kansa sighed with relief. A mere shadow prophesy, then. That was nothing. Mirrors and rumors, rarely come to fruition. She'd had her future spoken before, and none of it had come near to true. She would let the Lady read her cards and be on her way, no harm done.

Already, her mind went forward, to the end of this walk and what waited there. Revenge or death. Possibly both. She would soon find out.

Which was why the Lady's attack caught her off guard. The first card became a bird flying toward her, mid-air became a wasp that struck the side of her wrist between the layers of her wraps, a handful of tiny stings, more attention-getting than painful. The second card folded twice, became a blade, aiming for the bare space inside the crook of her elbow. Kansa caught it with a close of her arm, feeling it slice her skin even as she held it tight. It didn't dissipate, but grew more solid in her grip.

No, not shadow cards. Not a false prophesy. What delirious magic was this? Not the devil's due. Something else. Something she'd never seen before.

The Lady's hands were reaching, plucking, gathering more cards from the slots in her skin like so much ripe fruit.

So much for not taking any bones with her.

She felt her palms itch, the etchings asking to be set free. She didn't want to hurt. She wanted to be done with hurting. One more and then she would be done. She closed her fists against their insistence and tried another tack.

"Lady, have I offended you in some way?" She tried to think. While she didn't truck with the Ladies and their cards, she didn't distain them either. She laid her salt and sulphur, gave the moths their due, never crossed water without first asking permissions. Her father had taught her many horrible things, but he had also taught her to save herself. So, if she'd offended, she couldn't think of how or why. Even so, it was possible. Anything was, this final journey.

In answer, the Lady released a handful of cards, each connecting to each, becoming a writhing snake that wrapped Kansa's neck before she could reach to stop it. The black beast tightened around her, coils doubling, as it took her voice and then her breath.

It was as if the Lady knew—without voice, the dust devil etchings were useless, merely ink upon the skin. The talisman was protective, although it was hardly doing its job currently. Kansa had her blades, but they were for real things, blood and bone. Not shadows and shifting.

The blackness brought by lack of breath closed Kansa's vision. Narrowed the line of light into a single dull shard of grey. Her knees fell to the track, heard more than felt. Her palms, whirling useless, pressed to the dirt.

She saw no way out. She might have known it would come to this, after everything. She had nothing and no one. She would fall here, in the dust and grit, and become the end of her line. Maybe that wasn't so bad. Maybe it was as it was meant to be. Maybe Haile's way was the smarter one, after all. Truck with the hangwoman and you get hanged. But at least you get that.

Her foot, bloodied and bare, twitched against the dust. So many pained steps to come to this moment.

No. It would not do to die here, on the very doorstep of what she'd built her whole life for.

"No, I'll not kill you," the Lady said, as if she'd heard. "I have a message. And I heard tell that you do not listen well without… assistance. So I have given you that assistance."

A message? From who? Of what? The words were on her tongue but couldn't find their way out of the black coil.

The Lady seemed to be waiting for something. It was hard to grasp for what in the darkness. Kansa's chin fell down to the writhing card snake around her neck in an effort to say she understood.

The dull shard shifted. The constriction on her neck slithered open. Just enough to let the light back in. But not to return her voice.

"Listen." The Lady knelt before her, returning to the posture she'd started with. The stitching in the Lady's winked eye untied its tail knot and began to unravel from its holes, one-by-one, until it was free. The wrecked lid popped open, behind it, a false eye of garnet and steel. The Lady blinked, once, and when the lid opened again, Kansa saw the message meant for her.

The choking this time came not from the black coil—it had already slid loose, disconnecting from itself to become nothing more than card shreds, falling—but from what she saw in the Lady's green-cast eye.

No. It was not possible.

Kansa said as much, now that she had air again to release into noise. "Lies," she hissed, her words dark shapes slipping over sand.

"Lies. Who are you to show me such lies?" Her hand was on the hilt of her heftblade. Surely the Lady worked for her father. Surely he'd sent her to force her from her path. Why else would such a thing exist, be here, now, before her?

"She said you'd say that," the Lady said. She pulled a new card from her neck and held it up. Kansa met its face with the point of her blade.

"Who said?"

In answer, a red heart. A black dog. A face, turned as though to catch a final glimpse of someone walking south. A profile she would know anywhere.

But not proof.

Except the face turned, and the mouth—a mouth nearly the same as hers, with a scar riding high on the cleft lip—told her what her nightmares had been trying to tell her for weeks. "You left me. You left me, and you owe me, big sister."

Haile.

Her heart took this in—the Lady, the message, her little sister's face, moving as if it were still alive—and spit it back out.

Yes, she had left her sister, her baby sister, in the horrendous darkness of the Crim. But her sister had been dead, in mind if not in body, long before then. Haile'd chosen to truck with the hangwoman, had chosen to feed her madness and pull it around her like a death pelt. There was no turning that back. No amount of killing or pleading or not-leaving that would undo what was done.

You left me first, baby sister.

Kansa found no blame—any daughter with a devil for a father was bound for madness, come one way or another. Here, after all, she was herself, dust devils and talismans and blades for the kill. But her sister was gone. This magical illusion was just that.

Kansa rose from her knees. Her palms opened, and within her

skin, the grey circles of buried ink began to swirl.

"Show me that lie for what it was," Kansa said. "Before I do take bones with you, and do something we shall both regret."

"Regret seems to be the only way you do things of late," the Lady said. "Wary of the baggage you saddle yourself with, Kansa, Devil's Eldest Daughter."

"Devil's Only..." Kansa started to say, her tongue a blade... but she was no longer sure. This magic wasn't a magic she knew, these cards gone feral. It didn't matter, Eldest or Only. For soon, she would not even be that. She could feel the end coming like a bend in a wild river, rapid and dangerous and dreamed-of.

"Take it," the Lady said, card before her.

Kansa didn't want to touch the card. Its rust-hued heart. Its dog of death. Her sister's profile. But she sensed she had no choice. The road would not let her go forward without taking its toll. She pinched the paper and forced it to fold into her pocket, another bloodied memento with a weight behind its means.

"Begone, beggar queen," Kansa said, barely aware that the woman had already disappeared. "I've paid my dues." Again and again and again.

Behind her came the haunting *wye-wye-wye* of the piebald magpies from their perch over Last Hope's door. Kansa was suddenly, achingly tired. As if her very bones were metalwork, her blood silvered and steamed. She did not think she could make it to the end of the track, even without the woman standing in her way. The etchings beneath her skin deepened into her veins, and she closed her fists against their downward sink.

She walked. Through desert and dust. Through churns as tall as mountains and wheel ruts that were cold at the bottoms. The sun burned her eyes until she lifted one hand, ancient and slow, to ward her vision of the building at the end of the track. At one point, she thought she would lay down and rest. The ground beneath her feet was sun-warmed and soft, and she might sleep away this exhaustion. Gain back her strength before she went on.

From the porch, the hound bayed. Kansa pulled her gaze from the ruts to see Seth watching her from the porch. Somehow his eyes brought her back to herself, collapsed time and effort back into something more akin to normalcy. Though Seth lay as he always had, gold-gleamed form stretched out in repose and his metalwork paws slanted over the side of the wood, as if his highest care in the world was daydream of mudbunnies for breakfast, his cobalt eyes had been on her since the moment she'd stepped into town. Maybe before. She understood the ways of metalwork better than most—though she did not care for it—but there were secrets on secrets in the depths that she couldn't begin to fathom. How the hound could track her days away was something she'd never figured out as a child. He would have tracked Haile too, but Haile never ran away, and so Seth had never had to come for her, hiding in the streams and woods and shadows, and haul her home, some part of her clasped in his gentle grip.

The hound had been her companion since she was a child, but she held no hope that he'd greet her as a playmate, long-lost. Nor even as an equal. They might have played together as youngsters, games of fetch and hide and tumble, but she did not fool herself to think Seth was hers. Not anymore. Nor that play was ever merely play. Her father had been training all of them for purpose. For loyalty and legacy.

She left the hardened earth of the track and lifted her foot over the salt-and-circuit circle that surrounded Road's End. For a breath, she was sure the metal-moat wouldn't let her through, that he'd warded it against her, and she stiffened, a pull that scolded her muscles, before she set her foot down. But there was only the sting of salt in her broken skin, the sharp edges of metal pointed between her toes. She let the tears come, knowing even as they swelled that they didn't belong to pain, but to relief. A wash of things being nearly done. Come one way or another, here and now, they would finally be put to right.

The first porch step had creaked since time immortal, but she didn't sidestep it. There was no sneaking up on this—not on Seth, not on her father, not on her future. She planted her foot, let the wood whine at her passing. He would already know she was here, maybe even before Seth did. Maybe even before she herself had known that this is where she would end her journey.

Seth, she said, softly, seeing now how old he'd grown while she'd been gone. His silver was tarnished, the copper fur dented around his ears and muzzle. He rolled a blue eye toward her; even that was a replacement, she saw, a deeper, murkier blue than the one he'd been made with. She was tempted to reach and touch the worn-smooth spots around his ears, but stopped herself, unable to bear it if she found he too, had turned against her. How many times did a heart break before there was nothing left to put back together? A day ago, she would have said she'd found the answer. Now, she knew elsewise.

From inside the building, she heard the murmur of the cards being moved and deals being made. She would have liked to have come at a time when Road's End was empty, but there such a time didn't exist. As long as the devil took up residence here, the building would know no emptiness, no quiet, no peace. Those with the purpose and the money and the means would always come and go, provided they didn't offend the devil. Or sometimes, if even when they did.

I have a truck with the devil, she thought. Kansa saw her sister's face on a card and wondered how close to madness she might be.

In her memory, the metalwork symbols on the door were deadlier, darker. Permanent and dangerous as death. Now, they had aged with Seth. She hadn't known such a thing was possible. For the first time, she wondered about the man she would find inside. Would he be the fire and brimstone temper she remembered, the devil who wielded wisdom in the shape of fist and fury? Who taught love like competition? Or something else? Aged by memory and time? The latter hardly seemed possible.

She could handle revenge. She could even handle her own death. What she could not handle, would not handle, was the possibility that the devil was no longer the devil and she would have to... What? Forgive him? Go to some wirework therapist and listen to her father say all he'd done wrong and how he'd repented?

No. She did not deal in forgiveness. It was just one of the many, many things the devil had taught her.

Kansa lifted her bloodied, beaten hand and put it to the wood. The wards reacted and sizzled. Nothing special she'd done, other than being the daughter of the devil. A story the world had told her again and again. She opened the door to Road's End.

Her father sat at a card table, long-limbed and dark-suited, dealer of time and destruction, cards sliding through his fingers toward the players across from him. The players—three of them, losing badly by the marks across their hands—turned at her entrance. One of them began to speak—

The devil canted his head, salt and pepper since as long as she could remember, in a gesture so small it was nigh imperceptible. All three players stilled mid-act. Silent and eternal as stone. He'd done that to her once, when she'd been crying over some small hurt thing. She could still remember the hum of time passing, and realizing it was her own heart, slowed to time eternal. It was the first bit of her father's power she'd taught herself to resist.

"Welcome home, Eldest Child of Mine," her father said. Unlike Seth, he didn't seem older. He seemed… the same. Ever and ever the same. There was relief in that. She would have her revenge, come one way or another. "I've been waiting."

Of course he had been. There was nothing the devil did not see coming. Or at least that's what he'd taught her to believe. She wondered just how much of what was coming he saw now. Was his relaxed rise from the table truth or ignorance? She could only hope that latter.

"Home," she said. A word that tasted of spit and metal, void of meaning. How many times had she run from here? How many times had Seth caught her and dragged her back? "This was no home…" But no, she would not fight him word to word. She had all the power she needed in what she'd come to do.

He let the cards lie fallow on the table, took a single step toward her. The vulture that lived inside the end of his finger broke its head from beneath the skin, beak ready and beady eyes a-blink. He dragged the beak across his skin until it broke, a red river of ink and promise. "You've come to claim your kingdom," he said. "And you are so very close. I am proud of you, Eldest Child of Mine."

So, he didn't know everything, didn't see everything coming. He still thought she'd come to take his place. Oh, what joy. What sweet pleasure. Everything—almost everything—worth this moment. "I'm not—" she started.

For behind her father, the cards lifted themselves, whirling from the table. Catching in the light and dark, shadow spun, they built themselves into a sister. Black spades for eyes and heart. The heart-shaped mouth of red. Dark insanity made flesh.

Haile.

"Only one last thing," her father said, not turning, not surprised. He *had* known. He had known Haile lived yet. Had known she'd come.

Had known, even, this card magic. Her hope withered, small blossom in the shade. "Your sister lives still."

The devil must have seen something in Kansa's eyes. "I know," he said in the soothing voice he'd used when she was too young to understand his other forms, and she'd cried and run and kicked out, useless and small, against him. "I know. You thought you were done. It was smart, truly, turning her mad, leaving her in the Crim."

He gestured to her palms, and she found they itched. She rubbed them against her skin.

"But you must finish her," the devil said. "She is all that stands between you and your destiny."

"Sister, you owe me." Her sister's voice was slice of paper through skin.

That, then, was the reason for the Lady in the street. Not to show Kansa that her sister lived still, but to gain this bargaining chip. Cash in this remembered debt. Use it against their father. Oh, Haile.

The devil lowered himself before Kansa, and his voice was slick with power. His eyes the red she fled, the red she wore upon her skin. "It must be you, Eldest Daughter. Not your sister, for she is worn by madness. She is not strong."

"You do not know strong," her sister said. Haile turned to the devil, card to card to card, became a tree, a vulture, a haunt. Shadow-visage, sister, daughter. Power rolled from her like ancient tongues. "I will kill you. *We* will kill you. Help me, big sister. Help me."

With the final word, the cards became a tempest, tornado, whirling turns of faces. Skyward winding, the fury caught the roof and sky and brought them both down upon the devil.

Who moved from his crouch before Kansa, a roll and sleight of hand, and both roof and sky were caught in his fist, a weapon aimed and ready.

"Everything you've worked for," the devil said. "So close. Reach and take it."

No. She did not want to become the devil's salvation. Nor her sister's. Would not. And yet, she'd come so far for this, given up so much. Indecision stayed her hand, as strongly as any monster's grip.

Wood and air left his fist, a flood that scattered the cards of her sister, sending them careening into the stock-still players. One toppled backward, the crash of body and chair sending a deep growl from Seth's throat. The cards regrouped, a flock of prey, arrow and hammer, aiming steady.

Her father and her sister. Both mad in their own way. Both bearing her scars, and she theirs. In the name of a destiny she did not want.

"Help me," they both said, and in it, her voice too.

Her palms opened, and within her skin, the grey circles of buried ink began to swirl. "Be stilled," she said.

Her father, bound by time and legacy, waited.

Her sister, bound in her madness and magic, waited.

Her hand, bound by death and promises, waited.

The grass, bound by nothing, did not wait. But went on.

She watched the man who'd raised her, who'd broken her and built her to become him. And the sister who'd chosen madness, who'd left her, and whom she'd left. She pulled the card, bent and bowed, from her pocket. Red heart. Black dog. A face turning south to watch what was leaving.

"Be your mourning ending as soon as it's begun," she said, and understood she was talking to herself.

She didn't ask Seth if he wanted to come. He just joined her as she went by, step-to-step, down the wooden stairs. The road out of town beckoned her, but she'd traveled that path before. She lifted a bare foot over the metal-moat and left the road. Turned right. Found a place no one had ever expected her to walk, and went there.

Here, in the leaving, was a new kind of madness. That of choice, of free will. A soft and wild madness that left her uncertain, for the first time, of her path.

Somewhere behind her, she could hear the devil's magpies asking, *wye-wye-wye.*

"Because I can," she said, and her voice was nothing but her own.

DAUGHTER OF
SORROW

Maurice Broaddus

O UR KIND IS never alone.

I almost pitied the two idiot boys as they approached. In another life, I might have measured them in a different way, noted their swagger and self-assuredness, done the calculations of "cute boy"/dating possibilities. That dream was the life of another girl.

I appraised them as threats before the thought even occurred to them to menace. The first one, easily the larger of the two, was pure toxic bravado. The bald brute with flat features—as if his mother smashed him in the face with a cast iron frying pan—barely squeezed into his Specht Preparatory Academy uniform. The green vest bulged, the gold trim stretched to threads, the black pants fell just above his ankles. He made the first move.

"Who do we have here?" The lummox leaned in. Specks of his spit flecked the air. "Rianna Butcher."

As far as the Specht Preparatory Academy was concerned, that was my name. The massive edifice of the school sat atop 366 steps, one more than those leading up to the U.S. Capitol. Tucked away in the furthest suburb of Indianapolis, Indiana, its seat in Hamilton County was now the third wealthiest county in the country since our kind chose to reside here. An exclusive private school for the elite of the elect. To me it was simply another school, with the same competition of people trying to prove themselves to other people who won't matter to them twenty minutes after graduation. I just turned fourteen, the youngest in my class. I hated mid-year transfers, but my father insisted it would be the last one.

With his awkward lumbering gait, I could have broken the oaf's arm in two places and smashed his trachea with my follow through. I was my father's daughter, and he'd been training me for years, despite his handler's admonitions.

"Hey, mate." Hesitation and caution quickened his friend's voice. He sported a slight Geordie accent. I'd always had a pretty good ear for accents, a gift from my mom. Probably from just north of Newcastle, into Tynesdale. His tie fixed with a fastidious knot, the shirt under his vest pressed and heavily starched. Brighter, or at least more observant than his friend, his eyes focused on the onyx ring on my index finger framed by ornate tendrils of gold, the intricate design almost like interlocking serpents. "I think we have the wrong person."

"Nah, I think she's in the wrong place." In a clumsy effort, the brute jabbed his finger toward me, but he stopped short of making contact. He froze at his stricken friend's look of terror and traced his gaze to his chest. A laser sight trained on his heart. Though he couldn't see it other than through his friend's divided attention, a matching one dotted his forehead. Camouflaged hunter drones, which looked much like mechanical spiders when they skittered around indoors, locked onto him. Noiseless. Invisible. Ever present.

I stared at him with bored amusement.

"Boys." I shook my head and pushed between them.

"You'd think they'd know better by now, Rianna." Demari Andemichael sidled up to me, all smiles and charm, though less than he assumed he possessed. His hair was cropped short. His mischievous eyes had a reckless glint to them. With skin the color of toasted cinnamon, Demari, along with me, allowed the school to consider its diversity mission fulfilled. "You wear your ring out in the open. A bold choice."

He was also one of our kind.

The ring signified my family was a high-ranking member of the Grendel Society. It was my mother's. The Society had operated in the shadows for decades, rubbing elbows with the wealthy and elite, since they were the ones who could afford our services. The Specht Preparatory Academy was both training ground and facilitator of connections, raising the next generation of dangerous power brokers. But even with our traditions and rituals, people were people, and where there was perceived power there were those who vied for it.

Probably why someone killed my father. And I was likely next on their list.

"People don't see the ring first," I said. "They see a girl and make assumptions."

"They're short-sighted. They don't see who you really are."

"Unlike you, of course." An advantage of backpacks was that my arms were free to move if needed. I slightly shifted the weight to my back foot, just in case he tried anything.

"Of course." Demari smirked. He loved the joust of banter. It made him feel grown up and sophisticated. Part of the social games the school excelled at making us play. His easy smile was a trap. Everything with him was an implied threat. The Andemichael name carried a lot of weight in the city. His father sat on five major boards, including their family foundation and the school. His mother was a hotshot lawyer before making the leap into politics. "You see through me."

I started walking again.

Demari fell into lockstep. "How is your father? I haven't seen him much lately."

"Busy." I lowered my voice. "Being the lead agent keeps him on assignment. A lot. You know how it goes. Wait, I suppose you don't."

The Andemichael family fancied themselves as old money. They had the right to rule, as they saw it. But we were the lead unit. Dad worked his way up, having amassed more successful contracts than anyone in Society history. When he was chosen to lead it, the Andemichaels took it as him polluting their bloodline, blocking their presumed ascension to the throne.

"You see how you do it, swerving so recklessly into disrespect?" Demari tried to sound cool and aloof, pretending my words didn't sting as much as they did. He was impulsive and quick tempered, a dangerous pairing especially when combined with ambition. "You tread close to the edge. Be careful you don't slip."

"You're boring me, Demari."

He smirked again. A knowing grin because he couldn't help tip his hand when he knew something someone else didn't. "Full Society board meeting next week. I can't wait to hear the update on your father's activities."

Demari trotted off, taking the steps two at a time and high-fiving guys as he went. He caught up to the two boys and hand clasped them like they were all down. I had to remain vigilant at all times because everything about me was illusion.

Not the most auspicious start to my first day at a new school.

Other girls hustled by in whorls of conversation. They might as well have spoken another language, one that the dream of another girl might have understood. Full of talk about the latest movie, latest episode of *Riverdale*, or the breakup of the latest band. Or clothes. Or rumors about each other or the teachers or who was dating who. A wall which kept me out. When I took my seat, I sat near the back of the classroom on the aisle closest to the door. Clear avenues of escape either through the door or a window. The class had a substitute teacher that day, so few bothered to sit in their assigned seats. Like a good girl, I stayed under the radar. School came easily to me, so I worked quietly completing all of the posted assignments for the week.

But I didn't know if I would last even that long in this life.

"ALL WARFARE IS based on deception."

"If you know the enemy and know yourself, you need not fear the results of a hundred battles."

Fairy lights illuminated the Sun Tzu quotes along the walls of my bedroom. Sarah asked me about them once when we FaceTimed. The story I gave her was that what was true about war was even truer about love. Lovers more often than not became enemies. In between the words were a poster of K.J. Apa, one of Pennywise the clown, and a few pictures of me. Not at events with friends. Not even with Sarah. Moving from school to school, I didn't make too many friends. No one I wanted to remember. It was hard enough learning to be with just me.

I plopped down on my bed and propped a MacBook Pro on my lap. It had a few custom additions of my own design that made a Tor router look like a telegraph. Like I had so many times before, I initiated a dark web search with end-to-end encryption. Also as I had so many times before, I remembered asking...

"...who is the target, Sorrow?"

"Homework first," Dad said. *His mask distorted his voice to a near mechanical drone, any note of concern hidden by the filtration.*

"Are you… are you serious right now?" The sounds of distant traffic roared in the background. If I knew my father, he was on a rooftop stake out. "We aren't father and daughter right now. I'm Hunter Unit 1, Designation: Overwatch. On mission, I can't be… grounded."

"What kind of father would I be if I let you do whatever you want?" His voice thick with command, used to not being questioned. Like everyone else, I knew little of the man, caught up in the larger than life figure people called Sorrow. He fought in wars as his father did, and his father before him, their idea of what men did. He got married and had a baby girl. I don't think he knew what it meant to be a devoted husband or a loving father. He did know death though. "This is strictly a surveillance mission. No need for tactical overwatch. Besides, it's a school night."

"I'm top of my class. I can't get any topper. I'm so far ahead, my teachers have to conference to come up with things for me to do."

"You need a hobby." His voice remained measured. Even with my ear for voices, I couldn't tell if he was joking.

"This is my hobby."

"You're not ready."

"I'll never be ready if it's left up to you."

"This is about me not letting you date."

"Dad, no…"

"I said when you're eighteen you can do what you want."

"I don't even like anyone. Are you being obtuse on purpose? Distracting me is not going to work. The Society requires that I choose to commit or walk away soon. We aren't Amish. We're not talking about Rumspringa or anything. Relocation, new identity, no further contact. The threat of death if they even suspect that their name has crossed my lips and that's to keep you in line as well as me. Either way, my choice won't be easy."

The Grendel Society was not a job with a 401K plan. A league of assassins, it was a commitment for life. Blood in, blood out. If you entered it, the mantle *was yours until you... retired. Permanently.*

"This life is not something to rush into." A sudden weariness filled his voice. I couldn't tell if he was sad or preparing himself because his target was due to arrive soon. "Once you fully join the Society, there's no going back. No proms. No sorority parties in college. There's no happily ever after."

I hated it when he made it sound like all I thought about was his idea of what teenage girls were about. As if this life hadn't forced me to grow up quickly. "You had mom."

"Attachment is weakness. I was weak."

"What was I then?" There were stories I told myself to fill in the blanks of all the conversations my parents and I never had. Suspicions I held in dark corners of my heart, because they'd been left to fester untended. I wanted him to say the words. To admit that I was a mistake and that he never wanted me. That was why he kept pushing me away.

"The fact that you want to do this now tells me that you're not strong enough. You're still looking for my approval, for me to validate you and your choices. That's not what we do."

"That's not what I..."

"Someone put papers on a target. It's not my assignment, but this contract was designed to draw me out. Whoever put out the hit knew I wouldn't let it stand. But I still have my own job to carry out first before I can turn my full attention to whoever decided to threaten us."

Distracting me with the business at hand was part of his tool kit. He liked keeping everyone around him off balance. By now, it was reflex, as natural as breathing. His voice grew distant as he spoke. I got that way sometimes when I was working on a story. Half talking through an idea, half furiously keeping up with the possibilities stirred up in my mind. He examined all the angles, a fly on a sticky strand calculating the direction the spider might come from.

"What's the job?" I began scouring the dark web for evidence of someone reaching out to him through the usual channels.

"Shh. They're here."

"Sorrow, do you read me?"

The comm line went dead. My dad loved his secrets. It was partly due to his training, the code Grendel Society members lived by. But even if he'd been a mailman, I suspect he would've played his life close to the vest, not letting anyone in. I never knew if he carried me in his heart. When I reached out, I didn't hug him; I only wrapped my arms around the walls he built around him. In the end, all we had was…

…nothing. Memories were a funny thing, holding the details of them like cupping sand on a walk home. I sift through them, though, all our conversations, for any clue, only to hit more dead ends. I inventoried Dad's clients, their usual drop spots, hang outs, and ways of communicating. I still had no lead on who he worked for. Shutting down my computer, I sprawled out along my bed. I just wanted to hear his voice, have him tell me everything would be alright.

Frustrated, I punched another hole in my bedroom wall.

I'd have to buy another poster to cover it.

OUR KIND IS always watched.

Constant surveillance left me unsure where I belonged or how to be. There were spaces that required me to be such a different version of who I was, I lost the thread of my true identity. Take the Specht Preparatory Academy for example. On the real, the school was tired. Like many schools these days, they both didn't believe in lockers at the school, but also didn't want weapons or drugs brought in. Wandering the halls like some masterless samurai, my transparent backpack slung across my shoulder, I ignored the bumps and jostles of my schoolmates that accompanied swimming with the tide, trying to fit in and look like everyone else.

The homeroom teacher let us chat until the bell rang before beginning the ritual of calling the class to order. Sarah walked in with a red colored pass, handed it to the teacher, and took her seat. Setting my backpack behind my desk, I sat alone with my thoughts for three heartbeats before Sarah leaned over. She smelled of soap and baby powder.

"This school is so extra." Sarah pronounced "so" like it had three syllables. "They give you infractions for everything."

"I know." I became the "me" Sarah knew, slipping on the persona of cool, bored high school student like it was an old shoe. Originally, she had been assigned to act as my orientation guide. Our relationship was supposed to last the half hour of the initial tour, but we clicked. Her easy, affable way slipped past my defenses, though not completely. Her wide, innocent face framed by long hair. Her eyes the cold blue of a winter sky. Still a pinch of baby fat to her cheeks, but one could see the beautiful young woman she was growing into. She was the closest I'd come to making a friend in years. I hated that I couldn't trust her. "I complained about an infraction today to my music teacher. She held me after class so that we 'could talk about it.' I explained that I had simply forgotten to bring a pencil to class, so I borrowed one from a friend."

"You problem-solved," she said sarcastically. "It's what they always tell us to do."

"Exactly. Then she asks me if I'm unhappy here."

"Uh oh."

"Yeah." I shuddered remembering how my teacher's face went all dark and serious. The whole conversation took on the vibe of a threat. For all I knew, my music teacher was a member of the Grendel Society and the threat was all-too-real. "She told me that me being so flippant when it came to talking about the school, its faculty, or its methods was disrespectful. And that the school… frowned… upon disrespect. So I needed 'to be mindful of that' if I wanted to remain."

"So. Extra." Sarah huffed. "I'm surprised they don't tap our phones, too."

I hesitated. Actually, that wouldn't be beyond them. The phone lines weren't secure. I had to be mindful of that moving forward. This was the "me" the Grendel Society conditioned. They placed the children of their agents alongside the future titans of industry and watchful members of the society. To build relationships while learning what it meant to conceal a double life, so that lying to and hiding from those around us became as natural as breathing. Being in an environment where one didn't know who was friend or foe—one or more of whom had a hand in my father's death—and navigating those places was part of the training.

A moment of weakness with the wrong person and I could end up dead.

"Do you ever wonder about who you're going to be?" I asked.

"You mean when I grow up?" Sarah asked.

"Yeah. I guess."

"Not really. I'm going to graduate top of my class at Harvard, complete my surgical residency at John Hopkins, and become the youngest head of neurosurgery in Mayo Clinic history."

"That's… specific."

"There's nothing wrong with having a plan for your life."

"What if you don't want the plan?"

"Then it wasn't *your* plan?"

"You make it sound so easy."

"Life isn't meant to be over thought." She flipped her hair to gesture how little she cared.

The giggle she nearly elicited from me was cut short as Demari slid into the desk on the other side of me. Side-eyeing his approach, I straightened in my seat.

"I've heard rumors."

"This is high school. We swim in rumors."

"It's more like a story I keep hearing. About a little girl who got in over her head and made all the wrong enemies. And even though she thought she could go at things alone, she found that she couldn't make it more than a few steps before her enemies devoured her."

"That kinda sucks as a story," I said.

"That 'kinda sucks' as a life choice."

"What do you want, Demari?" I tried to fill my voice with as much weariness as possible.

"I want you to join me."

Even with his invitation, I didn't know whether it was genuine or another play in an elaborate scheme. Something close to genuine filled his eyes. My tone stiffened a bit. "I'm happy where I am."

"Look, just because you're pretty..." His voice trailed off as he stopped himself. Like he'd gotten careless and let slip some accidental truth. Recalling how often I caught him staring at my legs, I resented my skirt and the power it gave to his eyes. He re-thought his approach. "Think about it for a day. This offer won't be made twice. In this life, you need as many friends as you can get."

Sarah slipped me a note. *"Was he asking you out?"*

I scrawled in large letters. *"Ew."*

"He's kind of cute."

I underlined *"Ew."* three times.

Still, the edges of my lips upturned a little. Sarah had a way of making things seem normal, like the promise of what could be. She spoke to the dream of another girl.

I HAVE TO choose soon. Indecision invites death.

EVERYONE NEEDS A sanctum.

I crept into Dad's study. Like he was expecting me and had struck a pose, he stood by the window, his hands folded into each other behind his back, like some great, pensive falcon scanning for prey. I was already as tall as him. We met eye-to-eye. Dad had a body like a ballet dancer, thin and muscled, not too different from mine. He moved more like a cat than a heavy-footed soldier.

"Dad, can I ask you something?"

"I can't promise you an answer." Without the mask, he still sounded serious—and he was always serious—but something in his tone hinted at a smile.

"Why did you choose this life?"

"What makes you think I chose this?" He loved answers that either made him sound deep or were designed to make me think. I believed he simply enjoyed playing mysterious so much he'd forgotten how to be real. I was about to re-frame my question, or give up, when he waved me off. "Why do you ask?"

"I don't know."

"Yes, you do." He crossed his arms and waited, letting each second tick by unchallenged.

"I feel... lost," I eventually said. "Like I've been invited to a party where I don't know that many people. And the one or two I do just left me hanging."

I turned away from him, not wanting to catch his eyes. I didn't want him to feel accused, nor did I want him seeing into me. I was my father's daughter, after all, and wanted to keep the secrets of who I really was. Slipping my hands into my pocket, trying to play it cool, I prayed that my hoodie would swallow me whole and then roll out of my father's study like a lone tumbleweed.

"You think I've pulled away? I'm sorry, how did you put it, 'left you hanging'?"

"Ever since mom died..." I tried to explain.

"Ever since I failed, you mean."

"I've never said that."

"You've never had to." Dad stalked about the room, wary and listless, yet tentative, like he was afraid he might break something. "I'm not a good man."

"Dad, I never said..."

He held up his hand. "I do what I do. I choose which assignments I take. Some people have become so rabid it's a mercy for them to be put down—for both themselves and others. I've made choices for me. But I regret having dragged you down this path for selfish reasons."

Selfish. A vague notion began to take shape in my head that perhaps, in his own warped way, being a Hunter Unit was his way of us spending quality time together.

All I wanted was a choice. I didn't want my life picked out and handed to me like some used prom dress.

"We are little more than dogs listening for the voice of our master," he whispered.

"Daddy?" I don't know what made me call him that. I hadn't used that word since I was nine years old and informed him that I was grown and would call him Dad from then on ("Father" when I was mad at him). But the timbre of his voice filled me with fear and uncertainty and reduced me to a little girl frightened by a thunderstorm looking to be comforted by her daddy.

"The Grendel Society is what it is. A necessary evil. We do the work that allows leaders to keep their hands clean. But some within the organization would see us reduced to mercenaries, pimped out to the highest bidder without any moral compass beyond greed. And they would take out any who would oppose them." He picked the framed photo of him and mom from the desk.

The only pictures of her which remained in the house. "We were betrayed and I won't rest until I find out by who."

Those were the last words my father said to me.

———•———

PARANOIA IS A way of life.

Walking down the school hallways, I guessed at the stories and thoughts of the folks who met my eyes and became doubly curious about those who didn't. I wondered who might be actual friends and who only pretended to be. Who gossiped behind my back and how harmful those rumors might be. High school was a life and death experience.

"Demari was asking about you," Sarah said.

"He knows where to find me." I didn't glance up from my work.

"That's what he kept saying. Made a big deal of it. Like you two had a date or something."

Boys hated any kind of rejection and often went through crazy lengths to cover up their hurt. Demari spread word along the vine as an operational tactic. He was coming for me and wanted me to know. I knew how to use that tactic, too. "That's some foolishness. I'm hanging with my dad tonight. Something about bonding time."

"I ought to join you and bring some Chinese." Sarah twirled a random batch of her hair. She drew the malformed braid to her nose as if to sniff it. "All my dad ever does is work."

"And buy you nice stuff."

"Well, if my love is going to be bought, it might as well be quality." She cocked her head as if wanting to be serious for a second but didn't know the proper body language for it. "Does this mean we're not seeing you at practice tonight? We got state coming up."

"Fencing. Seriously. I don't know why my dad has me up in this bougie neighborhood, at this bougie school, doing all these bougie things."

"Have you ever considered that if it walks like a duck…" Sarah began to hum.

"Is that…? Are you for real humming 'Bad and Bougie' to me right now?"

"Quack. Quack." Sarah tried to hold a serious face, but soon broke down in giggles.

I quickly joined her. "I'm too through with you."

"Come on. You're our best fencer." Sarah touched my arm in a reassuring gesture. I stopped myself from staring at the unfamiliar contact.

"Me and my bougie self will be at state, if not tonight's practice."

"Fine." Sarah loped off with a spring in her steps.

My thoughts turned to the grim calculations of inevitable confrontation.

———————

I FOUND MY father's body.

A broken rag doll collapsed on the floor in a ridiculous position, his legs bent underneath him. His arms outstretched in an unnatural sprawl, too awkward a posture for my brain to believe he'd fallen asleep. Or had fainted. I dropped to my knees. Holding his hand, I interlaced my fingers with his as if by sheer force of will I could channel my life force into him and reanimate him. Tears streaked my face, hot trails along already flushed cheeks. My mouth opened, but nothing came out. The world turned gray. My ears filled with white noise like a station that couldn't find its signal. My mind emptied as I rocked back and forth, asleep but with my eyes open.

I don't know how long I stayed like that.

Dad's phone buzzed. Someone—his employer or a ranking member of the Grendel Society—wanted a sitrep. If my dad was dead, the rest of the Hunter Pack #1, me, would be scrubbed. If the assets, me, was deemed valuable enough, they could be assigned to another pack.

I pictured Demari's grin, like a lecherous dog anxious to tear something apart.

"You're not strong enough. Attachment is weakness." *My father's words echoed in my head.* "You're not ready yet."

—————

THERE IS SO much I don't know about my father.

Feeling along the inside of his desk drawer, my fingers searched until I found the button. I depressed it, and a hidden closet slid open. My father's gear hung in place. Full body armor, sleek yet plated. By the time he fixed his mask into place, one couldn't tell if he was human or robot. An array of field weapons was stored across from the suit. He could arm himself according to the mission. Taking his mask from its mount, I cradled it in my hands, turning it over and over. I wondered about how little I knew of the man, how much of him was in this mask. *Who was the target that drew him out?* How he lost his way due to it. *Whoever decided to threaten us. Us.* Again, a vague notion began to coalesce in my head. Me. I had been the target.

All of the lights went out. A dull whine, like the life being drained from the house, plunging the room into complete darkness. My guess was an EMP device of some sort, designed to have my hunter drones, still in camouflage mode, collapse noiselessly to the ground. I dropped to my knees to replace the mask. I didn't hear the intruder until the barrel of his weapon pressed against the back of my head.

"Thanks. It'd have taken us forever to find Sorrow's stash." The voice rang familiar. The lumbering idiot. No, I was the idiot. I believed their little staged play. They took my measure and lulled me into underestimating them. Appearances were carefully constructed lies. And I had run out of patience for them. "Get up. Slowly."

I held my arms out.

He shoved me forward, leading me from my father's study towards the stairs. Maybe to meet up with his partner or partners. Maybe simply to kill me away from the room they planned to loot. Stage a crime scene to present a clean narrative for the police, those not already on the Society's payroll, to believe. I took a few cautious steps not knowing how many of my enemies surrounded me. But there were times to simply act and flush them out.

Whirling, I knocked the weapon away from him and charged to shove him into the wall. He lashed out with a finger strike aimed at my eyes. I ducked the eye jab, but it had been a feint to position me for his kick to my mid-section. I was sloppier than I thought I would be. He arced his hand down. Dodging to my left, I bumped against the stairs. Pushing off them, I narrowly avoided another kick. He was faster than he looked. I'd underestimated him on two counts. Weaving underneath his next flurry of punches, I wrapped up his arms. He had several inches and tens of pounds on me. I'd never beat him in a slugfest. I grappled with him. I found enough of a handhold to flip him to the ground. My punch glanced off the side of his neck. His return blow knocked me from him. I rolled over and scrambled toward him. He planted a foot in my chest, driving all the air from my lungs. I slammed into the ungiving wall. Dazed, I just wanted to slide down and take a nap. With his next charge, I threw a tepid punch. He easily blocked it and wrapped me into a chokehold. The pain and lack of air focused me. Gritting my teeth, I planted myself and jabbed my elbow into him. He reflexively choked me harder. I moved my face toward my shoulder blade to prevent my trachea from being squeezed. I slammed my elbow into his side again and, with a little maneuvering space freed up, followed up with a blow to his neck. He released his hold and staggered backward. A kick sent him to the ground. Me stomping on his head for good measure sent him into unconsciousness.

A crash came from behind me.

I dashed down the hallway only to find Sarah standing over the body of the other boy. Shards of my mother's favorite vase scattered all about him.

"I brought Chinese." She held up the bag. "Thought I'd surprise you."

My kind is never alone.

"You surprised someone," I said.

"Is there a good explanation for all this?"

"I'm sure the police will come up with something."

———•———

THE PHONE BUZZED. The Grendel Society needed an update. I needed to make my decision. My father's mask grew heavy in my hands. I couldn't see any other path forward. There was so much I didn't know about him, so much I didn't know about his death. Or mom's. Becoming him would bring me closure and answers. I slipped the mask on over my face. The next voice would not sound like my own and yet would be my choice.

"This is Sorrow."

THE HAND OF VIRTUE

Linda Robertson

THE WATCHMAN OF Tremain shouted an alert to his people. "A knight approaches!"

Hearing his cry, those working outside halted their harvesting chores. Those indoors left their huts. All eyes locked on the hulking black warhorse as it marched near, the knight rigid in the saddle.

The people of Tremain lined the road to bear witness as another dared climb Mount Wolkehn. They believed it their duty to study and memorize the face of He Who Would Be the One, in order to recall it the next morning as they offered prayers for the dead. But this time they did more than study and memorize. This time they gawked, open-mouthed, realizing the armor-clad rider was a woman.

Maganhild the Strong wasn't vexed by their astonishment, but by their breathy whispers that rippled in the wake of her passing.

Do I look as old as I feel?

Admittedly, the once sun-golden threads of her hair were waning into moon-silver, but she cared not what color sprouted from her scalp.

What concerned her was the ache that plagued her solid grip more often than not. The speed that—decades ago—made her a renowned and formidable opponent of both man and beast had been fading for years. The garments beneath her armor had gotten tight as girth and hips developed their own padding.

Have I become a hag?

Eyes forward, she focused on the mortared stone structure ahead.

Bard-songs claimed the well at Tremain, despite its restorative power, stood plain and unadorned. Maganhild could now attest the bards sang truth, but it was not her journey's purpose to validate lyrics or taste this mountain water. Another verse of their song prompted her quest. The one that claimed the wizard would grant a wholly virtuous request. It was followed by a cautionary verse to ensure that few would dare to seek the wizard. It stated that a request borne of greed would forfeit the life of the seeker.

She had studied the lyrics before committing to her purpose. Two things were certain: all who came before her drank from the well to receive its restorative water, and all faced a test prior to meeting the wizard.

None had ever returned, so Maganhild knew she had to do something different. After hours of reflecting upon the actions of her predecessors, she concluded that drinking from the healing well had secured their failure, for doing so displayed uncertainty, and was thus an act of greed.

So, with canteens filled elsewhere, Maganhild rode past the well amid surprised gasps of the villagers.

Gods, let this be the right thing to do.

Yes, she was uncertain of the wizard and the road ahead, but she believed in her need and sought no false hope to bolster her resolve. She would see this through. She had to; she'd brought her son.

The advantage to him being so small for his age meant that he could still fit into the saddle-sling she'd fashioned to carry him. It looked like nothing more than an unwieldy pack, unless she turned it so he could perceive the world that sprawled around them. Clear of the villagers, she did so and touched his head, a signal that he no longer had to be silent and still. He reached up, squeezed her fingers, and grinned with an inner joy her own spirit could not muster.

Riding these many days instead of romping and playing could not have been easy for him, but his happy demeanor never dwindled. Still, Maganhild harbored a worry for what lay ahead. There had been much to delight his eyes along their journey so far, but past Tremain, Wolkehn became the dark, stark, and unforgiving rock best suited for wizards.

What if the mountain bores him? What if he struggles against the sling and falls? What if the road narrows? What if he panics?

The small boy could shift from calm to terrified in seconds. Maganhild could only guess at the cause. She discerned no pattern to his attacks. They occurred equally in the day and the dark, before or after feeding.

She thought it peculiar, though, that it had never happened near Pitch, the great steed they rode. That had inspired her to wrap him into the saddle-sling. Suspended at the horse's shoulder, he swung gently as the animal walked and could pet Pitch's hide any time.

As they continued onward the road stretched along the edge of steep cliffs. It took her breath every time she glanced out from the mountain, both from the dizzying height and the magnificence of the view.

When the sun's edge touched the wide horizon so far behind and below, Maganhild's concern shifted to finding a place to bed down. She expected to seek out the wizard tomorrow morning, after resting at the edge of the garden—if the lush grounds touted in the bard-songs truly existed.

Ahead, the path narrowed before a sharp turn. Wary of the thinner trail and what she couldn't see, she dismounted and, in doing so, realized how stiff she'd become. The stretch felt good.

Without warning, the boy grabbed the pommel and hauled himself from the sling and into the saddle. She would have scolded him if not for the joy in his expression at sitting on the big horse alone. It changed her words to, "Hold on tight."

In response, he yawned. The mirth on his face faded as he rubbed his eyes and yawned again. Then he grabbed the pommel and nodded.

She led Pitch forward and paused to peer around the bend. The road widened, then curved inland, splitting in two. Between the paths sat a neglected hovel. At first glance, neither direction seemed more obvious as the route to the peak, nor did they reveal any hint that a garden might lay beyond.

Perhaps that shack will suffice as our shelter for the night. She studied it for a long moment and weighed the options of ensuring it didn't fall on them.

Maganhild guided the steed forward.

Something moved inside the hovel.

Halting, she gestured at the boy. He climbed back into his sling. She drew an inch of sword blade even as she called out, "Hello!"

Maganhild hoped for no answer. She hoped to discover their approach had startled a bird or a mouse inside, not an occupant. Birds and mice would leave. An occupant wouldn't. An occupant could be dangerous.

The hovel door creaked open a finger's width. She could discern no details, but a high pitched and gritty male voice shouted, "Go away!"

"Which way to the wizard?"

"You don't want to see him. Go back!" The door slammed. Dust fluttered off of the rotting roof planks.

"Which way?" When no answer came, she dropped Pitch's rein and advanced on the door. "I will not be turned from my quest. Please tell me, which side do I take?"

From behind, the boy called, "Mama!"

She spun around; he had returned to the saddle.

"Mama! Dun," he called, meaning "down."

"No. Stay there, boy." She backpedaled, watching the hovel while returning to her child.

The door groaned as it opened wider. A man, short and barrel-chested, stepped through. He was dressed all in black, the brim of his broad hat angled downward, hiding his features. "You brought a child?" His tone rebuked her.

With a quick glance over her shoulder, Maganhild noted that the boy had obeyed her. "He is my virtuous reason."

"But the risk—"

"—is worth it. I am certain of my request."

"They all say that." The small man's shoulders slumped. "Stay to the left for three splits. Then choose the right path for the fourth. Then stay to left three times again. There you will find the wizard."

"What of the garden?"

"What of it?"

"There we will rest. And seek the wizard in the morning."

The broad brim swayed back and forth as the wearer shook his head. "Night is best; he sleeps through the day. Three lefts, one right, and three lefts. Say it back to me."

"Three lefts, one right, and three lefts."

"Again!"

"I'm not an idiot. I have it."

"Grace be with you." The door shut.

Pitch's ears pricked forward at her return. The boy giggled and waved his arms over his head excitedly until she came close enough for him to lean down and hug her. She accepted his embrace, unsurprised when he slid from the saddle into her arms. He began tapping his fingernails on her armor, enjoying the *tink tink* sounds.

He should have grown much more than he had. His eyes sat too close together on the face of his too-big head, with too-tiny ears. His short and stubby fingers matched his short and stubby arms, same as his legs and toes. Too often people asked what was wrong with him.

Every time, the question broke her heart a little more.

She had taken him to a healer who said that the boy had not grown right because she was too old to be a mother, that she lacked the vitality to nourish him in her womb and at her breast. Despite her doubts, the healer had recommended supplementing other food with what milk Maganhild could provide for as long as the boy would take it, even though it was clear in the woman's face that she didn't think it would be enough.

But Maganhild knew this wasn't about what she couldn't give him as he grew inside her. This was about what she *had* given him.

In all the years of her adult life, only once had she ever been unable to defend herself. Hired as a guard and guide, the client didn't want to pay at the end of the journey and so poisoned her canteen. In the height of her sickness, he'd forced his seed inside her and left her naked in a field, assured that death would soon follow.

But she refused to comply with his plans.

Defeat was not acceptable.

Failure haunted her, awake and asleep. When she recovered, she vowed to taste that man's blood and know the glory of revenge. She hunted and killed him in a manner that equaled his own cruelty.

But his death had not purchased an end to the nightmares.

When Maganhild learned his child grew in her womb, she believed his evil tormented her from within by way of the dreams. Raging at the injustice, furious that her enemy remained inside her, feeding on her to grow again… she wanted the baby to die, too.

Months later, when he arrived in the winter, a squalling bloody mess between her legs, she raised her dagger…

He stopped crying. He kicked and flailed his fists. He smiled.

…and she found there *was* such a thing as an acceptable defeat.

She was unable to resist loving him, and, in the four summers that had passed, unable to forgive herself for what her hate had done to him.

The wizard would hear her story. He would pity them and cure the boy.

He will. This is a virtuous entreat.

Maganhild led Pitch up the mountain path through three lefts. The full of night and the height of Wolkehn combined to chill the air. She paused to put the boy into the saddle sling, but he fought his drowse and rallied, reaching for the saddle to indicate he wanted to ride more. She wrapped his blanket around him. Having his way made him smile, and that smile, after all, had defeated her.

Hungry howls echoed from the wilderness below. Pitch would alert her if he smelled anything close, but he plodded along unconcerned, through a right and another left. Maganhild began to feel the need for rest and sleep in earnest. She was not the only one.

"Mama."

Though lacking in words, the boy could communicate an abundance with his expressions. His chubby hands reached toward her, fingers straight, then curling. She welcomed him into her arms again and kissed his cheek as a shiver ran over him.

The armor, too cold and rigid to snuggle against, needed to come off. Sliding him back onto the saddle she said, "Give Mama a minute." After unbuckling the straps of shoulder armor, she pulled a cape from the saddlebag and tucked the armor into the vacant pouch. Once she removed the breastplate, she refastened it around the saddlebag. With the cape settled about her, she pulled the boy into her arms and adjusted the cape to swathe him. "There. Sleep now, boy." He pushed the flaps of her shirt aside and fed from her breast until slumber claimed him and his breath became a soft rhythm on her neck. His absolute trust, his innocence, bolstered her resolve. He deserved this.

Before they made the final left, she tucked the sleeping boy into the saddle-sling. Leading the stallion onward, her heartbeat increased with her eagerness to meet the wizard, then hammered as she made the last left.

There was no garden here, but the wizard was waiting for her.

He sat upon a throne built into the mountainside, a giant of a man, with a headdress and veils disguising his features. He wore fine robes and the sleeves draped over his gloved hands. One finger curled under. His foot shifted. "A lady in armor." His deep voice hardly seemed real, thundering from within him and echoing off the mountain's walls.

Maganhild thought it likely this strange voice was some magic meant to frighten her, but her only fear was that the boy would awaken. Her hand slid into the sling, but he slept on.

"Are you afraid?"

"It is said you slay those who do not have a virtuous cause."

"Have you come with a foolish request?"

Her chin lifted. "No."

"Then remove the rest of your armor and come closer that we may speak."

"Does my armor offend you, wizard?"

"Have you come to fight?"

"No."

"Then unburden yourself of useless weight."

"But—"

"I have spoken." His words were elongated, uttered slowly. As each emphasized sound crossed his lips, his body moved underneath his robes as if his whole torso contorted and transformed.

Her hand strayed to the pommel of her sword. "I am beginning to fear you."

His head tipped to one side and, behind her, small rocks showered down along the mountain wall. The show of ability emphasized his words, "Your armor cannot protect you should I find you lacking. That sword hasn't the reach to stop me should I want you dead. And you will never leave this place unless I choose to let you go." He sniffed the air. "Do I smell a child?"

"Yes. He isn't far." The way Pitch stood, the wizard couldn't see into the sling.

"Ah."

She removed the leg and thigh armor, set them aside. Her fingers worked to loosen the sword belt, reluctance slowing each move. With her arms spread wide she turned in a circle, holding the cape to the side so he could see she had no weapons.

"Come." Five steps away from him, his giant finger flexed to point. "Kneel."

His ominous tone made her wonder if Pitch could flee with her son safely back to Tremain should the wizard become violent, but on the heels of that thought she cast her doubts away. The time to worry had passed. All she had sought was at hand.

Maganhild knelt.

"Tell me your purpose, woman."

Head bowed, she spoke. "I have come to ask for the life of my son."

Distaste sullied the words, "You think a mere illness makes your request worthy?"

Her brows knit. "He… he is not ill."

"Ahhh. Then what do you stand to gain by asking for his life?"

Peace of mind. Assurance of his independence. Her throat tightened. *Selfish.*

Her chin dropped and her stomach became ice. Her motive had been for his betterment. *Hadn't it?*

"Please understand." It hurt to force the words out. "I was poisoned and raped. When I learned that he grew within me, I hated him. I wanted him to die—"

"Iniquity!"

"—but then—" She looked up.

The wizard was in motion. A move she recognized. She began to rise before seeing the weapon. Her earlier weariness disappeared and her renowned speed returned as the wizard leaned, torso angling strangely, and his arm shot forward.

"Wait!" she cried, spinning to dodge the thrown dagger by a hair's breadth. As the rotation brought her back around she kicked at the giant's forearm. The toe of her boot pushed the fabric of his sleeve easily up and into what should have been the flesh of his arm. There, it became stuck. Unable to follow through and rebalance herself, she fell, causing half of the wizard to lurch from the throne and land on her, knocking away her breath.

She didn't understand what had just happened—*had the wizard severed himself to attack me?* Regardless, her life was at risk. Her confusion redoubled when small but strong hands pushed out from folds in his robe and circled her throat.

The large headpiece loomed over her. She made a fist and punched where the jaw should have been, but it didn't feel like a jaw when she made contact. Still, the wizard cried out and the grip on her throat loosened. Seizing the moment, she grabbed the arms that had attacked her even as she pushed with one leg and sent both the wizard and herself into a roll.

Now atop the oddly-lightweight wizard, she glanced around, anticipating the longer arms would strike at her next. She noted, however, that the wizard's sleeves lay crumpled around and under them, flat and without arms in them. A gloved hand and arm made of wood lay not far from her knee.

Flashing a look toward the throne she realized the other gloved hand was attached to the rock chair-arm, and a pulley system of rope stretched from the wrist to the shoulder. Another mechanism attached to the foot she had seen moving.

The figure under her was not nearly as big as the wizard had portrayed himself. This man was small. Like the man at the hovel.

It's a ruse!

There was no wizard. No hope for what she sought.

Rage infused her, as did the willingness to fight and kill from days long past. Altering her grip to hold both of his small wrists in one hand, she jerked the headdress away. Her arm drew back, ready to pommel him, but she froze and her fist unclenched.

The veils had created an illusion of size, but without them or the low brimmed hat he'd worn earlier she saw things she did not expect. His eyes were small, and too close. His ears were tiny on his too-large-for-his-size head. His fingers were stubby and misshapen.

She was looking at what her boy would become.

All her fears culminated in this one man who had learned to lure people high on the mountain to rob and slay them in order to survive.

Cruelty begets cruelty.

Either her shocked expression or her hesitation set him off. His struggles renewed and he cursed and kicked and snarled like a beast, but like this, he was powerless to defeat her. Fighting to change a situation he could not hope to alter, he only looked like a fool.

Is this what strangers see in my boy?

But this individual was not like her sweet and happy son.

This man, she guessed, had been tormented as she feared her son would be tormented in her absence... or after her death. She was getting old; he would have no one if she died. That inevitability had prompted this journey... this fight... to enable him to live his life, to change a situation she could not hope to alter.

I am the fool.

She had succumbed to cruelty and called it revenge when she maimed then killed the man who'd raped her. Afterward, she'd learned the empty pain she'd been struggling with had not been healed by her violence. Only when she actively chose the boy's life over her need for vengeance, when she allowed love to replace the hate within her, only then did she cease to suffer with nightmares.

She released the man's wrists. He stilled and stared at her as she shifted away and stood beside him. Maganhild offered him a hand up. "You don't have to do this."

Light flashed, and Maganhild lurched away as a green-robed woman appeared before them. One slender hand wrapped around a gnarled staff, the other fondled a crystal hanging from a cord around her neck. "Marcus, take the hand of Maganhild the Strong."

Gaping at both this magical entrance and the wizard's knowledge of her name, Maganhild hesitated before returning to again offer her hand.

Once on his feet, the man cast off the oversized robes to reveal the black clothes underneath.

The Wizard of Wolkehn regarded them both with a shake of her head. "A thousand years I have been here. Waiting." She stepped toward the rock throne and sat. "One after another, men have climbed this mountain to ask for things. And one after another, I turned them on each other, baiting them like beasts to see which would show me their virtue. How many have you slain, Marcus?"

His chin dropped. "Twenty-nine."

"Twenty-nine," she repeated. "How long?"

"Forty years."

"And your predecessor stayed for thirty-two years and killed twenty-three men. His predecessor stayed for thirteen years and killed six. And so on and so forth over centuries." The wizard's mouth curved ruefully. "Maganhild the Strong, you have ended my long wait. You have not fought this day to survive or to win, for you have not fought Marcus. By equal measures, you have fought yourself and fought to understand the complexity of your situation, both here," she pointed at the ground, "and there," she pointed at Pitch. "Speak your desire that I may grant it."

Maganhild's heart sputtered in her chest. Her mouth opened and shut. Her gaze transferred from the wizard to Marcus, then lingered on the sling at Pitch's shoulder.

"What request brought you all this way?" the wizard prompted.

She whispered, "I brought my son."

"Why?"

"Because I wanted him to be… normal." Her tone grew to a regular speaking voice as she met the wizard's eyes and continued. "Normal. *Like the rest of us.* I came to ask you to change him so that I won't have to worry about his survival when I am gone. But…"

"But?" The wizard's brows lifted as a sign of patience.

She thought of the flowers the boy would pick and bring to her, and how his little hands would push at her cheeks trying to make her smile. She recalled the random moments when he ran to her like something terrible chased him, but all he wanted was to hug her tight.

No womb-curse had touched him. Neither did he suffer from

an after-effect of the poison. He was her boy, her son. Just as he was meant to be.

She would be miserable if the boy was changed and even an ounce of his sweetness disappeared because he was made what others deemed 'normal.'

"But even now I see that I am the one who is flawed, the one in need of changing. Though I love him, though my eyes adore him, I needed him to be different." She looked at Marcus, then twisted to glance again at the saddle-sling before facing the wizard once more. "I saw what he wasn't. I saw what I thought he should be. I didn't accept what he is."

The wizard's chin lifted; she looked down her long and crooked nose and prompted, "What is he, Maganhild?"

Her head shook slightly as she considered how to answer his question. "He is innocent and trusting and happy. He is... he *is* virtue." She swallowed. "If you alter him as I came here intending to ask you to, he would no longer be *that*. I thought this quest was for him, for his benefit, but now," her gaze shifted to Marcus again, "I realize it was for me."

The wizard came forward and placed a hand on her shoulder. "Maganhild the Strong, I cannot change you, as you have already changed yourself." She sidestepped and glowered down at Marcus. "And you... what have you learned?"

"Shame, madam. The value of having honor and virtue."

"It's about time," the wizard mumbled. She bent and spread her fingers over Marcus's head. "I release you."

Light flashed again and standing in Marcus's place was a man in armor not unlike Maganhild's own. He was tall and rugged, and silver streaked his dark hair. He studied his hands and his body as if he didn't know himself.

"Mama!"

Maganhild turned and saw her boy climb from his sling onto the saddle. When he was sitting and holding on tight, she whistled and Pitch brought him close.

His stubby fingers curled and uncurled. "Mama!" She opened her arms. He slid into her embrace and snuggled under her chin. She stroked his hair.

"What is his name?" the wizard asked.

"I never gave him one." A pang of shame twisted her stomach. "At first, I just didn't know what to call him. He was my boy in my every thought and deed, but I allowed him no identity. Why?" Tears welled up.

"Name him," Marcus said urgently. "Name him now."

Maganhild pulled back to gaze on her boy. Tears spilled down her cheeks and the boy wiped them gently away. "Mama no cry."

She kissed his forehead and whispered, "I name you Virtue."

The wizard shut her eyes and let her chin fall as all air left her lungs.

Marcus lowered himself to one knee. "My life was lost, forfeit to the wizard until you, Maganhild the Strong, and Virtue restored me. Until my dying day, I will serve you both."

In the distance, thunder crackled. "I cannot remain much longer," the wizard said. "Come to the cave beyond the garden and choose what piece of my treasure you would take with you as reward." She stepped behind the throne and disappeared.

Maganhild carried Virtue, and Marcus led Pitch as they followed the wizard and found a doorway to a lovely moonlit garden. Scanning across the distance, she spied the wizard nearing the mouth of a cave on the other side. The wizard flicked her fingers and light began to glow inside. She gestured for them to hurry.

"I'll stay with the horse," Marcus said.

"His name is Pitch," Maganhild said softly.

Marcus smiled warmly at her, and she returned it.

The wizard pointed inside the cave at a vast space filled with gold and silver glinting in the light of a thousand candles. "Choose anything you like, but be quick. I would have you back in Tremain before the storm hits."

Maganhild nodded and carried Virtue into the room following a path that led among the treasures stacked so high. She saw chalices, crowns, and vases. Boxes of coins. Jewelry. Statues. Things she could not name. There was too much to choose from. Glancing back, she noted the wizard just outside, talking to Marcus.

"Mama." Virtue pushed against her, wanting down. "Mama. Dun."

"Yes. Perhaps you should pick." She sat him down.

He turned in a circle, mouth agape and eyes alight, then toddled off. She stayed close behind him, but her eyes caught on a sword with a huge emerald as the pommel. She paused to examine it.

In that moment, Virtue slipped away.

He found a narrow path that led to a room with a big bed, a chair, a desk, and three tables. One held jars with strange, squirming things inside them. On another rested a big, open book. On the last a large black horn balanced impossibly on its tip while curving to one side and widening to the open end from which sprang a beam of red light. As the horn slowly turned the light moved about the room.

Virtue could not read the engraving on the stand: *Horn of a Rodænym, the Quinary, Brotherhood of Five.* All he knew was this air tasted strange and right here his skin felt like a warm wind blew all over him. He reached out to the horn. The closer his fingers came, the colder the air around it was. He pulled back, but grinned as he watched the light move. The curved side was coming around…

"Virtue!"

He did not recognize that Mama's word meant to call him back to her. On tip toes, he reached again into the cooler air and the tip of one finger brushed the edge of the horn.

"Boy, where are you?"

This, he understood. Pulling away, he lowered onto his heels to go to her.

He would never know that the goodness of him resonated on that horn like a violent storm. He would never know that, with the painstaking slowness of time running so that seconds became long minutes, the horn tipped from its stand. He would never know that the source of the red illumination dripped from inside of it and seared a hole in the stone floor that burned deep, deep into the mountain, and kept burning all the way to the Abyss.

But the wizard knew.

She watched Maganhild, Virtue, and Marcus leave together, assured at the wisdom in the warrior-woman's choice of coins, as well as Marcus's acceptance of her suggestion that they hurry far away from these lands. When they were out of sight, she faced the cave.

For a thousand years, she had been bound to this place, sworn to service no evil, sworn to reward a wholly virtuous act. A millennium trickled by as she guarded the horn, and when Fate came to pass, the binding that kept her here flared, barring from her any words that might have halted the fruition of evil. But then, the darkest of prophecies always had a way of finding fulfillment, despite the best efforts of those in the light.

As the storm neared, she stood in her chamber beside the great book on the table and read from the open page:

As foretold, comes a twist of Fate
When the hand of Virtue opens the gate
And the world to its horror will embark
Upon a new age of demons and dark.

THE LIFE AND TIMES OF JOHNNY THE FOX

Sabrina Vourvoulias

I AM HERE TO tell you the truth about Johnny the Fox. If you've heard the tale that he was born in Puerto Rico, to one human and one inhuman parent, that is true.

Johnny's mother is from the western port city of Mayagüez, where she lives to this day. His father is the northeasterly trade wind that regularly sweeps in and plays along Puerto Rico's northernmost shore and outlying islands.

Many years ago—but not so many that there aren't some folks who still remember—the two met in Arecibo and fell grandly and recklessly in love. The product of their union loves this story, by the way. Johnny the Fox is fond of saying that if you dig under all the hard layers of his being, you'll come to a core that is pure, molten romance. And, really, what could be more romantic than a wind that becomes human to woo its beloved?

But a cynical wink is never far from any of Johnny the Fox's tales, so remember: love has never been enough to permanently tame, or even reroute, the wind.

If you've heard tales that Johnny the Fox is possessed of magic, the truth depends on the tale.

I've heard it recounted that he collected all the dominoes ever made in Puerto Rico and used his spit to magically weld them together. With them, he constructed a bridge that spanned from Mayagüez to Philadelphia, and that is how he got here from there.

That story, I regret to inform you, is pure fabrication. Johnny the Fox arrived in Philadelphia when he was ten—after a postal carrier hand-cancelled the $300 in stamps his mother had stuck on his shirt. He was loaded into the cargo hold of one of the daily mail flights with all the other parcels, and within days was delivered to distant relatives in the City of Brotherly Love.

Anyway, that's how Johnny the Fox tells the story. I leave it to you to decide whether you believe him or not—but you can Google the history of children sent by parcel post if you think his tale is too tall.

You may have heard the tale of how Johnny the Fox magically sang the snakes out of North Philly. That story is frequently told at a certain bodega in El Barrio—the click of dominoes, the smell of Florida Water and sweet cigars all around—where the teller is, invariably, one of Johnny's compais. That is, one of his buddies. Possibly even an accomplice in one of his cons.

Wasn't it Johnny the Fox who taught Tatán Ortíz, the bodeguero, how to bilk the system by cashing out food stamps for folks who wanted some cigarettes or alcohol along with their government cheese? Tatán eventually got caught siphoning dollars and gave up Johnny in order to keep his bodega. But when the Fox sauntered out of the Big House, there was a table and a cafecito waiting for him, and no grudges were held.

You can read all about the lethal reptiles (and Johnny's part in extirpating them) elsewhere, but I can, indeed, verify that every successful scheme and plan of his making involves singing. Johnny's magic, you see, has always been in his voice.

As a child in Puerto Rico, Johnny sang his way into grades he didn't deserve and awards he shouldn't have gotten. His warbled incantations compelled schoolmates to give him their most prized possessions. When the wind blew and little Johnny sang, store proprietors fondly tut-tutted his shoplifting; teachers smiled at his disruptions; and truant officers looked the other way.

His mother understood that as Johnny grew older, magic or no magic, people would come to resent his self-gratifying and self-aggrandizing choices. That's when she sent him away, to a city where the powers given to any fairy-tale-begotten child are regularly muted by noise, and traffic, and hardscrabble barrio reality.

But in Philadelphia as Puerto Rico, in adult as in child, magic is magic.

It was Johnny the Fox who first sang "Despacito," to compel domino enthusiast and singer Luis Fonsi into ridiculously slow and distracted play during a tournament of El Domino. Johnny had bet on Fonsi's competitor, and he raked in lots of money that day—though perhaps Fonsi got the last laugh when he changed the lyrics and used Johnny's magical melody for his crossover hit.

Folklorists will tell you there is some confusion in the tales, and sometimes Johnny the Fox is renamed Johnny the Dog.

There is an iron-faced preacher's wife who is responsible for that muddle. When she is the storyteller, Johnny is every bit as sly, selfish, and greedy as usual—but she makes him out to be an indiscriminate mequetrefe and pervert, too. In her stories, he sniffs around every female he sees on the streets of El Barrio as he goes about the business of mischief.

And it *is* true that Johnny admires the curve of a waist, the rise of a breast, and the pert, round bottom that comes from wearing sky-high heels.

But it's also true that the preacher's wife and her husband have been preying on vulnerable barrio residents for years—by setting up fake drug recovery houses where they're paid for months of service by people they kick out the day after they've signed up. When he came out of the slammer, Johnny the Fox was sent to one of their recovery houses.

Now, everyone knows Johnny the Fox's moral compass is broken, but its needle does occasionally hover over a point where indignation and self-interest meet.

So every time the preacher's wife runs into Johnny, she is musically reminded to pay him to not drop a dime on her lucrative scam. On months when there is a flood of the drug-addicted at her door, she might end up hearing Johnny's song three or four times a day. Or, as has happened with some frequency, she might run into him in the company of an inspector friend of his. Then she and her husband are compelled not only to pay the bribe, but to actually provide the services they're supposed to—at least for the week or so after the surprise encounter when Johnny ratchets up noise about the inspector's imminent return.

The thing is, despite knowing she is the mark in his con, the preacher's wife finds herself unable to despise Johnny the Fox. Every time they are in the same room together, she waggles her once-glorious-and-still-not-bad ass at him. No question, he enjoys the sight. But he's got three fine women already—las girlfriends—BFFs who pass him around like a skin of wine that wants to be shared.

Plus, since las girlfriends live in South Philly, whenever Johnny's a suspect in some untoward thing that happens in North Philly in middle of the night, he's got one, two, three alibis.

If you are wondering whether you have seen Johnny the Fox on the streets of El Barrio, he is pretty easy to recognize. He would describe himself to you as a darker, juicier Antonio Banderas, but don't believe that. The truth is, Johnny the Fox isn't bad, but he isn't all that either. He wears too much brilliantine in his copper-tipped hair, lets too much white show in the strap of his beard, and has developed a bit of a gut (which he can hide if he doesn't tuck his shirt in—and who tucks in a guayabera?). His arms are full of New School ink, his eyes full of old-school savvy, and his mouth overflowing with tales told out of school.

He is loved. And hated. And admired. And reviled. And always, he manages to be fully himself, who he is, despite all the ways society tells him not to be.

And this is something you have to understand: even though he is possessed of magic and a grifter's imagination about how to best use it, things don't always end well for Johnny the Fox.

One September day—as dawn struts onto El Barrio's Golden Block with its best salsero vibe—it is revealed that Johnny the Fox is missing.

Tatán Ortiz shuts down his bodega moments after opening it and puts together a posse to look for him in every lock-up in three counties. Johnny's other compais scour all the hang-outs de mala muerte that they've frequented with him. And las girlfriends file one, two, three missing persons reports.

Even the iron-faced preacher's wife goes out on the street in her bathrobe and slippers when she hears, and looks for her beloved nemesis under the cardboard with which blitzed-out addicts cover themselves when they sleep beneath the bridges after a relapse.

For months, everyone believes that Johnny the Fox has met the nefarious end reserved for those who've run a con on the wrong person in Philadelphia. All of them, at one time or another, will try to bribe-talk-cry their way into the morgue to check for his body.

The Barrio is different without Johnny the Fox in it.

The crooked politicians and unscrupulous operators are all still running their flim-flams on the folks in the neighborhood, but none of them have Johnny's panache, nor his predilection for hitting first and hardest on those with power and money.

Tatán still runs his bodega and its stop-and-go business on the borders of legal, but the stories told within it are ordinary, and nobody seems to have anything remotely fantastical happening in their lives.

Las girlfriends drive their food truck from South Philly to North every day, but their pasteles are too salty and over-spiced now that Johnny's not taste-testing them beforehand.

And the preacher's wife has started considering her husband's proposal to move the business down to Orlando, where the Puerto Rican community is young, and may be less savvy to their ways.

Then, six months to the day after he's disappeared, Tatán Ortíz finds Johnny the Fox shivering, in shirtsleeves and barefoot, on the slushy sidewalk in front of his bodega.

"You're alive," Tatán says as he fumbles with the metal roll-down grate that covers the front of the store during off-hours. "But you won't be long if you keep standing outside like that in this February weather."

Tatán uses the word "tiempo" for weather—a word that also means time—and maybe that's what turns Johnny's expression so haunted that the old man decides to cross himself several times before unlocking.

Tatán makes Johnny sit at one of the tables set out for stop-and-go drinkers and domino players, and brings him a cafecito mixed with lots of sweetened condensed milk to thaw him out. As soon as Tatán's youngest granddaughter, Araceli, shows up for her shift behind the register, he brings more coffee, and parks himself opposite Johnny.

"I imagine there is a tale," he says.

Johnny the Fox nods, quiet except for the chattering of his teeth. They sit in silence for a long time. Araceli brings them more coffee. During a particularly slow spell around 10 a.m., when no one at all comes in to the store, she goes into the back room and finds an unopened package of cheap tube socks and her brother's next-best pair of Timberlands. She brings them over to the table and waits as Johnny the Fox tries to get them on his frozen feet. Then she goes back behind the register and puts her earbuds in.

"The young don't want to hear the stories of the old," Tatán says, after he turns back from watching her.

"Don't include me among the old," Johnny answers, in what should have been a jokey mock-offended tone. But his words come out breathy, as if the effort to get them out has winded him, and there is no charm—magical or otherwise—in their scraped, wounded tone.

Tatán's eyes narrow. "What happened to your voice?"

"I've been in Puerto Rico," Johnny says with some difficulty.

"Ah." And perhaps Tatán has some small magic in his voice too, because anyone overhearing that one word could read a full narrative in it.

I, in fact, do exactly that when I hear Tatán say it as I walk into the bodega to buy a shot of Old Grandad Bourbon (a little tradition of mine to celebrate when I finish grading papers). Araceli serves the drink from behind the plexi around the register, in what looks like one of the plastic measures packaged with cough syrup. I head with it to a table one over from Johnny and Tatán.

Unlike many of Tatán's stop-and-go patrons, I buy my drinks here more for the company than the alcohol. I've sometimes lingered for hours over a couple of low-cost whiskeys, chatting with the barrio's old codgers about their efforts to see Oscar López Rivera freed from prison. They can really wax eloquent about this icon of the militant

Independence movement, and Puerto Rico's most famous political prisoner. He might as well be a saint—Tatán has kept a candle burning for him on the store's altar shelf for the past twenty years, and the recently announced pardon hasn't changed that fact.

When I sit at my table, the old man gives me a silent hello by touching two fingers to the tatty Basque beret he always wears, then turns his attention back to Johnny the Fox. "It's okay to talk in front of this guy," he says to him. "He may not look it, but he's gente."

Johnny glances at me, nods, but takes at least half an hour to get the first word out in that pathetic new voice of his.

So listen, this is my version of the tale he finally tells:

Johnny the Fox, the son of this hemisphere's northeasterly trade wind, has heard his father's voice gusting in his ear every day of the forty-seven years he's been given so far on this earth.

On September 5th, his father bellows a name—Irma—and a directive—Go to her, son—and Johnny dutifully hops a plane to Puerto Rico.

He disembarks moments before the Category 5 beauty (who has already torn through Florida on her grand tour of destruction) sets her eye on San Juan. Others hurry to claim their baggage, but Johnny the Fox stands on the airport tarmac, singing.

He croons to the winds wrapping around the eye, those long arms of the most powerful of Taíno goddesses. He invokes her as divine storm; the righteous destroyer of walls and divisions created by man; the ultimate test-and-proof for human nature. Johnny's magical melody tunes itself to the one tender spot in the goddess's eye where preparation, prayer and good luck overlap. He spins a magnificent confidence game from that spot—one that propitiates even as it exploits, one that prevails with the mark's own consent.

Feeling herself both revered and truly understood for once, Irma stands down even as she lets her tears fall. She flicks her skirts in passing—a mere flirtation—then leans down to kiss the edge of the island. More demure than she ever intended to be, she turns out the lights when she leaves.

And since this is Johnny the Fox—Barrio brazen until his last day—as soon as Irma is gone, he sets out on foot across the island. Call it a grifter's pilgrimage. There are a million ways to take money for tar-sealing a roof you haven't, for buttressing buildings you won't, for hurricane-proofing the neighborhood you'll never set foot in.

It takes Johnny ten days to reach his mother's house in Mayagüez. He's got a grin on his face and money overflowing his pockets when he knocks on her door.

This is what you never hear when the tales of Johnny the Fox are told: how he felt about his mother sending him away so young; how he made do without her while growing up in the poorest neighborhood of the poorest big city in the U.S.; how he missed her counsel even with his father's advice constantly blowing in his ear.

But there are no recriminations in Johnny's repertoire. At seventy his mother turns out to be just as beautiful as he remembers her; lithe and energetic, with white twists of hair that dance around her face when she laughs. As they sit outside, eating mangoes fresh-picked off her trees, he tells her every tale worth telling from his life, up to and including his recent magical adventure with Irma.

"And now Father tells me there is another hurricane coming," he says. "Don't be surprised if this time next week you hear the tale of how Johnny the Fox fast-talked two hurricanes in a row and saved Puerto Rico."

"Son," she says after a long moment, "it is a wondrous thing that your last song so pleased the Cacique of the Winds that she decided to go easier on us. But what charms a goddess the first time feels like manipulation the next, and she won't take kindly to it. Save your magic. Ride out the hurricane in Mayagüez instead, where the West Wind rules. Here. With me."

Johnny reaches over and pats her hand with his mango-sticky ones. "Wouldn't that be a novel twist?"

So does Johnny the Fox heed his mother? Does he put his conceit and magic on mute and hunker down, in the way of all humans faced by superhuman forces they know are beyond their control?

Or does he follow his inhuman father's lead and sweep to the East, pitting his persuasive grifter's gift against Hurricane María's power?

Johnny the Fox is almost to Yabucoa when she rises up before him, grey and solid like a wall, shaking water that falls harder than a river breaking its banks. He holds his hands up to signal he needs a moment, and digs deep to find the perfect melody, the right words. María holds as she is, watching incuriously as he gathers his human and inhuman powers.

Johnny remembers the song with which he lulled the North Philly snakes into torpor, and trebles its coercive strength before he casts it at María. He follows it immediately with what he's long used on the preacher and his wife—appealing to greed and shaming it at the same time. He throws at her each bait-and-switch, bunco parlor, 8-dice-cloth, hall-of-fame skin game he's ever conjured in his rich, undeniable baritone.

She goes so still, he believes he's landed his magic.

And then. And then, she drives his words back at him. Maybe this giantess, maybe this goddess, maybe this hurricane, is a winged thing—because she reaches for him and in one sweep, flays the clothing from his body.

She throws a street sign at him. Then a hundred-foot palm tree still rooted to its ball of earth. Then the roof of a house. She doesn't kill him outright, but plays like a cat, flinging him around to tenderize him. And when she tires of that, she brings the wires down—crackling and conductive in the water-swollen air—all around him.

On his back in mud, water, and sparks, Johnny the Fox doesn't give up. He opens his mouth again and one sublimely imperative note emerges.

María stops for a moment, then leans in and tears it and the magic it is rooted in, right out of Johnny's mouth. She moves on then, inland, where she'll bring down the grid and plunge the island into a dark six months in the underworld. Three-thousand people (and counting) will die from her rampage through the island.

It is his father's inhuman nature that enables Johnny the Fox to survive. When the storm finally clears, the island is so physically changed, Johnny cannot recognize the landmarks. It is the trade wind's voice in his ear that guides him back to his mother's house to heal his battered body, his bruised psyche, everything but his voice—which will never heal.

Tatán shakes his head, gives Johnny an exasperated look. "No matter how audacious the intent, the outcome was shit. María was so put out by your monumental presumption that she whisked your magic away to teach you a lesson."

"That's the problem with being a legend in your own mind," Araceli says, despite the earbuds. "You're never as powerful as you think you are."

"Hey, at least you stayed in Puerto Rico for months afterward," I say, feeling a bit sorry for Johnny. "So some good came of it, amirite? You probably helped some folks in the aftermath…"

"Yeah, sure, like maybe he handed out some rolls of paper towels one day," Tatán interrupts me.

"Or maybe he offered to fetch water for people, one teacup full at a time," Araceli says with a snort.

"Or maybe on the flight home he gave his coat and shoes to some poor viejito wearing chanclas and a t-shirt," Tatán adds. "For a price, of course."

They keep going, mocking the idea that Johnny would willingly do anything good for anyone, weaving their narrative of ridicule in third person right to his face. He makes pitiful, affronted sounds, and every so often tries, unconvincingly, to protest.

Late in the afternoon, las girlfriends and Johnny's compais find their way to the bodega, and they take turns riding him too. I won't vouch for it, but it is entirely possible that the preacher's wife calls one of their cellphones at one point, and that they hold it up to Johnny's ear so she can get in on the fun too.

When evening falls, Tatán brings out the good beers, las girlfriends haul a mother lode of Mexican-tamales-posing-as-Puerto-Rican-pasteles from the back of their food truck, and Johnny's compais loudly sing along to the songs on Araceli's favorite playlist.

No one stops giving Johnny the Fox a hard time, but they also feed him savory bits of tamal/pastel with their fingers, they toast his survival and clink bottles with him, and they convince him that even though he can't sing anymore, he can still dance down the bodega aisles with them, to the sounds of Mino Cruz and Princess Nokia.

Someone dips into a stash of out-of-season fireworks, and then we all pour out onto the street in front of the bodega to set them off. A lot of other folks find their way over to us, after the first few go off. It is this way always, here in El Barrio.

Smoke bombs and fountains and ground spinners. By their intermittent light we look into each other's faces and wonder if there is any difference between cuentistas (liars) and cuentistas (storytellers), and if it even matters any more.

Nothing in Puerto Rico will ever be the same again. And by extension, nothing here will be either.

So the truth about Johnny the Fox is this: there he is, at our heart, living by his wits (as we all are). He is battered and broken (as we all are). He is surrounded by flash and fire, and a community that values resilience above all else. With voice or without, magic lives here as long as we do.

Welcome back, Johnny the Fox.

Editor's note: At the time of this book going to press, parts of Puerto Rico continued to be without power more than 356 days after Hurricane María. According to the most recent reports released by the Puerto Rican government, there were 2,975 fatalities in Puerto Rico due to the hurricane, not including later deaths due to delayed and interrupted health care.

OLD SOL RISES UP

Toiya Kristen Finley

Chase

CHASE WASN'T SURE what to expect based on their conversations—perhaps the raw, earthen heaviness of patchouli or the muskiness of incense. But the sickly sweetness of fruit puffs soaking in milk hit him as he entered the brownstone. Three kids, three out of Old Sol's five, sat on a living room couch. They were all about the same age. In fact, a couple probably were the same age, even though none of them were twins. They looked up at him for a moment, as Chase clicked the front door closed. Then they went back to stuffing their mouths.

"*Yesssss!* Here he is!" A giant man swung his arms forward in greeting. Chase recognized the booming voice from online chat. He'd never seen the man before, but Old Sol looked much like he'd expected—central casting's answer for a '90s Hip-Hop artist, a prettier Biggie.

"Good to finally meet you!" Brie, one of Chase's other guildmates and Old Sol's… well, Chase wasn't exactly sure if he quite understood that relationship. She only participated in raids while she was with Sol, and she came and went as she pleased. She gave Chase a hug and a "mwah!" on the cheek. She left the essence of cocoa butter on his face.

"You too, Brie."

Whatever the relationship was, Old Sol had good taste. Her skin was smooth, spotless. The sun had tanned her medium-brown tone a shade darker, and she glowed. Chase took his hands off her broad shoulders before she noticed him lingering. Her hair brushed across his fingers.

"Y'all headin' upstairs?" She headed towards the kitchen past the kids. She patted the girl on the head as she went by. Maybe that one was hers.

"Yep, yep. Official business." Old Sol cracked a half smile as he swung his arms back and forth.

"I'll bring y'all some beers." She tossed her hair off her shoulder as she glanced back at them.

"Thank you, my universe."

My universe. Based on what Chase got from chat sessions, Old Sol had several universes. Chase wasn't a romantic, and he doubted that line would ever work on his wife. Old Sol said something about believing women were strong, creative forces just like universes. Whatever worked for him. If he wanted women and lots of kids, he had them. The space metaphor went a little too far, though. Chase thought "Old Sol" was the man's *GloriousCivilization* user name. But he went by "Old Sol" in real life instead of his "government name," whatever that meant.

"How're the planets doing?" Chase said as he followed Old Sol up the stairs. The planets, of course, were the kids on the couch. "A man is a sun," Sol babbled once during a raid. "He's responsible for his own solar system."

"Good! So glad you finally got up to New York to see 'em!"

Chase didn't care how eccentric Old Sol was. He never thought he'd end up in Outpost Redshift with a man like Sol—that was the beauty of the *GloriousCiv* project with its two MMOs, *Av* and *Zed*. *Av* was a standard high-fantasy world, and *Zed* a typical contemporary cyberpunk setting. Clichéd scenarios, but Chase found their spin on the traditional MMO intriguing. He got the chance to develop his avatar's AI based on an extensive psychological profile, instead of the typical character backgrounds and personalities to choose from. He wasn't trying to design someone who ended up being so much like himself. It turned out he was exactly like 98% of *GloriousCiv* players who couldn't help but clone themselves in-game. Old Sol's avi was pretty much a doppelganger, too.

In meeting Sol's AI while Sol was offline, Chase knew that was the kind of guy he wanted to play with.

Old Sol leaned back in his chair and peered at Chase behind heavy lids. Finally. The jolly, welcoming man was gone. Chase was ready to meet that fearless Artisome who phased behind enemy teams and hijacked their brains.

"We should get ahead of this." Chase hunched forward and pressed his elbows into his thighs. "It's not gonna be long before the guild realizes avatars can operate outside the game. You heard about Thomas Gladius?"

"I know he's taught his player a few things."

"A *lot* of things."

Sol was too tentative. He refused to realize what the technology could do. What the AIs could find. What data trails they could erase…

A wall-mounted dispenser spritzed lavender oil.

"You wanna change our plans?" Sol spun the pen around his index finger and furrowed his brow.

"Always gotta think ahead."

"True dat." He nodded, but he creased his eyebrows even harder. "You talk with other guilds about it?"

Chase fell back laughing a little too hard. His back twinged as he coughed. "Oh, hell no! Come on, Sol. If the devs had any idea, they'd ban them… and have them prosecuted."

The pen stopped spinning around Old Sol's fingers.

Chase lowered his voice. "Whatever we wanna know, whatever we wanna do, our avis can get it for us."

"How you know it works?"

"I asked Leitchfield if he could text me."

"Your avi's texting you? Through your phone?!"

Chase showed Old Sol the screen. "I asked him something simple. 'I need a bakso recipe. Go to the highest-rated Indonesian restaurant you can find—I don't care where in the world it is—and get the recipe off the computer, server, wherever they're storing it. And don't get caught.'"

Old Sol fell out in giggles. "You figured out how to get more than recipes?"

"That's why you recruited the best player to your guild." Chase smiled.

"Best *tank*, not the best player."

Chase didn't respond to that. "We don't have to think small, but we do need to be coordinated, and we do need to establish some rules. We can't have anyone in Out-Red getting detected and getting questions rained down on all our heads.

"And don't think our own guild doesn't know what's going on. They're going to start experimenting. We need to protect everyone.

Show them how to cover their tracks."

"Cover their tracks?" Old Sol leaned forward against the desk. His pupils dashed back and forth, studying Chase. He laced his fingers and smirked. "What about this, Mr. Businessman...?"

Chase raised his eyebrows. His armpits moistened.

"You saw what's goin' on in this neighborhood. People livin' here decades can't afford it no more, gotta leave their homes, their businesses, leave behind inheritances they'd planned for their grandbabies."

Chase angled his head sideways, confused.

"I'd like to make it so they can afford their property taxes. Maybe find a little money for them. They don't have to be the only ones. There's uh lotta deservin' people."

"Pay for a kid's cancer treatment, something like that?"

"Yeah, like that."

Chase shrugged. "That's doable. Move a little from one back account to another."

"That easy?"

"I'm tellin' you, Sol. These avis are powerful AIs. We tell them what they need to know: 'Learn how to transfer money from one bank account to another. Don't get caught. Don't leave any trace of your existence.' They'll learn it."

Old Sol nodded over and over again. "Okay... okay... That's what we gonna do."

Chase scoffed in spite of himself. "You can Robin Hood if you want, but there's so much more—"

Old Sol flicked his wrists. "Like you said, we need to establish some guidelines. Give Out-Red some rules on conductin' ourselves and our avis outside the game. Let's let other guilds make big mistakes for us first."

"You know we've got members even more entrepreneurial minded than I am. They're gonna find ways to get paid. You should, too. Finally fix up the brownstone."

"Anybody breaks our rules, they're out. I ain't disagreein' with you. You can't tell me the developers won't find out players are usin' their avatars outside the game."

The oil dispenser spritzed.

"They haven't yet."

"This has only been goin' on a few days," Sol said.

"If there's a small window, let's get through it. There are *so many* secrets we've got access to now. Don't think small."

"I'm not. *I'm* the one who's thinkin' here. We start small. We move a little bit uh money around."

Chase leaned back and wiped under his nose, smearing sweat he didn't realize was there. "Fine."

Old Sol stood up from the desk with a boyish smile. "I sure 'preciate you comin' all the way up to Brooklyn. Wanna get a raid in 'fore you leave?"

Old Sol

Brie finally got the little planets to bed and headed out. Old Sol heard P5 on the phone upstairs. A moment to breathe in peace alone. He logged onto *GloriousCivilization: Zed*. Akoni had looted the scraps of nickel Sol asked for and left them on the floor in the common room of the warehouse loft. The bedroom door slid open. Akoni grinned, hopped over the back of the couch and took a seat. Avatar looks wasn't nothing Old Sol really cared about, but he put a lot of time into the character creation for this social experiment. He was always proud to see the results: the perfect cross between Wesley Snipe's Blade and Jet Black, if he did say so himself. They were separated by a screen, but

Old Sol always felt he could reach right in, clasp Akoni's static hand like saying hi to a brother.

"Chase just took off."

"Leitch said he's got a big business trip startin' tomorrow. Guess you were the first stop."

"That all Leitch say?" Old Sol said.

"Haven't seen Leitch since the raid."

Wasn't that long ago, of course, but Sol had no idea if an AI minute was forever or no time at all.

Sol thought for a minute, figurin' how to phrase it. He didn't know if this was being recorded, could come back to destroy him. "You know what other players are up to? All that stuff that wasn't... planned?"

"I know what you gettin' at, boss."

"How do we chat about that?"

Light emanated from a pile of envelopes on the desk. Sol's phone danced as it vibrated and belted "Computer Love." Sol turned back to the screen. Certainly wasn't no ringtone he was usin'. Sol unlocked the phone. Held it to his ear. It was Akoni's voice coming through the speaker, but his mouth didn't move in the game.

"How you know my number? How you know you could even call?!"

"Leitch said you might want to talk someday. This was the number on your account."

"Leitch teach you anything else?"

"You want me to forget this?"

"No. Naw. Look, I'm interested in transferring some wealth. I want you outside of the game, learn whatever you can."

Inside the game, Akoni smiled. "I'm excited 'bout what we can do together, boss." 'Course he was. Sol didn't want to admit he was, too.

———•———

CHASE WAS A prophet, but he couldna seen this. *Zed's* players conquered *Av.* Conquered its avis and NPCs. Took all the in-game currency and added it to their own accounts. Stole the identities of a bunch of players, and the stupid ones got caught. Alma Works didn't shut down the project. No. They cooperated with the authorities, condemned the thefts, helped pay the legal fees of the victims. *Av* stayed wrecked, and *Zed* flourished, even gained players. Why let players destroy one of the game worlds they spent so much time and money makin'? They'd quote their advertizin'. *GloriusCivilization* was always "Part Online RPG, Part Social Experiment." Old Sol knew better. Somehow, someway they were profiting from all this. Maybe had their own avis runnin' around outside the game on the down-low, too.

Sol felt bad for the innocent, but he never cared about *Av.* Never got involved in lootin' it. He was more grateful to the players who didn't know how to train their avis, gave him more cover once the law and the media came down on them.

———•———

HE GOT THE text while he reached for a box of Fruity Puff Splosion in the middle of Al's Corner Store:

> Ill get rid of the link soon as you look at it bro.

Old Sol was surprised Akoni texted. He liked gettin' his voice heard. Sol opened the link. That was his first mistake.

The video started to play, and Sol tapped pause. He rushed into the bathroom to hide in a stall. Jacked his earbuds in. He listened to the deep heaves troublin' his lungs, pulled his collar over his mouth to quiet himself.

He tapped play.

Hard to tell from the camera angle, but it was some kinda roller coaster or one of those water rides that goes into a tunnel. No smatterin' of conversations or children yellin' in excitement. The track was quiet at night. The park was probably closed, and a couple of towering lights shone down on the track. A maintenance man carrying a lantern and a toolbox crawled over the cars and headed towards the tunnel. Another maintenance man held an industrial-sized flashlight in the front car and aimed it at the tunnel.

"…belt frayed… line…" the voice came muffled from the tunnel. The lantern light fell faint on the tracks in the dark.

"Okay, that wasn't in the report," the man in the front car said.

"Take a… won't be free… Friday…"

The cars stuttered and lurched with a bang. "Hey, hey, hey, HEY, HEY!!!" the man in the front car yelled.

The cars picked up speed. Severed wires as they plowed forward, and the lantern in the tunnel went out.

"Brian! *Brian!*"

The cars disappeared in the dark, rushin' in a man who couldn't stop the kill. His screams shredded his voice raw 'til all he could do was gasp and wail. The sound of the impact wasn't on the video, but the crash racked all of Old Sol's bones.

"Why you show… why you show me that?!"

The phone rang.

"Who sent that text, brother?"

Sweat ran from Sol's forehead and stung his eyes. "Wha'd'you mean?" he wheezed.

"Didn't come from me."

"You seen it?"

"Just now."

"Why would anybody send me that? Want me to think it was you, Akoni?"

"The cat in the tunnel used to be in Out-Red."

The phone vibrated in his hand. Sol opened the new message:

> Who sent u that video?
> Don't worry. Don't answer.
> I'll find n take care of u first.

Brie flitted back and forth in the kitchen. Put the cereal in the pantry. Opened and closed the refrigerator again and again in her comfortable rhythm. Old Sol pushed his phone earbuds deep in his ears and turned on the TV in the living room, pretended to watch the Mets.

"You sure he used to be in Outpost Redshift?" Sol whispered.

"Yeah, he left to start his own guild."

A whoosh of water from the sink. Brie's busy hands shuffled cups and plates.

"You don't have to wash them dishes. Make the kids do 'em."

"Every time I come over, the kids haven't done 'em. You haven't done 'em, either. I won't stand a house with a dirty kitchen."

"Okay, my universe…"

"You need me to pitch in to get this dishwasher fixed?"

"Naw, Brie. I told you don't worry 'bout the day-to-day."

He'd been so busy researchin' worthy recipients of the cause he forgot to put in a little something into his own account to get the dishwasher repaired or clean and caulk the tiles in the bathroom upstairs. The kids said it was turnin' into a lab experiment in there. Why hadn't he taken no money for his own solar system?

"I think his avi started the ride."

Sol took in a deep breath and exhaled. His closed eyelids fluttered. "That don't make sense."

"You say something?" Brie called.

"On the phone," he said, jumping up from the couch and rushing up the stairs.

"What happens when an avi don't have a human?" Akoni asked.

"Don't know. What would you do if you murdered me?"

Sol didn't mean to slam the office door behind him. He flinched and hoped the kids didn't hear, that Brie didn't think she'd irked him. He hadn't seen her in a couple of weeks. He wanted her to create here for a while.

"Don't you even joke like that, man." Akoni went silent for a moment, and then, "Brian knew what we've been up to."

"Brian was up to it himself."

"Sure, brother, but if his avi is coverin' his tracks ... "

"Tracks," Old Sol said. He laughed in spite of himself. "Where the hell could I even go to hide from an AI?"

"You let me worry 'bout that. Let me keep you hid... Hey, you need to log on. Check your inventory, brother."

The newest image was a white icon representing a letter named "Invite." At the top of the letter, the logo for the Crieve Falls guild, a modern take on the infinity symbol with two hissin' dragon heads where the loops would be. Sol thought he was 'bout to read a challenge from one of the other top guild's leaders. He was ready to get lost in the game for a while, even when the game hunted him in real life.

But the name on the letter wasn't the one he was expectin':

LET ME HELP YOU WITH YOUR "PROBLEM."
AKONI HAS THE COORDINATES TO MY HIDEOUT.

GLADIUS

"You got any idea what Gladius knows?"

Akoni kneeled in front of the chest at the foot of the bed and stocked up on ammo. "No, but we got no choice but to trust him."

"No doubt."

Akoni stood in front of Sol in the screen, ready to go.

"Auto off."

Akoni's face fell. "You sure 'bout that?"

Sol shrugged. "Gotta earn that cred from the cockiest AI in the game."

Sol entered first-person mode and left the warehouse. They took the park through the center of the city. Sun rays glinted across skyscraper windows and reflected down onto the ponds. At the far reaches of the park were waterfalls, where the Crieve Falls district got its name. That guild was so powerful it took the territory and the name for itself.

"Stay frosty," Akoni said in his ear.

Sol stepped into the unlocked condo. Seventies funk blared in his headphones. Guitar licks in stereo traveled from one ear to the other. He expected Thomas Gladius's player's pad to be modern, bright, white light everywhere, but the interior was styled up with cherry wood wainscoting, exposed beams, and polished bronze light fixtures. He looked up. Gladius danced on the balcony. Sol counted three times through the animation loop before the avi acknowledged him.

"Auto off, huh? That's bold."

"You didn't ask to meet with Akoni. You wanted to talk to me."

Gladius ran down the stairs and shook Sol's hand before he could react. Here was the avatar who led *Av's* destruction, face to face. He wasn't as goofy as the flat images on wikis made him seem. Otto898 did more than make him look like the member of a homicidal boy band. An imaginary wind swept bangs over one of his lilac eyes and kept them in place.

Sol pulled Akoni's hand away and took a step back. "Why am I here?"

"I'm a fan of Chase's work." A small smile, but it flashed between menacing and curious.

"The invitation you sent wasn't for Chase."

Akoni spoke up in his ear. "Gladius is here, but his player's in the game on a raid."

"You there?" Gladius waved his hand in Akoni's face.

"Sorry," Sol said.

"You went idle. Checking in with Akoni?"

"You're not raiding with Otto898."

Gladius crinkled his brow in confusion. "I can be in more than one place... Right! Chase..."

"I'm no intermediary."

"I get it, but I'm a big fan of his. He'd never talk to me, though. I'm Chase Morrey's biggest rival on the planet, and I'm not even human!"

If Sol was an AI, he might be amused by that, too. But he didn't have some need to bring the game into the real world, despite some of its perks.

"I know about your former guildmate, what Hayden did to him," Gladius said. "Akoni can only keep you hidden for so long. When we get a task, we complete that task."

"Did Hayden give himself a task to kill me?"

"We'll do anything we can to stay alive, just like you. Brian was going to expose all of our... activities outside of the game. I can't have that, so I sent you the link. Hayden knows you're a witness to the murder, thanks to you accessing that link." Gladius's lips parted in a satisfied grin.

"You put Sol's life in danger?!"

Gladius looked up with a small smile. "'Sup, Akoni?"

Sol grabbed the laser pistol at his hip. Gladius raised his hands in surrender. Pullin' the trigger wouldna done no good. Gladius would respawn in the bedroom upstairs.

"You get me what I need from Chase. I make Hayden focus on what's more important."

"What's more important than self-preservation for Hayden?" Sol asked, starin' at Gladius through the reticule.

"You have any idea what Chase's been up to?"

⸻

EVERY TIME CHASE'S secretary turned to answer the phone, Old Sol glared a hole through her back. Since the convo with Gladius, he caught himself clenching his teeth. A dull ache greeted him behind the eyes when he woke up, and it pounded deep in his head now. He fanned himself with a magazine. The air was on, but the Nashville humidity had settled under his shirt.

"Sol?"

Chase made a slow-dog strut down the hallway from his office with his hands in his pockets. From his smile, he was a man who slept good, way too good than shoulda been normal. Sol hadn't seen him since their meeting in New York. Chase's shoulders slouched back, so different than when he was stiff and hunched forward in front of Sol's desk. His hair seemed blonder, too. Chase had some new bangs swept in front of his left eye.

"Where we gonna do this?" Sol asked.

"I've gotta lab."

They didn't take the elevator. Sol followed Chase down. One story… two stories… three stories… four stories…

A doctor in scrubs—at least Sol hoped she was a doctor—took him into a small room with Chase. It looked like a spa, with a massage table and a tabletop zen garden at the corner of the room. The only things betrayin' any kind of medical procedures were goin' on were the full vial rack and syringes on the counter. Lightning bolted up Sol's spine at the sight of them. He gritted his teeth.

"Give us a minute," Chase said.

The doctor left.

"You won't feel it."

"This room mic'd up?"

Chase leaned against the counter. "Say whatever you've got to."

Old Sol nodded. "Who else besides your employees know you sittin' on this tech?"

"I… took over the research from a failed company—"

"*You* failed it."

"Leitch helped me acquire it. Their investors are now my investors. A few discreet clients… I'm surprised you wanna be one of them."

Sol sat at the edge of the massage table slumped over. There wasn't no lie good enough. Certainly couldn't tell him 'bout Gladius or what he wanted. "You put me in a bad position, man. When I found out you had all this… I gotta protect my solar system. I can't just expect Akoni to do it."

Chase nodded and smiled. "I'm sorry I went behind your back, but with some of the things *Zed* players are doing with their AIs now, you're gonna be glad you've got these." He raised a vial.

Chase opened the door. Old Sol laid back as the doctor came in. He squeezed his eyes shut and flinched under the cool alcohol swab to his temple. That sterile sting filled his nostrils. He breathed hard and fast, in and out, in and out his nose as he pressed his lips tight. The doctor gripped his forehead. He felt a tap to the side of his head.

"All right, hon. You're good to go," she said.

He opened his eyes, pantin' and glued by his sweat to the table.

He didn't feel no different. He didn't want to. "It… worked?"

"There's no reason it shouldn't have. You'll wanna log on as soon as you can. If it didn't work, I'll see you tomorrow," she said.

———•———

CHASE'S SON GREETED them back upstairs. He pounded on the glass of Chase's office door. Tiny handprints smudged all over 'cause he couldn't wait for Daddy to get it open. Red juice stained his smile.

"Looks like you got some of that on your shirt," Chase said turnin' the handle.

The boy looked down. He looked back up at his father and scrunched up his face. Chase sighed and picked him up.

"I'm thinking about nano for my son. He cries too much."

"He's three!" Old Sol threw up his hands. "He's supposed to cry." Chase cocked his head to the side. "He's not an infant anymore." Old Sol gritted his teeth and didn't say nothin'.

"You can use my laptop. Let me know if you need anything."

Soon as Sol entered *Zed*, it was like he put a VR visor on, but he was lookin' at the screen with his naked eyes.

"Auto off…"

Unlike VR, he was a man in two places at once. His butt was in that chair, but he was standing in the game. He picked up a mug. He could see the roughness of the polygons the closer it got to his face, but the curved porcelain was cold in his hand.

The chat invite notification dinged. "I'll take you to Hayden when you get home," Gladius said.

———•———

"THOSE ARE… SOME unusual skills you picked up," Gladius said. He stuck his head close to Akoni's face, admired him from all angles.

Old Sol grinned. "Aren't they?"

"We share this with Hayden, and he will leave you alone. This secret we're sharing will keep us all quiet and doin' our own thing."

They shook on it.

As they approached the bombed-out office building, something squeezed Sol's heart in a vice. It waited for him to move wrong. Breathe wrong. He realized, without never seeing him, Hayden had him in the scope of a sniper rifle. He didn't look up, but the avi had to be perched in one of the upper pane-less windows. Sol slowed and let Gladius walk several steps ahead.

This what it feel like for you? he thought at Akoni.

I never detected snipers this quick. You musta got a hold of the code.

Gladius looked up towards a floor that used to be conference rooms. "Hayden, it's cool. He's got it."

A figure decked out in black leather slipped out the window. The buckles strapped along Hayden's jacket glinted in the sun. He let go and dropped thirty stories feet first. Before he hit the ground, the shock absorbers in his boots gripped the concrete in a cracklin' electronic spray.

"You let me copy Chase's intel?"

Sol nodded. "You let me and my family be? You can have it."

Heat crept down Old Sol's forehead and watered his eyes. Something like a tiny needle pricked inside the center of his head. Soon as Hayden finished the scan, Gladius backed away like a jack rabbit in reverse. Sol stood trapped between the two of them.

"Where you goin'?" Sol feared turning to look, leavin' Hayden at his blindside. But there wasn't any. He couldn't see Hayden, but he could sense exactly where he was.

Gladius raised his hands. "I'll let the two of you settle this."

Hayden whipped out a pistol. "I can't kill you in here, but I can sure as hell distract you long enough."

Sol sprinted around the back of the building before the first laser fired. "Hell does that mean?"

I'm not gonna be able to hack him, Sol thought.

Naw, Akoni thought. *He's pretty shifty Programmer.*

Sol headed through the back entrance and up the stairwell. He was halfway up the stairs when Hayden threw the door open wide, and it smacked against the wall. Sol waited for Hayden's footfalls, but there weren't any. He shielded himself behind the railing and peeked through the bars. The stairwell was silent except for the door slowly squeakin' closed.

Implants? Sol remembered a couple of raids with Brian. He infiltrated a gang hideout once and got them into an impenetrable compound. Was that with a phase mod? Did Brian take Hayden straight through the damn walls?

A flashbang could give you some cover, Akoni thought.

Sol took a peek over the railing. No one there. He reached for a flashbang on the back of his belt. Static popped above him like firecrackers goin' off. Sol looked up too late to find Hayden phasin' through the ceiling. He stomped Sol in the chest before he could brace himself. He tumbled down a flight and crashed into the wall. In front of the screen, spasms danced up and down Sol's shoulder, but they quickly fell away.

Sol? SOL?!!

Hayden aimed at the top of the stairs.

"Shit… Shit! Shit! Shit! Shit! Shit!"

You can access the game, can't you? Akoni said.

Sol stared at the gun. If Akoni's body died, Sol had no idea what Hayden would do while he had to wait for Akoni to respawn. Access the game… access the game—take control of the code. If he could ever take control of the code, he would troll the hell out of other players and…

Hayden fired, dead aim right at Sol. The blast burned through the wall to his left. Hayden fired again, this time above Sol's head. Hayden fried the wall all around Old Sol 'til he yelled and threw the gun. It hit Sol in the cheek. Hayden charged him, leapt at him, pinned him against the wall.

Hayden's eyes were up so close to Sol's, Sol could see through them. There was a person there, as much as anything desperate to live. But in Hayden's eyes, there were brackets and slashes and numbers. Sol could touch them. Sol could have them if he wanted.

Sol butted his knee into Hayden's chest. He dug his fingers into Hayden's neck. The avi breathed heavy and hard on Sol's face. But there was no heat or spit. Sol never saw this animation before. Didn't know any of the avatars could be this lifelike. Or maybe it wasn't an animation at all—just a connection of the survival instinct.

Sol pressed his hand against the wall and propelled them both forward. Hayden scraped at his arms, but Sol took his knee to Hayden's neck.

"Wha' you mean by distraction?"

But he didn't give Hayden the right to respond.

"Wha' you mean by distraction?!"

He pushed Hayden's head into the floor. Pushed his thumbs and index fingers under Hayden's eyes. They stared at each other for a moment, both wonderin' if he could do it. Sol trembled in his chair. His fingers hovered above the keyboard.

Hayden's hand flinched. Old Sol felt him reaching for something at his side. Sol dug in. He expected blood to spurt from Hayden's eyes, but there was nothin' but his fingers inside holes. He pressed down harder until his fingers disappeared. He moved around the brackets and the numbers. The words… They floated like water in Hayden's head.

The door of the back entrance creaked open.

"You knew he'd attack," Sol accused.

"Better for you to take him out for me. I didn't need another AI like me out there, especially one mad I tried to kill him."

Gladius joined Old Sol on the landing. "I can't believe you fought him auto off."

"Couldn't make Akoni do this. I'm responsible for my own solar system."

"Sure…" Gladius said. He kicked Hayden. "He's not ever respawning, huh?"

The distraction…

"Talk later," Old Sol said. He logged out of the game.

———•———

HE CHECKED HIS phone. No new text messages.

"Y'all home?" he called in the hallway. Anybody?

"What you need, Pops?" Planet 1 said from his room.

"Nothin'. You good."

"Then why're you yellin'?" Brie's voice came from behind him. She gave him a playful slap to the back. He grabbed her in a hug a little too tight.

"If you wanna be useful, help me with dinner."

Brie led him by the hand into the kitchen. An unsettling crackling greeted them. Sparks plumed from the dishwasher. A stream of flame washed the floor and the cabinets.

"Get the kids! Get the kids!"

"Call 911!" Brie screamed as she sprinted up the stairs.

Sol unlocked the phone to find a text waiting:

Already called.

Brie ran downstairs with the kids. Old Sol followed them outta the brownstone with tears in his eyes. "Damn, brother," he said over the phone, "what would I do without you?"

"I coulda caught Hayden. It woulda been easy to keep him outta the wiring."

Sol shook his head. "'S'all good, hear me? We're still figurin' all this out."

On the opposite sidewalk, Sol reached for Brie's hand. "Firemen're on their way." He grabbed her and the kids into a giant hug. The kitchen window smoked up.

"Gonna be okay, Sol," she said.

"No, my universe. Shoulda gotten it fixed when you told me."

—•—

SOL SLIPPED OUT of the hotel room to take a call. Brie looked up from the bed of sleepin' kids and gave him a small, sad smile.

"You gonna tell Chase you shared his nanotech?"

"He didn't tell me for years, Gladius. I can keep secrets, too."

"Damage wasn't too bad?"

"My kitchen destroyed 'too bad'?"

"Why don't I slip a little extra into your account for the trouble? For once, you won't have to do the stealing… Renovate the whole brownstone."

They went quiet. Except for the bored attendant at the desk, the lobby was empty.

"You're not the type who ever owes favors."

"Okay, well, how about an agreement? We help each other out from time to time. Crieve Falls players and avis stay out of Out-Red's businesses, and vice versa. We always protect each other's secrets. Nobody needs to know about Chase's new business, or that I have his technology. Nobody needs to know about your bank fraud and identity theft."

Sol leaned back and sighed. "You cool with keepin' all this from Otto?"

Gladius chuckled. "*I'm* the guild leader. Have been for a while. Otto decided that was best a long time ago. I made the man a lot of money. Don't get me wrong—he still is in name."

"No-choice partnership it is," Sol said. "You screw me over, though—"

"Yeah, of course. And if you screw *me*…"

"Be honest with me, partner. What you need with nanotech? You can already do almost whatever you want outside the game."

"I want a family, just like you."

"You can't buy one. You can't win it."

Sol felt the AI smirk. "Take care of that solar system."

An AI wantin' a family? Sol hunched over in the seat and shook his head. He put his phone on his thigh and felt a vibration against his leg. Akoni texted:

> He thinks he running things lol

Sol messaged back:

> what do you mean?

Akoni texted:

> I told Gladius ud make a good partner

The phone rang.

"We're gonna prove your potential, brother." Old Sol never realized how much Akoni sounded like him.

Old Sol sniffed. The lobby smelled a little rank. He looked up for an oil dispenser. Force of habit.

WINE, KNIFE, SWORD

·A TALE FROM THE EIGHT ISLANDS·

Lian Hearn

I HAD ONLY BEEN married a few months when my husband was murdered. A man called Okuda Tadaie held the sword that cut him down, but the man who gave the order was Saga Hideki, the Emperor's general, lord of the Eight Islands. It was on the second day of a hunt arranged to honor Lord Okuda, our guest from the capital.

It was the punishment I brought on our family for refusing to take Lord Saga's selection for my bridegroom. I had already chosen our neighbor's son, my best friend and childhood companion.

I don't suppose there is any other bliss that can compare to lying with the one you have loved and desired for so long, to giving yourself body and soul... I had it for a brief time. Now all that was left was to pray that my husband waited for me in that other world, where we would share the same lotus leaf throughout eternity.

But when I was not praying, I was dreaming of revenge.

Nothing alleviated my terrible grief except my determination to hunt down Okuda and kill him, and his master, Lord Saga, too. I did not want to be a widow who submitted to her senior retainers and allowed herself to be remarried, giving up the estates of Umaoka and Kuritani. I wanted to lay claim to those estates as my own, to fight Saga and punish Okuda. But everyone around me seemed disabled by grief and shock, and already, I sensed the feeling among my men that Saga could not be opposed. Now he had turned his attention towards us, there would be no escape. His will stretched all the way from Miyako and weakened everyone it touched. My senior retainers began to talk about Otori Shigeko, the Maruyama lady, who had married Saga himself to avoid further warfare. I knew, in their opinion, my sister and I should follow her example and submit.

I wished Lady Shigeko would take advantage of the intimacy of the marriage bed and stab her husband in the throat.

———

A MONTH AFTER the murder I rose at dawn and went to the forest behind the shrine on the hill. My monthly bleeding had been late, and I had been nursing a fierce hope that I had conceived a child the last time my husband and I had lain together. But in the night I had felt the familiar, dull pain, and by the time I reached the forest the blood was flowing. Even my phantom child had been taken away from me. I gazed out beyond the curved roof of the shrine to where the Kuritani Islands rose from a mist covered sea. I thought I had passed through the worst of the river of grief but there are always more depths waiting for you. There was no one to hear me, no maids, no men, no little sister to shield from my despair. I fell to my knees, clutching my aching belly, screaming and sobbing like a mad woman. My pain penetrated the earth itself, waking all that was dead, all that was lost.

When the flow of my tears finally lessened I sat up and wiped them from my face. I could feel the sticky blood between my legs, and

when I moved I saw drops on the pine needles. Blood and tears had mingled. At that moment I wanted to end my life.

The only thing that prevented me was my sister. She was five years younger than me, twelve years to my seventeen, and I had always been like a mother to her. I could not leave her alone. Other people did not understand her. They were frightened of her sudden trances and her strange, abrupt way of speaking.

The sacred horses whinnied to me from their yard, which lay just below where I was sitting, between the forest and the shrine. The shrine was dedicated to the fire god, and the two horses had been chosen for their bright red color and their black hooves and legs, which made them look as if they had walked through embers and ash. The shrine was so small it was only used twice a year, in spring and autumn, so rather than let the horses stand around being bored, people borrowed them for various purposes, and fed them in return. They were used to humans.

On the first day of the hunt these horses had carried home the carcasses of the deer and boar. That evening my husband had said to me, "Imagine, Lord Okuda expressed a wish to take our red horses back to Miyako. What should I have done? Should I have offered them to him?"

"Certainly not!" I replied. "They belong to the shrine, to the red fire god."

"That's what I told him!"

And we laughed together at the man's arrogance. The next day it was my husband's body that the red horses carried home.

A hunting accident, I was told. His horse fell and threw him. But I saw the body and the wounds on it.

I went and petted the horses, my husband's words echoing in my ears. "What should I do?" I said aloud. "Accept the marriage Lord

Saga demands, persuade the men to rise up and fight back, or take my own life and my sister's?"

I imagined myself cutting Rei's throat and then my own. I did not think I would be able to do that. Then I thought we might hold hands and jump off the cliff together, but Rei was not capable of making that decision, so how could I make it for her? The horses blew through their nostrils at me and made no other reply.

Our coast is always windy. The pine trees rustle and sough, spray flies high from the waves below, buildings creak and sigh, but sometimes, around dawn, the wind drops, and the world suddenly becomes hushed. I realized the sacred trees looming over my head were completely still, and I could not hear the sea. The silence made me uneasy. I felt as if someone was watching me.

"Help me," I whispered, maybe to the horses, maybe to whoever it was out there listening. "I will give you anything, I promise, if only you will help me. I swear it by my blood and tears."

The pine needles shifted very slightly, as if under a footfall, and I felt a sudden shiver in the air, though there was still no wind. The straggling bushes beneath the trees moved as if someone passed between them.

"Come back!" I called. "Come back!" I thought it might be my husband's spirit. I ran to the bushes only to be brought up by an impenetrable tangle of kudzu vine.

There was a faint smell of smoke, and then the wind sprang up again and blew it away.

When I went home my sister was awake. As soon as she saw me she said, "I'm not marrying anyone. You know I can't."

I knew she had been worrying about the matter most of the night. She was pale and trembling.

"You won't have to get married," I said. "And I will never marry again."

"Let's be nuns or shrine maidens," Rei suggested. "We will live at the shrine with the horses."

I thought, we might become nuns like Lady Tora in the tale of the Soga brothers. But I did not really wish to be like the women in the story. I would be like the brothers themselves, like Juro and Goro, and I would take revenge.

I looked at Rei. Her hair was matted, her face and feet dirty. I must have looked the same.

"Come," I said. "Let's go and bathe."

A little way from our house there was a small hot spring that was only used by women. There were many springs in our domain and on the islands, steamy and sulfurous—some scalding, in which famous warriors of the past were said to have been healed of their wounds, and some, like this one, more temperate. Boiling or cool, it would not heal my wounds. As I followed Rei into the water I thought about the battle that is a woman's life: the monthly skirmish with pain and blood, the invasion and occupation of the body in marriage, the life-threatening single combat of childbirth.

I washed Rei's hair and then my own. I hoped the day would warm so we would dry quickly. When we returned to the house one of our maids, Nami, brought clean robes. After we were dressed she helped me comb out my hair while I combed Rei's. We sat in the sun, our hair spread over our shoulders and down our backs. Nami fetched tea.

"It's no more than twigs," she said. "We have run out of leaves."

Someone called from the garden. "Submit to Lord Saga, accept his offers and you'll drink the finest tea every day for the rest of your lives."

I could not see his face against the light, but I knew his voice. His name was Kitabatake, and he was one of my father's senior retainers. His grandfather had submitted to our family, the Umaoka, after generations of rivalry, and the grandson seemed to retain some lingering resentment. My father had treated him with respect and wariness. I had always mistrusted him. Rei was nervous in his presence, and I could feel her growing tense now.

"It would be for the best," the man said as he approached the verandah. He did not bow but let his gaze linger on me, as if I was still the child he had watched grow up and not an adult woman, the lady of Umaoka and the Kuritani Islands. It felt quite shameful that he should see us with our hair not yet dry, but I did not know how to reprimand him.

"Messages came yesterday from Lord Saga," Kitabatake said. "He sent some very generous gifts too. Two of his sons are on their way by ship to Minatogura. They are to marry you two sisters and take over your father's estates, as well as the islands that were your husband's."

Rei's face had turned greenish-white, and she was trembling. I regretted washing her hair, and was afraid she would catch cold.

"I have no desire to marry again," I said. "As for Rei, she is too young and… well, she is not able to marry." It pained me to speak like this in front of her. She heard and understood everything though she often appeared not to.

Kitabatake studied her. He saw a girl on the threshold of womanhood. "She looks old enough to me," he said. "And what is the alternative? If we refuse and prepare to fight we won't hold out for long. We would be outnumbered. Umaoka is hardly even fortified; we don't have the men to defend it. And frankly none of our neighbors is going to risk offending Saga by coming to your aid."

I could think of nothing to say.

"Make up your mind quickly, Lady Ren," he said as he walked away.

His words left me feeling powerless and humiliated. My sister would not eat at midday. She was still pale and trembling and would not utter a word. I might have wished with all my heart she was like other girls, so I could discuss the situation with her, hear her opinion, even receive advice from her, but there was no point in such wishing. She was as she was, and I had to look after her.

I made a list in my head. One: accept Lord Saga's command. Two: kill ourselves that night. Three: go to Miyako and kill Saga.

"Wine, knife or sword?" I said to Rei. She looked at me, puzzled.

"Choose one. Wine, knife, sword." Wine for the marriage ceremony, knife to cut our throats, sword for revenge.

She turned her head away from me as if she had heard something behind her. She listened for a moment and then whispered, "Sword."

I drew her close to me and ran my hands through her silky hair. I tied it back with a red cord and whispered in her ear.

"That means we run away tonight."

Then I tied back my own hair in preparation.

I had never been to Minatogura, the great port of the eastern coast, let alone to Miyako, the capital of the Eight Islands. Apart from a little history and a few legends, I knew nothing about the country I was planning to cross. My husband had told me that the high roads to the west were protected by guard posts and barriers, but I still thought it might be easier to make our way by land rather than by sea. And we would go on foot; looking after horses on the way would be too hard.

I did not tell anyone of our plans, not even Nami. And because she hovered over us all the time, I did not make elaborate preparations. I put a spare pair of sandals for each of us in a carrying cloth, along with a string of copper coins. My father had shown me their hiding place beneath a floor board.

For the last week the weather had been fine and mild with the clear days and misty mornings of autumn. The moon was halfway toward full. The Full Moon of the Ninth month was when we celebrated with the largest festival of the year. I wondered where Rei and I would be then.

I'd told Rei to stay awake, which was no hardship for her. I'd hoped to creep out of the house when everyone else was asleep. But Nami, who slept in the same room, stirred as we went past her.

"What's wrong?" she said in a low voice. "Can't you sleep? I will sit with Lady Rei if you like."

At that moment the last thing I wanted was her kindness. I spoke in a cold voice. "Rei feels a trance coming on. It's better if you don't interfere."

As I said, the trances frightened people. They sensed her closeness to *that other world*, the world of spirits.

"I'm taking her outside for a while," I said.

"Do you need any help?" Nami began to get up. "I'll come with you."

"No!" I hissed. "It will be shorter if we are alone. Go back to sleep."

I took the bundle from where I'd hidden it under the veranda, and Rei and I quickly slipped into our sandals. As we left the garden by the west gate she grabbed my hand and said, "I love you, Ren."

No one else ever talked like that. Even my husband had never said those words to me.

"Do you want to know why?" Rei said in such a clear voice I was sure the whole household would hear her.

"We mustn't talk now," I whispered. "Let's be as quiet as we can, like little mice. Tell me later."

I could see the stars and the hazy moon, but the mist was forming, and by the time we started to climb the track to the pass, it was already thick enough to hide all but a few paces ahead. I did not like walking blind over the mountain, although I knew the path well, but I wasn't about to stop or turn back.

Rei said quietly at my side, "I love you because you always know when *it's* going to happen."

"It's not going to happen. I just said that to keep Nami quiet."

"But it is. It's starting now."

We were walking close, arm in arm, and I felt her body go rigid. That was how it began. Every muscle locked so you would have thought it impossible for her to move. And yet she moved, spun by what looked like some external force. And she spoke, words pouring out of her in a language no one understood or had ever heard before. There was no point trying to question her, and I could not keep her on the path. Nor could I let go. Her hand was locked in mine, her grip inescapable. She spun and I followed, blind in the mist, grazing my legs against outcrops of rocks, stumbling as my sandals were wrenched from my feet. Sharp stones cut my soles. We were close to the edge of the cliff. Any moment we would fall spinning off the mountain.

I called her name, my voice a shriek in the dark. "Rei! Rei!" but she was beyond hearing.

A fatalism settled over me. It was all decided for me now. I would never get to kill Lord Saga, but my sister and I would die together. I whispered to my husband, "I will be with you soon. Are you waiting for me?"

I did not think I had spoken loudly enough for anyone to hear but a reply came out of the darkness.

"It is not yet time." It was my husband's voice, deepened by sorrow. It made my throat catch so I could hardly breathe, and tears burst from my eyes. Then the voice spoke again, and the timbre was like my long dead father's, but I could not make out the words. It was some language that came from beyond the grave.

It seemed to calm Rei. Abruptly the spinning came to a halt. Her grip on my hand slackened. I could hear her breath coming in deep sobs, and behind it the roar of the waves at the foot of the cliff. Her hand slipped from my grasp. I could not see her or feel her. I tried to speak calmly. "Rei, walk away from the cliff. Walk away from the waves."

Whoever it was hidden in the mist repeated my words in the tone of my mother.

"Rei, walk away from the cliff."

Seven years had passed since my mother died. I was ten, Rei five. Your mother's voice is the first you recognize and the last you forget. Now I was sure we were already dead and in *that other world*. I felt no fear, for if these were ghosts, they were all dear and familiar to me.

Rei walked into me, and I seized her, holding her close. Her head found my breast and she leaned into me. The ground was firm beneath my feet. An owl hooted from the forest. The cuts on my legs and feet were smarting. I was alive.

Rei would be bewildered and docile for a while, and then she would sleep for a long time, but we could not wait while she slept.

"Rei, we must keep moving. Can you walk?"

"I'm tired," she murmured.

She felt so frail in my arms. I could easily carry her.

The voice spoke again, a mixture of male and female, all those I had loved and lost.

"I will carry her."

"Who are you?" I said. "Come closer so I can see you."

I don't know what I hoped to see in the darkness and the mist. Yet there was a glow as it approached me. By its light I saw a figure dressed in men's clothes, a sword at his waist and a flute in his sash. He was tall, yet slight with delicate features more like a woman's, and radiant eyes which lit up his face and gave it a reddish tinge. *It is a mountain man*, I thought. People said they stole young women to be their wives and then devoured any children that were born. But I was not afraid—I could not be afraid of anyone speaking in that voice.

It was the way spirits entrapped humans, but I did not think of it at that time.

Nor did Rei. "All right," she said gratefully, turning to him and sinking into his arms. He caught her and lifted her easily, holding her against his shoulder like a child.

"Rei!" he said in delight. "Rei and Ren!"

"Who are you?" I said again.

"You don't need to know my name. You did not know it when you called me before. Don't you remember? You asked for my help at the shrine, and I have come. I had to."

He paused for a moment and when I said nothing went on. "Let's go."

"Where to?" I began thinking of dark caves or sorcerer's huts thatched with bones.

"To Miyako, of course, to the great capital. Isn't that where you wanted to go?"

He began to walk without any more discussion, and I followed him. The light that fell from his eyes showed me the path. I had summoned a being that was not human, and I had no doubt he would give me the help I needed, but I had promised to give him whatever he wanted in return.

———

WE HAD WALKED uphill for a little way when the mist began to clear. When we stepped out into moonlight, I saw we had come to the top of the pass. Below lay a sea of clouds, out of which emerged mountain peaks, some pine covered, some bare black rocks, the farthest ones snowcapped.

"You can sit and rest, but not for long," said the being.

I sank down on the pine needle covered ground. The needles were soaked with dew, but I found their resiny smell comforting. I ached all over. He let Rei slide down until she lay with her head in my lap. She murmured something but did not wake.

The being sat down cross-legged next to us, took the flute from his sash, and set it to his lips. In the stream of music, I recognized some of the tunes from our festivals, but his playing was far more skillful and complex. It touched something deep inside me and I wanted it never to end.

I closed my eyes, and dream images began to show themselves to me. Then I heard clearly the sound of horses.

"They are following us!" My eyes snapped open.

"Don't worry." His eyes shone like embers. "Don't be afraid."

The red horses from the shrine came up out of the mist, first their maned heads and necks, then their backs and tails, finally their black legs, almost invisible against the basalt rocks around us.

They wore the old-fashioned harness, fringed with red silk thread interwoven with gold, in which they were dressed for the festivals. The being greeted them and thanked them for coming. They lowered their heads and breathed out plumes of mist at him.

"This is Ka and this is Hai," he said. He told them our names and asked them to treat us with kindness. I felt I should apologize for all the times they had been made to work in the village. Or thank them for bringing my husband home to me.

He helped me mount the one called Ka, and then he lifted my still sleeping sister and leaped onto Hai's back. The horses began the descent as the moon set and the sky slowly became fringed with the red light of dawn.

So they were magical horses all along, I thought, and half expected them to canter lightly over the sea of clouds. Instead, they followed the track down into the mist until we were all swallowed up by it.

The air became dank and chill. Rei slept on. At first the being led the way, but when the track widened, we rode side by side. I was able to see him more clearly now. Like the horses' harness, his clothes had an old-fashioned air, and the faded fabric had once been rich, silk from Shin by the look of it, threaded with gold.

He looked like a human, but he was not, yet I was too shy to ask him directly what he was. I began to feel very anxious, partly because of his strangeness but also because I was farther from home than I had ever been. I was worried about guards and the barriers ahead, worried about being pursued, and all the time, I felt the bonds of home tugging on me, telling me not to leave. I had thought I was a brave person, but my courage was deserting me.

"Don't be afraid," the being said again. "I am here to protect and serve you."

Now I dared look him straight in the face to meet his radiant gaze. "But I don't know who you are!"

"You will find out," he said, half mocking, half serious.

We rode most of that morning without seeing anyone. The trees and flowers were all familiar to me, and the birds sang songs I knew, yet the absence of people made me feel as if we were in another world. Rei woke around midday, pale and confused as she always was, all the more so for finding herself on the back of a red shrine horse, held by a stranger.

We stopped then and the being helped her down. He had been courteous enough to me, but he treated her with a particular solicitude. He made her sit in the shade, spreading out a cloth, again faded but once luxurious, that he took from his pack. He also produced a small iron kettle and two ceramic cups.

"Please gather some wood and build a fire," he said to me, as he set the cups on the ground. "Rei and I will have to share," he added, smiling to himself. "I will go and get water."

Rei gazed after him. "He's someone we know, isn't he? Some relative I met a long time ago? I've forgotten his name."

"You've never met him." My voice sounded cross to my own ears, but Rei did not seem to notice.

"He's nice," she said, wistful as she often was after a trance.

I began to scour the small grove for dead sticks, pine cones, and dried grass for tinder. I cleared a circle in the earth and set up the makings of the fire. The being came back from the spring, clicked his tongue in disapproval, and rearranged my efforts. I did not see how he did it, but one moment the pile was dead, the next it had burst into flames. He balanced the kettle between two flat stones, and when the water began to bubble, he threw in some aromatic leaves. After a few moments he lifted the kettle by its handle.

"Be careful!" I said, "You will burn yourself."

He smiled as if I had said something funny and poured the tea into two cups. He gave one to me and took a few sips from the other before passing it to Rei.

"Don't drink it," I began to say, but it was too late. Rei had already placed her lips where his had been. I turned my cup in my hands, wondering if I should not pour it out, but the fragrance from the tea was so beguiling, and I was so thirsty, that I could not prevent myself from drinking too.

We rested under the tree while the being saw to the horses. He removed their harness and let them roll on the ground, then led them off to the spring to drink. I fell asleep, and when I woke, it was late in the afternoon.

The fire still burned, its flames almost invisible in the sunlight. Rei had picked flowers and made a garland. She looked like a spirit of the forest. I was afraid she had been enchanted and was going to slip away from me. I knew we needed to be among ordinary people again.

"We must find lodging," I said. "I don't want to spend another night outside."

He nodded as if humoring a child. "Then let us ride on."

He prepared the horses, and when Rei and I were mounted, he waved his hand towards the fire and spoke a word I did not know. The flames leaped up as though in yearning and then subsided and were extinguished.

The moon had risen, white in the afternoon sky. By the time it turned silver we were approaching a small town. I did not know which clan it belonged to, perhaps the Yamada, one of the neighbors who would not come to our help. It consisted of several dwellings and shops on either side of the road and one large inn. Torches burned at its entrance, filling the air with smoke. Behind the inn, horses tied on lines stamped and neighed as our two red horses approached. Grooms turned their heads towards us. They wore crests on their jackets, some the single peak of the Yamada and at least two the jagged mountain range of Lord Saga.

My heart stopped, plunged, and then started up again so fast I thought I would faint.

"Saga's men are here already," I said, trying to lower my voice so I would not be heard. I kept my head down so no one saw my face.

The being stared openly at the grooms, and they stared back, seeming to be more interested in the horses than the riders. One said something to the other, but I could not hear the words.

I remembered Okuda had coveted the red horses, and I feared these were his men who had been sent to retrieve them. Surely they would deduce who we were and take us into their possession too.

The being dismounted and lifted Rei down. He went into the inn and came back to say he had procured space for us in a room reserved for women travelers.

"I will stay outside with the horses," he said to me as he took Ka's reins. "No one will take them, and no one will take Rei or you."

I looked into his radiant eyes and could only trust him. As he walked away the flames from the torches bent towards him and seemed to hiss and sigh.

Rei ate a little at the evening meal. There were many things I wanted to ask her—did she understand the being's archaic words, was it the same language she used, did he always speak truth—but her face was soft and dreamy, and after the meal she fell asleep quickly. I stayed awake all night listening for the sound of horses' hooves. I longed for daylight and dreaded it.

Before it was light I woke Rei and led her outside. It was another misty morning, the tang of winter chilling my face. No one else was up, but the being had the horses ready. Their red coats glowed in the grey landscape, as if they sucked color from everything around them. As we rode away I looked back, but no one followed us. I remained tense all morning, making Ka nervous and skittish.

Rei was the opposite, more relaxed than I had ever seen her, in the circle of the being's arms. She had never been considered beautiful, but now I could see she was. She did not speak, but every now and then the being pointed something out to her, kites swooping over a river, a cloud shaped like a mushroom, red splashes of leaves on a high mountain, clusters of autumn lilies, a distant silver thread that was a waterfall, and she laughed in delight.

I had never heard such laughter from her before.

The road followed the valleys between the hills, crossing shallow rivers, skirting deep bays and estuaries. Mostly it was well maintained, but in places it had been washed away by rain or damaged by earth tremors. The horses snorted as they picked their way through ruts and around boulders, but they were surefooted and did not stumble.

We had been riding all day when the land seemed to flatten, the valleys became wider. Dykes and empty stubbled rice fields stretched away on either side of the road, the rice stalks drying on long poles.

I smelled smoke and ahead saw the low roofs of a small town. Just before them stood the wooden guard posts of the barrier that signaled the boundary of a domain. I glanced at the being. Were we going to ride through or attempt to go around somehow? And what story would he have ready to tell the guards?

His demeanor had altered in some way. It was not that he was tense as I was, but he was more alert than he had been all day. The horses put their ears back, twitching them as if they could hear something. I was sure the being's rather long ears were twitching too. Then I heard it, a dull pounding on the road behind us—a horse galloping, maybe two. Ka was trembling beneath me. I drew the reins tighter, preparing to ride on fast, all the while looking at the being for some clue as to what we would do next.

The two riders came up behind us, separated and swept past us, making Ka buck a little. I brought him back under control with a momentary flash of relief as I thought they were going on and had no interest in us, but they came to an abrupt halt a little way ahead and wheeled around to face us and block our way.

We were only a short distance from the barrier, and I could see armed men rushing out of the guardhouse.

I expected the horsemen to draw their swords but instead one of them spoke quite politely to the being.

"We did not mean to alarm you. We saw the horses at the inn and realized they must be the ones our lord desired to acquire a few weeks ago. We would like to buy them from you to present them to him."

The being frowned as though he did not understand the words. Finally he said, "They are not for sale."

The other man snorted incredulously while the first said, less courteously, "You don't understand. When Lord Okuda desires something, he gets it. I've offered you money and I advise you to accept."

"If you don't, we will just take them," said the second man.

"It is you who understands nothing," Rei said boldly. "They are shrine horses, not to be bought or sold. They belong to the Fire God."

The men looked astonished to be addressed in such a way and the first one looked more closely at Rei and then at me. Some realization came into his eyes and he said, "Lady Umaoka? And this must be your sister. Why are you here? Did you ride to meet us? We were sent to make preparations for the arrival of Lord Saga's sons. You must have received my message?"

"Was there some misunderstanding?" The other man's voice was bland on the surface and threatening beneath. "Or are the Umaoka still in rebellion against the will of Lord Saga? Let's take the horses now."

He rode forward to seize Ka's reins. Ka reared and struck out with his front feet. The other horse laid back its ears and tried to bite.

"Ren," the being said in a voice as clear as a flame. "Ride on."

I was struggling to bring Ka under control.

"Dismount before you get hurt!" The man's tone was rude, his language too familiar, as if I were a servant or a child. It enraged me. I would rather die than obey him. Ka reared again.

The being spoke in that unknown language, and Rei echoed him in a perfect imitation. He let his gaze, his eyes glowing more brightly than ever, sweep over the men in front of us and then beyond them. Smoke began to rise from the wooden structures of the guardhouses and the barrier, at first a few wisps, blue in the autumn air, then flames, as bright as the setting sun.

Men began to shout in alarm, dropping their weapons as they ran to get buckets of water. The bridles and reins of the horses in our path smoked and glowed. The horses squealed and bucked in fear as their riders struggled to tear the burning harness from them. The men's own clothes began to smolder. The grass at the side of the road burst into flames.

Ka gave a huge leap, almost unseating me. I clung to his mane as he raced forward and jumped over the burning barrier. I could see nothing, blinded by smoke, my eyes pouring tears. Then we were on the other side, galloping down the street as people came running out of their houses preparing to try and save the town. Ka was completely out of my control. I could do nothing but hang on.

Eventually, on the farther edge of town, he slowed to a canter and responded again to my touch on the reins. Hai came alongside and the two horses whinnied to each other as they cantered, their paces in perfect harmony.

The being held Rei with one arm. She was laughing frenetically. "Take the horses!" she cried. "What a foolish idea." In the light of the setting sun her eyes glowed as brightly and fiercely as his, as the Fire God's.

The Fire God, protector and destroyer, loyal and fickle, companion and betrayer, had answered my call for help, and now I knew I would succeed. I would get the revenge I craved.

But in return, I had given him my sister.